## THE AUTHOR

Richard Wagamese, an Ojibway from the Wabaseemoong First Nation in northwestern Ontario, was one of Canada's foremost writers. His acclaimed, bestselling novels included *Keeper'n Me*; *Indian Horse*, which was a Canada Reads finalist, winner of the inaugural Burt Award for First Nations, Métis and Inuit Literature, and made into a feature film; and *Medicine Walk*. He was also the author of acclaimed memoirs, including *For Joshua*; *One Native Life*; and *One Story, One Song*, which won the George Ryga Award for Social Awareness in Literature; as well as a collection of personal reflections, *Embers*, which received the Bill Duthie Booksellers' Choice Award. He won numerous awards and recognition for his writing, including the National Aboriginal Achievement Award for Media and Communications, the Molson Prize for the Arts, the Canada Reads People's Choice Award, and the Writers' Trust of Canada's Matt Cohen Award.

Wagamese died at the age of 61, on March 10, 2017, in Kamloops, B.C. *Starlight* was his final work of fiction.

## BY RICHARD WAGAMESE

### FICTION

*A Quality of Light*

*Dream Wheels*

*For Joshua: An Ojibway Father Teaches His Son*

*Him Standing*

*Indian Horse*

*Keeper'n Me*

*Medicine Walk*

*Ragged Company*

*Starlight*

*The Next Sure Thing*

### POEMS

*Runaway Dreams: Poems*

### NON-FICTION

*Embers: One Ojibway's Meditation*

*One Native Life*

*One Story, One Song*

*The Terrible Summer*

# KEEPER'N ME

RICHARD
WAGAMESE

PENGUIN MODERN CLASSICS EDITION, © 2018



This book was first published by Doubleday Canada in 1994
Anchor Canada edition published 2006



Library and Archives Canada Cataloguing in Publication Data
is available upon request.

ISBN 978-0-385-69325-7

Cover image: Graham Bezant/Getty
Front Cover Design: Andrew Roberts

Printed and bound in the U.S.A.

Penguin Modern Canadian Classics
Penguin Random House Canada Limited,
a Penguin Random House Company

www.penguinrandomhouse.ca

1 2 3 4 5 22 21 20 19 18

There are those who believe that the root of our aboriginal belief lies in the realm of magic and mysticism. *Keeper'n Me* shows that those roots are the gentler qualities of respect, honor, kindness, sharing and much, much love. These are the Indians that I have met, known and shared with . . .

RICHARD WAGAMESE 1993

*To my mother, Marjorie Nabish,*
*for giving me the gift of stories,*

*and my brother Charles Wagamese,*
*the best writer I have ever known.*

## ACKNOWLEDGEMENTS

We are granted vision in this life through the territories we navigate with those we share the planet with. I've moved through varied geographies in this short lifetime, and along the way there have been many amazing personalities who have added to the fabric and texture of this life. This book and this story could not have been born without their influence. Saying "thank you" seems so insignificant when people have helped me realize a dream, but thanks anyway to all of these people who are in here somewhere and with me always.

First and foremost, to the Spence family, Dave,

Doreen and Kim, who gave me a haven during a very stormy time, shelter from a variety of demons and a home in which to write this book. I owe it all to you.

To my editor at Doubleday, Jill Lambert, who came looking for a story one day and found only a writer who carried one but needed a hand getting it out. I thank you for your dedication, patience, honesty, insight and friendship.

To all the native organizations, groups and individuals that ever sat down and talked with me through sixteen long years of communications work, I thank you for giving so openly of yourselves so that I could understand and one day bring this story to your homes and offices.

To the elders who guided this work and have asked to remain nameless, I thank you for your encouragement, guidance, prayers and support. Without you there is no story.

And finally, to these people, who have populated each of the territories I've navigated, who convinced me I had stories inside me: Morningstar Mercredi, Bill Park, Lorna Crozier, John Cuthand, Carolyn Deby, Maria Campbell, Ray Fox, Paulette Jiles, Tomson Highway, Chief Leonard George, Buffy, Tantoo Cardinal, Norval Morrisseau, Lorraine Sinclair, Helene Kakakaway, Wil Campbell, Gord Enno, Diane Meilli, Gary Fry, Karen Huggins, the *Calgary Herald*, Viola McLure, Marlena Dolan, Brad Braun.

There are more, of course, many, many more, but there's a story waiting to be told . . .

BOOK ONE

# BIH'KEE'-YAN, BIH'KEE'-YAN, BIH'KEE'-YAN

## KEEPER: A PROLOGUE

*Get a lotta tourists this way now. Never used to be. When I was a boy this here country was still Ojibway land. Anishanabe we called ourselves. Lotsa huntin' and trappin', fishin' still good in the rivers. Not like now. Everywhere there's big expensive fishin' and huntin' lodges for rich Americans that don't know the difference between a good pickerel and a bad one. Only fish for the photographs them. Us we used everythin', every part of everythin'. They come up here year round now with their guns and rods and reels, big boats and Kodaks makin' lotta noise, botherin' ev'ryone.*

*Okay for me, I'm an old man now. I just play dumb Indyun*

*and they leave me alone. But it's hard on the young ones. Kinda caught between two things them. Want the big boats, big guns, big money, same time as they want the culture. Hard to find your way sometimes in life. Me, I'm just an old man that's been down many trails. How they say in them movies? The ones that got lotsa Mexicans bein' Indyuns? I lived many winters? Heh, heh, heh. Guess that's true, only me, I don't talk so romantic anymore 'less some of them rich Americans are ready to dish out cash to hear a real Indyun talk 'bout the old days.*

*Funny thing is, like I told the boy, the old days never really gone. Not for us. The outside world goes crazy all the time, findin' new ways to do old things, forget the teachin's their own old ones taught. But us we listen all the time. To old guys like me. Always talkin' anyway, might as well listen, eh? Heh, heh, heh.*

*What I mean is, us we always had our storytellers. The ones who come and listen to the old men and the old women when they talk. Listen hard, learn the stories, then go tell everyone same thing. That way the old days are never gone for us, see? Always got a storyteller to pass those old teachin's down. Works good long as there's old guys like me. And we got it good us. Young ones bringin' us fresh fish, fresh meat, driving us here and there, doin' all kinda work around the place, hanging around all the time. Not just rich Americans got hired help, eh? Heh, heh, heh. Nope. Us old guys had 'em beat years ago. Anishanabe got a good word no one ever argues with, Indyun or not, makes everything right and okay. We say—*TRA-DISH-UNN*. Heh, heh, heh. Wanna make white people believe what you tell 'em? Say its* TRA-DISH-UNN*. Same thing with young ones round* *here. You gotta do it, we say, it's* TRA-DISH-UNN. *Good word that. Makes life easy.*

*Don't mind me. Been around as long as me get kinda busy in the head and talk all kindsa things at the same time. Gotta listen though—it's* TRA-DISH-UNN! *Heh, heh, heh.*

*Boy's got some stories he wants to tell. Stories 'bout this reserve, this country, our people, how it feels to be a tourist. How it feels to need someone to show you the way. We all of us are tourists. All of us. That's my theory. Us we hitchin' and complainin' all the time about these American tourists that invade our land regular. But there's teachin's in evervthin'. They come to our docks, our camps, right onto the reserve sometimes, lookin' for a guide so they can get what they're lookin' for. Fish, bear, moose, anything. When they find one they're happy and when they get what they're lookin' for they're even happier still. Just like life, I say, even for us Indyuns. 'Specially the young ones. 'Specially now, in this world, in this time. That's why I told the boy that we're all tourists. Everyone. Same thing. Indyun or not, we're all lookin' for a guide to help us find our way through. It's tough. Takes a long time sometimes and not lots of people find one either. Them that do, well, they really got something to say then.*

*See, things changed too fast and us we got a diff'rent way with time. Never had no punchclocks like the whiteman uses, never had nothin' like time management stuff I heard about one time, nothin' like that. Us we lived with the seasons. Always knew what needed doin' by time of the year not time of day. Always got things done, always survived. Was like that long time here.*

*But the whiteman's been inventin' things for a long time now. They kinda got used to the speed of their world gettin' faster'n faster with each new invention. Got used to dealin' with time diff'rent even though they were just like us once. Them they lost touch with the rhythm of the earth, left their drums behind long time ago, forgot their old songs, their old teachings and got lost in the speed of things. But when they got here Anishanabe still lived the old way. My father was still trappin' the same territory been trapped by my family for a long, long time. Kinda seemed like the rest of the country got swept up in the whiteman's progress sooner'n us. But it's been only 'bout fifty years that things really started to change around here and maybe even lots less since the young people really started feelin' that lost kinda feelin'. Now they gotta choose between worlds. Wanna listen to that rap dance instead of the pow-wow drum, watch the television instead of hearin' stories, make up their own minds instead of hearin' the teachin's. It's hard. Wanna be part of one world cause it's all shiny and fast but afraid to let go of the other world that's slower and more familiar. It's not their fault. Us Indyuns we always like shiny things.*

*Lotsa good things like school and workin' that the whiteman brought here but still, those young ones need a guide to bring 'em where they wanna bc. Always lookin' for the sign, buyin' diff'rent maps, goin' here and there all the time. Got the old slidey foot. Always on the move and lookin'. Wanderin' around all owl-eyed lookin' for something.*

*The boy knows this. He come here lookin' around too not so long ago. Funny-lookin' sight he was then, too. Fresh outta the city, not even really knowin' he was an Indyun, especially not an Anishanabe. Learned lots though. But he was a real tourist that one. Coulda got lost in a bathtub then. Heh, heh, heh. But he learned and that's why I told him to write all of this down. Be a story teller. Any damn fool can get people's attention but it takes a storyteller to get their attention and hold it. Lots of people out there gotta know what happened, how you found your way and what it takes to be an Indyun these days. Real Indyun, not that Hollywood kind. That's what I told him. He's a good boy, you'll see. Me, I'll just come along for the ride, make sure he's doin' right. Besides, lotta stuff's my story too and maybe if you listen hard, pay close attention, you'll see that they're your stories too. Our stories all work like that. Its* TRA-DISH-UNN. *Heh, heh, heh.*

You gotta drive for miles on this bumpy as hell gravel road to reach White Dog. You turn off the Trans-Canada Highway a few kilometres outside Kenora and head north. Heading towards the little railroad town of Minaki, you follow this curving little paved highway as far as the White Dog turnoff, and that's about where you leave things like cottages, road signs, picnic tables and civilization behind. From there it's an agonizing trip on this washboard road that's hard as dusted steel in summer, soupy as a poor stew in autumn and slippery as the Department of Indian Affairs at funding time in winter. Calling it a road's a stretch even by White Dog standards, but it's the only way in here unless you care to boat it up the Winnipeg River about a hundred k. The only thing that makes the trip bearable is the country.

And what country. The trees come right out to the very shoulders of the road in places and are so tall and green it'll make you blink and just when you're getting used to that a big silver lake'll flash into view like a big mercury platter in the sunlight. My favorite thing is how on summer days the sun'll throw big stretches of shadows from those trees across the road and when you drive through 'em, all shadows and light, it's kinda like seein' the world through a strobe light. Anyway, about halfway in there's a huge cliff that looks like it's about a mile high leaning out over the road. The old people used to go there to pray, and I always wondered how they ever managed to climb the thing. We climbed it once, my brother Stanley and I, and it took all morning and all the gumption we had to get up there. But once you're up top the view is amazing. Looking away across any direction you can see miles and miles of green kinda pockmarked with drops of blue where the lakes sit. It's like a big green carpet rolling up and down like waves as far as you can see. You miss that from the road but you can still get an idea of the size of it all when you top one of the hills.

But the further and further you get into this country the more and more the feeling of mystery starts to surround you. Kinda like that cliff is the signpost to another world and I guess maybe this is another world. Not Another World like the soap opera my ma watches every time we hit Winnipeg, although there's been a few episodes around here'd be good watchin' sometime, but another world where things like time and moving and living itself are diff'rent. It's a feeling more than anything. Nothing you can reach out and put your finger on, but if you spend any time at all up here wandering around you can feel it start to work on your bones. Pay attention and you feel it slipping through your car windows driving up here. People that live here get used to that feeling of mystery and magic but not many outside people visit White Dog unless they got business and frankly, we like it that way. Maybe it's just the pure wild spirit of this land seeping through, I don't know, but it sure beats the hell out anything I ever saw or felt before. Every now and again you'll see moose way off in the marshes or bears skipping outta view in the berry patches and Keeper'n me seen a cougar one time too. Just a flash like a well-tanned deer hide through the trees and gone. No wonder Ojibways called cougars bush ghosts. They're a part of the mystery too.

There's a small band of Ojibways that call White Dog home and have for a few hundred years now accordin' to my ma. It's home to me too now but I was gone for a long, long time, kinda lost in the outside world. Most people never hearda the Ojibway. Probably because we never raided wagon trains or got shot offa horses by John Wayne. The Ojibways' big claim to fame is a few centuries back when we chased the Sioux outta Minnesota. Had some kinda squabble over territory and we ended up putting them to rout and chased them out onto the plains where they raided wagon trains and got shot off their horses by The Duke. Yeah, right outta the backwoods and into the movies. You'd think they'd be grateful but they're still pissed about that. Every now and then at a pow-wow some Ojibway will tell a Sioux that the only way they can recognize them is from behind. Or they'll be sharing deer hunting stories around a campfire one night and an Ojibway will describe a deer running through the bush faster'n the east end of a westbound Sioux. It's all in fun and nobody gets offended but them Sioux take a lotta pride in their warrior tradition and they don't talk too much about their bush days anymore. Nobody ever hearda that tussle on accounta it all happened before the whiteman got here. Funny thing about them white historians is they always figure North American history started when Columbus landed here. Us we know better. The Ojibway people have been bush Indians forever and kinda settled into northern Ontario long before Columbus even hearda Columbus.

Sociologists call us hunting and gathering Indians. Or else northern woodlands people or something like that. Us we just call ourselves Anishanabe. Means the good people in Ojibway. Most of our history's about fishing, hunting and trapping on accounta that's what we do. Or at least that's what we did before "the settlement of North America" as the books say. Nowadays there's still a lotta that happening but no one's making a living off it anymore. Most of the time there's just welfare. Every once in a while the government will surprise the hell outta everyone and give us work cutting scrub timber or something. A few jobs are created by the band council once in a while too and the American tourists fly in to hire guides, but it's mostly a poor reserve with not lots to do for people used to the fast pace of the outside world. Took me a long time to get used to walking down to the dock behind my ma's place on winter mornings, chopping a hole in the ice and hauling up the day's water in a five-gallon lard pail. Or even hanging my wool socks up to dry on the pipes of the pot-bellied stove that heats the place or worse yet, making the forty-yard dash to the outhouse through the pourin' rain. Things like that are just facts of life around here and you get used to it and pretty soon you discover that you'd really rather live like this anyway. Ma says she's seen too many families get split apart by the "electircal invasion" as she puts it. It's true. I've been here five years and I learned more about things than I woulda if we had electricity and TV. You get to know each other pretty good when all you got is each other for entertainment. Guess that's the strongest point about this reserve and the people here. Even though we're poor we still got spirit and heart and we look out for each other. Lotsa other places can't say that.

My name's Garnet Raven. The Raven family's been a fixture on the White Dog Reserve ever since they signed Treaty Three across the northern part of Ontario in the 1870s. Raven's also the name of one of our people's messengers in the animal world, so I guess old Keeper telling me I was supposed to be some kind of a storyteller's gotta make some sense. I don't know. But ever since I've been here I've been listening to what that old guy's been telling me and pretty much trying to do what he says and it's all worked out fine. So who am I to argue?

I live here with my ma. We've got a small cabin on the west end of the townsite. This reserve's built on the shore of White Dog Lake and it's the kind of rocky, bushy territory you'd expect. So the houses are all spread apart and built on top of rocky little hills. They're not houses like city folk are used to. They're just small one-story jobbies with maybe four rooms that all empty into the main room where the stove is. Not much insulation, and some of the poorer people here still use clear plastic instead of glass on their windows. The townsite's called that on accounta the band office, school, medical building, store and garage are all clustered around the only clear, flat place around. There's about half a dozen houses down there where the only electricity and telephones are. That's where the chief and a few band councillors live along with the white teachers from the school and Doc Tacknyk and Mrs. Tacknyk, our Ukrainian medical team. There's a ball diamond that doubles as the pow-wow grounds four days every summer, a boarded hockey rink with a couple of rickety light poles, and a small aluminum trailer where the Ontario Provincial Police sit drinking coffee the few times they get out this way. Ma's cabin sits above the end of the dirt track that serves as the main drag out here. Beyond us is just bush trails leading to other houses deeper in the woods near Shotgun Bay.

We like to sit out back where the trail leads down to the dock where I keep my boat. My uncle Archie got me that boat with money he won at the big blackout bingo in Winnipeg two summers ago. It's a fourteen-foot aluminum with a thirty-five-horsepower motor, nice waterproof cushions and a built-in cooler for the fish. Ma and I take lotsa rides in that boat in the evenings and she's always pointing out places on the shore where big things happened either to our family or our people. When I think about my life these days the thing I think about most is my ma's wrinkled brown face in the front of that boat, all squinty-eyed into the wind, smiling, pointing and gabbing away, her voice rising and falling through the sound of loons and ducks and wind. But we also sit out back late into the evening watching the land. If you sit there long enough while the sun's going down behind the hills you'd swear you can see those hills move. Like they're breathing. It's a trick of the light really. Something caused by distance and time and a quiet yearning of magic we all carry around inside us. That's what Ma says. Says that magic's born of the land and the ones who go places in life are the ones who take the time to let that magic seep inside them. Sitting there, all quiet and watching, listening, learning. That's how the magic seeps in. Anishanabe are pretty big on magic, she says. Not so much the pullin' rabbits outta hats kinda of magic but more the pullin' learning outta everything around 'em. A common magic that teaches you how to live with each other. Seeing them hills breathe, and believing it, is making yourself available to that magic. Like leaving the door to your insides unlocked, she says.

So we watch that land through the twilight and wait for the first shakings of the northern lights before we'll head on inside to sleep with our heads fulla dreams about this land, our people, a place called White Dog and a certain common magic born of all of it that brought us all together.

When I was three I disappeared. Disappeared into foster homes and never made it back until I was twenty-five. I'm thirty now, been here five years but it feels like longer so much has happened.

See, when I was born my family still lived the old way. There was a small clan of us Ravens that lived across Shotgun Bay in a few canvas army tents on what was my grampa's trapline. My ma, pa, two brothers and sister all lived together with my grandparents and a few aunts, uncles and cousins. We trapped, hunted and fished and pretty much lived off the land like our people had for centuries, and according to everyone we were a pretty happy clan. The first words I spoke were Ojibway words and the first sounds I heard when I was born were the sound of the wind in the trees, water and the gentle murmur of Ojibway voices all around me.

According to Ma, they got an idea I was gonna be one of the wandering kind real early. I guess I was a rambunctious little kid and got to crawling around real good. In fact, I got so good at it that I'd crawl right on outta the tent and be heading off towards the woods to look for my pa and grampa when my ma or granny would have to charge out and put the scoop on me. Guess it happened so many times that my granny finally got tired of chasing me around and made me a little harness out of moose hide, which they tied to a tree with about a ten-foot lead for me to crawl around on. Kept me out of trouble but I disappeared anyway.

What happened was a couple of guys from the Ontario Hydro showed up one day with a big sheaf of papers. They told my family they were planning on building a big dam downriver and that the reservoir behind it would be flooding right back over our traditional trapline. Even though the Ravens had trapped that area for generations no one had ever told them anything about ownership or title. It was outside the reserve lands that were ours by treaty and was actually owned by the Hydro company. So my family had to move, and since there was no work or even houses available on White Dog at the time their only choice was to head for Minaki, the nearest town.

Now according to Ma, learning to live by the clock sure was a hell of a lot tougher than living by the sun and the seasons the way they'd been used to. Finding work was tough. You gotta understand that northern Ontario around the middle 1950s was a pretty uptight racist community and Ojibways weren't exactly the toast of the towns then. So Ma and Pa spent lotsa time away from the small shack we lived in at the edge of town and we kids were left in the care of our granny who would have been about sixty-five then.

Now, Indians got a whole different way of looking at things like family. When you're a kid around here everyone's always picking you up, feeding you and generally taking good care of you. Sociologists call it the extended family concept. When you're born you got a whole built-in family consisting of ev'ryone around. So it was natural in my parents' eyes to leave us with the old lady while they were out trying to make a living. But the Ontario Children's Aid Society had a different set of eyes and all they seen was a bunch of rowdy little Indian kids terrorizing a bent-up old lady. Now anybody who knows anything about Indians knows that if there was any terrorizin' being done at all it was being done by the old lady. We were being raised just fine, but it wasn't long before they showed up with a plan for all of us.

According to my sister, Jane, who's the oldest of us and the one who remembers the most from those days, they showed up one afternoon, a young woman and an older white-haired man. They pulled up while we kids were playin' tag and swinging from an old tire hung from a tree in the front yard. My granny was out back doin' something or other. Anyway, they called us over to this big green station wagon and handed out chocolates all around. Well, for some wild little bush Indians raised on bannock and beaver, chocolate was pretty close to heaven, so when they offered us more if we hopped into their car, well, we all piled in.

We wound up in a group home on a farm outside of Kenora, in the custody of Children's Aid.

About a year later I was taken away from my brothers and sister and put in another home by myself. Jane tells it like this. See, the foster home we had on that farm had about six other kids in their care. We all stayed in a kind of dormitory on the third floor of their farmhouse in bunkbeds and we had to help out with the work around the farm too. Anyway, these people didn't exactly go out of their way to show us any kind of real welcome. At Christmastime while their kids were whooping it up in the living room the foster kids were made to sit at a long table in the porch. There weren't any gifts for us either. But my brothers and sisters had somehow managed to scrape up a little cash and bought me a toy truck for Christmas. They wrapped it up in plain brown paper and put it beside my pillow so I'd find it come Christmas morning.

It was just a little toy truck, nothing like the big Tonka trucks kids get these days that they can ride around, just a little blue and red truck with one wheel missing. Well, according to Jane I loved that little truck. I slept with it and carried it with me wherever I went. It never seemed to matter that it had one wheel missing. I'd be plowing roads, chasing bad guys and building cities all over the yard with that little truck.

Well, one morning I was sitting in the sandbox playing with my truck when the schoolbus came to pick up the other kids. I guess my brothers and sister had been told the night before that I was getting sent away and Jane said they all figured it was better to just let it happen rather than let me know about it. So, I'm out there playing that morning and Jane came and grabbed me up in a big, warm hug and just held on for a long, long time. I guess I got a little irritated and pushed her away finally and got back to my play.

"Jane, jeez," was all I said.

She says those were the last words she heard, and the last sight she had of me for twenty years was from the back window of that schoolbus. A little Ojibway boy all hunched over in the sandbox with a little red truck with one wheel missing, growin' smaller'n smaller, till it looked like the land just swallowed me up. When she got home that night the sandbox was empty except for that little blue and red truck, the wind already busy burying it in the sand. When we met again twenty years later she grabbed me in that same big, warm hug and just held on for a long, long time.

By the time I made it back here I was lost. At twenty-five years old I never figured on bein' no Indian. I didn't remember a thing about my earlier life and when I disappeared alone into the foster homes I disappeared completely from the Indian world. Everywhere they moved me I was the only Indian and no one ever took the time to tell me who I was, where I came from or even what the hell was going on. I mean, being from a nomadic culture is one thing but keeping a kid on the

move for twelve years is ridiculous. I was in and out of more homes than your average cat burglar.

Anyway, I lost touch with who I was pretty quick. Growing up in all-white homes, going to all-white schools, playing with all-white kids can get a guy to thinking and reacting all-white himself after a while. With no one pitching in any information I just figured I was a brown white guy.

Because around about the early sixties there was only a couple of ways for anybody to get to know about Indians, unless you knew a few of course, which I didn't. It was the same for white people as for those of us trying to be white. The most popular way of learning about Indians was television. Man, I remember Saturday mornings watching them Westerns and cheering like crazy for the cowboys like everyone else and getting all squirmy inside when the savages were threatening and feelin' the dread we were all supposed to feel when their drums would sound late at night. Injuns. Scary devils. Heathens. All of a sudden popping up at the top of a hill, taking scalps, stealin' horses, talking stupid English and always, always riding right into the guns of the pioneers. We tumbled off horses better'n anybody and that was about all the good you could say. It was embarrassing stuff to be watching.

Then there was books. Indians never got mentioned in any of the schoolbooks except for being the guides for the brave explorers busy discovering the country. I could never ever figure out how you could say you were

out discovering something when you needed a guide to help you find it. But Indians were always second to the explorers who were creating the real history of North America. Comic books and novels were just carbon copies of the textbook and TV and movie Indians. We were either heathen devils running around killing people or just simple savages who desperately needed the help of the missionaries in order to get straightened out and live like real people. There weren't any other kind of stories.

Of course, everyone was buying into these messages and I started hearing the usual stuff. Indians were lazy, no account, drunken bums, living on welfare, mooching change on street corners and really needing some direction. If white people hadn't got here when they did we'd have all died.

I remember one time after doing something against the rules in one home I was in, the man of the house drove me into the Indian section of town. He drove real slow, pointing out drunks and dirty-looking people reeling around on the sidewalks or sleeping crumpled up in alleys.

Then he said, "See. Those are Indians. Look at them. If you don't start shaping up and doing what you're told around here, that's what you're going to become!"

And the kids I played with were kinda the same—kids bein' kids and all. They were always on me with the usual "ugh, how, Tonto" stuff they learned from TV, their parents or both. Always asking me stuff like what's your tribe, how do you say such-and-such in Indian, what does dog taste like, you know, run-of-the-mill kid stuff.

One time we're busy getting up a neighborhood game of cowboys and Indians. Except back then it was "cowboys and itchybums"—kids bein' kids and all. Naturally being the only itchybum in the crowd my role was easily cast. No one could understand why I broke into tears that day. No one could understand why I dropped my little guns and holster and ran indoors and up to my room, and I, in turn, couldn't understand why everyone at the suppertable that night broke into uncontrollable laughter when I was asked about it and I explained, "'Cause I don't know how to be an Indian!"

And that's how it was for me growing up. I was embarrassed about being an Indian and I was afraid that if I ever met a real one I wouldn't know what to do or say. So I started trying to fit into that white world as best I could. I decided that I would try to learn to be anything other than what I was. I didn't want to be compared to any of the images I had of my own people, of myself. But this brown skin of mine was always a pretty good clue to most people that there must have been a redskin or two creeping around my mama's woodpile.

So at various times I was Hawaiian, Polynesian, Mexican or Chinese. Anything but Indian. Those people on the street that day still haunted me. Of course, if I got cornered on evidence then I'd become any one of four famous kinds of Indian. I was either Apache, Sioux, Cherokee or Commanche. Everyone had heard of those Indians. I mean, if you absolutely had to be an Indian, at least be one that everyone had heard of. Embarrassed as I was at the time I sure didn't want to be no Passamaquoddy, Flathead, Dogrib or Ojibway. Aiming for the romantic was my game plan.

I fell in love with the blues when I was twenty. Something in the music sorta bumped up against something deep inside me and made it move. Maybe it was the built-in lonely that got me, or the moving, searching, losing and fightin' for a living that good blues singers gotta do before they can really put it out there. I don't know for sure what it was, but the first time I heard it I was hooked. Still love the sound of the blues late at night. Kinda fits in with the sounds of the north. All that moanin' and cryin' goes real good with a dark, dark night, the wind howling through the trees and a fire going real good in the cabin. There's even a few White Dog folks starting to like it too now. Mostly folks up here like the old-time fiddle tunes like "The Red River Jig" and "Maple Sugar" or the pow-wow songs they tape during pow-wow season, but some have taken a liking to dropping by late at night and sitting on the porch listening to the blues on our battery tape player. Guess maybe us Indians have a lot in common with our black brothers and sisters when it comes to bein' blue about things.

Wally Red Sky pooh-poohs it all though. Wally's bound and determined to be known as the best Indian country-and-western singer ever. Spent too much time listening to his daddy's old country records and now he walks around with his hair all Brylcreemed up and swept back, wearing tasseled western shirts and smellin' of Old Spice. Says Indians are more tuned in to the country on accounta they're closer to the land and that things like wide-open spaces and riding horses are more Indian than gettin' drunk and crying over lost women. I tried to point out to him that most country songs are about those very same things, but he just grins and walks away shaking his shiny head all sad like.

"Catch on one o' these days, Garnet," he says. "One o' these days you'll be singin' 'I Saw the Light' 'steada 'Goin' Down That Road Feelin' Bad.'"

I spent a lotta time going down a lotta roads feelin' bad actually. When I heard the blues they just kinda fit right into my head and that was actually the first step in my getting back here. Funny how those insignificant little moments wind up being the biggest things in your life after you live some. Who'da ever thought that some black blues band in a tavern in downtown Toronto would be the first step on my road back to White Dog. Funny, but that's what happened.

See, I split the foster homes at sixteen and went wandering everywhere. I hitchhiked all over looking for something to do or just somewhere to be. Got around pretty good and saw a lotta country over the next four years but just couldn't find it in me to settle down anywhere. My friend Keeper calls it "havin' the old slidey foot." Well I had that old slidey foot thing going real good in my life until I hit T.O. in '77.

Back then I was running a lotta games past people. Reason I was moving around so much was because my games were pretty easy to see through actually and I'd always split just before I got called on my bull. I still didn't wanna be known as an Indian. Mostly on accounta the Indians I saw those years were pretty much the same kind my foster father'd shown me in the car that day. Scary-looking, dirty, drunk, fightin' in the street or passed out in the alley, and I sure didn't wanna be connected to them in any way. So I'd hit town and be anybody from anywhere when I'd meet up with folks.

I was a homeless Hawaiian for a while there in Niagara Falls. Had these flowered shirts I found at the Sally Ann, mirrored sunglasses on a rope around my neck, brushcut, and even got a beat up old ukulele at a pawnshop. We'd be drinkin' wine in the park and I'd be teaching people how to say things in fictitious Hawaiian and singing these dumb songs on that ukulele. Touching stuff like "KahmonIwannalayya," "Nookienookienow" or "The Best Leis Are Hawaiian" for the ladies present. Still don't know how that dumb stuff passed, probably the wine more'n anything, but I was a Hawaiian refugee there for a while.

Another time after seeing a couple of episodes of "Kung Fu" on TV I became a half-Chinese guy looking for my father all across North America. He was supposed to be some Canadian businessman knocked up my ma, little Wing Fey, while on a trip to the East. He left me'n Ma in desperate poverty in Shanghai. I was gonna use my considerable kung fu skills on him when I found him and avenge the death of Wing Fey, who'd succumbed to malaria finally after putting me through some monk temple in the mountains. That one ran pretty good in a few towns until I got too drunk in Sudbury and gave a traditional Chinese name to a big biker named Cow Pie. Guess he didn't like being referred to as Sum Dum Fuk. My kung fu skills failed me utterly.

Then there was the period I roamed around being Pancho Santilla, the Mexican/Apache boxer who'd quit fighting forever after kililin' some guy in a bar fight in Taos. Got the name Taos from watchin' "McCloud" on TV and figured it was a cool-soundin' name to be talking about. Taos. Kinda rolled right off your tongue and made whatever story you were running prettier and more believable, I thought. It was cool to be part Apache since there weren't any Apaches in Canada and I wasn't likely to run into any and Apaches were rated pretty highly on mainstream society's masculinity scale anyway. Anytime you had to be Indian, see, anytime the other shtick wasn't a go, well, you had to be one of the top-rated prime-time kinda Indians. Didn't dive into that one too often but the old Pancho Santilla routine was always worth a few draft somewhere.

Not being Indian was a full-time occupation and maybe me gravitating towards bein' a storyteller isn't that difficult a thing to understand now. Some of those tales were pretty wild back then, but when they say that the truth is sometimes stranger'n fiction they musta had me'n my life in mind.

When I discovered the blues I was pretty much ready for anything. I'd just gotten back from working a few months on a railroad gang tamping up big stretches of track across southern Ontario. So I hit Toronto with a lotta money and figured a new set of clothes and a girlfriend would make life pretty sweet for a while. Managed to find a rooming house close to the downtown strip and I remember thinking that life wasn't such a bad deal after all. I'd been kind of a Toronto regular over the years, stopping in for a few months every now and then. One night after supper I changed into my new duds and headed out for a big night on the town, not really sure where I was headed except I wasn't going anywhere near the Warwick Hotel or the Silver Dollar where all the Indians hung out. But something big was in the air and I set out just knowing that this was one a those nights that would go down in history.

That was the night I met Lonnie Flowers.

Lonnie Flowers was a tall, rangy black guy who hung out downtown selling pot and shooting pool. I'd heard of him from some of the other streeters but until that night never had anything to do with him. Hanging out on the street, you hear a lotta names but mostly you hang with those you know and circles can be pretty small there. Anyway, the way things turned out we'd both heard of each other but never crossed paths.

I was heading down Yonge thinking maybe I'd catch a few strippers at the Zanzibar and my mind was a few million miles away in the future when I heard this voice calling out to me.

"Say, my man, what it is? You lookin'?"

He was standing there in the doorway with this great big purple silk superfly hat on and an orange leisure suit with bell-bottoms and those platform shoes that were real big back then. Had a Fu Manchu mustache and an Afro sticking out from under the hat and he was smiling. Good-looking guy but giving off the air that tells you this isn't someone you mess with.

"Huh?" I said with all the cool of a downtown pro.

"What, you deaf foo'?" he said, leaning in a little closer. "You sorry ass need some mendin', my man. Bring your narrow tired-lookin' butt over here."

"Huh?" I said again, wondering where in the heck this guy had come from.

"Shit. You real downtown, ain'tcha? Got me a regular Jethro Bodine here. Man, c'mere!"

There wasn't anything else to do, so I edged into the doorway beside him. I'm about six feet even but Lonnie Flowers was head and shoulders taller than me even without the platform shoes. Besides, I kinda liked the way he talked, all fast and moving around, hands and feet going in rhythm with his speech. We stood there a moment and then he offered me a smoke. I don't smoke but I took one anyway and tucked it behind my ear like a lot of guys I knew. He watched me, smiling with his eyes and shaking his head.

"Damn, man, you got that Jimmy Dean shit down, don'tcha? Where you from? Buffalo?" He laughed at his own joke and it was one a those big rolling laughs that makes everyone feel good around it. "Don't mind me, man. I'm just funnin' witcha. What's your name, man, really?"

"Huey," I said, glad to be able to squeeze out something a little more cool-sounding than *huh*. "Huey Kolahey."

"Kolahey? Damn. Sound like junk food for cows or somethin'. Where you from, Kolahey?"

"Hawaii."

He slapped his thighs a little while he bent over in laughter. A few heads turned our way and I wished suddenly that I was anywhere but that doorway.

"Damn. You that dude runnin' that King Kahmaymaya shit around. Man, look at you. You be havin' them great big Sasquatch cheekbones, squinty little kung fu eyes and you got like two square feeta unused denim where you butt should be. Gotta get you a wallet or sumpthin' fill them cheeks out. Damn, one look tell people you a redskin man. But you runnin' aroun' bein' Hawaiian? Who the hell you think you are? Don-fucking-Arapa-HO? Shit."

This was the first time I'd ever been confronted with my own phoniness and I just wanted outta there fast.

He was laughing now but I'd heard and seen a lotta big black guys that turned mean real quick.

"Hey, look, man," I said, "I, uh, I gotta go. Gotta meet someone down the street a ways and I, uh, I'm kinda late."

"Damn, brother, only dude you gotta meet is yourself. Who you kiddin' gotta meet someone? Who you gotta meet? Hawaii Five-O? Shit. Where you goin' really?"

"Man, I don't even know you, okay," I said, getting kind of irritated myself and feeling pretty put down and scared. "I'm mindin' my own business here, okay? See ya."

"Wait wait wait," he said, holding out his hand. "You right, you right. I be runnin' track all over your ass, you don' even know my name, man. That ain't right. My name's Lonnie, man. Lonnie Flowers. How you doin'?"

We shook, exchanged a high-five, and I started to feel a little better about this strange-sounding guy in the doorway. We stood there, arms crossed, looking out over the street, moving up and down on our toes, heads bobbing and not saying anything.

"My name's really Garnet. Garnet Raven and I, uh, I guess I'm from here now, man."

"Hey, thass better, man. Garnet Raven's cool, man. Kinda got that spooky Indian shit workin' through it, y'know?"

"Yeah, never thoughta it that way before. Better'n fuckin' Tonto."

We both laughed and I remember thinking that this was the first time I'd ever really hit it off with someone without having to run a game on them. It didn't seem to matter to Lonnie Flowers that I was Indian and it sure didn't matter to me that he was black. If anything I was starting to wish that I was too.

"Say, man, look," he said, "I gotta meet with someone for a minute in this club see, but you wanna go do a rack of eightball or two, man? That is, if your social calendar got room for it, I mean."

"Sure. Pool ain't my thing but I'll shoot you if you want."

"Damn. 'Nother person wanna shoot a poor black man on sight. Tell you, it don't pay to be colored no more!" he said, laughing, slapping his thigh and pulling me outta the doorway and down the street. Follow me, Arapa-HO. Drag your pineapple-squeezin', hula-hoopin' redskin ass this way!"

We wound up in a tavern somewhere off the Yonge Street strip. Reason I don't know exactly where it was or the name of the place was because I was so fascinated watching Lonnie Flowers "doin' the locals" as he called it. The man was in constant motion, bobbing and weaving through groups of people, head nodding, waving, thumbs upping people and chatting with and to everyone. It was amazing to watch, especially for someone like me who tried to be invisible most of the time. I just tagged along in the background trying to look like I was with him but not doing too good a job of either keeping up or looking good.

It was worse when we got inside finally. People were calling out to him, laughing and whistling as soon as we walked in. He found us elbow room at the bar and ordered a couple beers from the bartender he introduced as Raoul.

"Gotta watch Raoul, my man, he be one of them John Wayne–lovin' niggers might wanna be shootin' your ass," he said, laughing and lighting another smoke. "My man Garnet here's a Hawaiian Injun, Raoul. Regular Don Arapa-HO," he said with a wink and a slap on my back.

"Meetcha." Raoul offered a handshake across the bar. "Really Injun?"

"Uh, yeah. Yeah, I am. Good to meetya." I was wondering whether this had been such a good idea.

Well, the place was full of black people. I'd been around colored people before in my travels but like everyone else at the time, I figured going into a black bar was tempting fate just a little too much and I'd avoided them. Back then there was three places you didn't go: gay bars, cowboy bars and black bars, and I guess if you ever heard about gay black cowboy bars you really gave them distance.

People were wandering over every minute or two to chat up my new friend and it was fun to watch. I was getting right into the loose way these people acted. For a guy always concerned with how he looked to people, watching a whole room fulla people acting so casual was a treat and I found myself wishing I could be like that and that maybe me'n Lonnie could become good enough friends that I could hang around for a long time here. I just leaned back against the bar with my beer in my hand eyeballing everything.

Two things happened real fast. First Lonnie starts whooping and slapping the bar in delight when three women and two men walked into the room together. He hustled me over to their table and there was a lotta hugging and squeezing and shoulder punchin' before we got sat down and he introduced me to his mother Delma, sisters Gladdie and Maddie and his brothers Truman and DeWayne. They all just kinda nodded politely in my direction, ordered a tableful of beer, lit up smokes and started talking to each other and laughing.

The second thing that happened was the music started. One vibrating note from an electric guitar that slid into another one and was followed by a bunch of notes all tumbling over each other before the drums, bass and horns kicked in behind it. It was like nothing I ever heard before and I turned in my chair to face the stage to see who was making this noise that made me shiver inside. Kinda got lost in it, forgetting where I was, who I was with or what I was doing. The music seemed so wild, so ancient and full of danger, pain and heartache that I fell, as Lonnie would later say, "head over heels, puppydog-eyed in love."

It was the close-up laughter that pulled me back.

"Oooo-eee shit!" Delma was saying, leaning forward in her chair and staring at me. "Lonnie, this boy's got the blues in a bad way! He be twitchin' around and bumpin' his ole leg up and down and shakin' his head around like a dog with a new bone! Damn! You sure he ain't no black man?"

"Maybe not now, Mama," Lonnie said, "but if he gets to likin' it too much he might try bein' one sooner or later for someone somewhere!" He winked at me.

"Lonnie says you Indian," said Gladdie. "That right?"

"Yeah, that's right," I said.

"What kinda Indian you be?" DeWayne asked, looking kinda impressed with this information.

I caught Lonnie's eye for just a second and he nodded slowly.

"Don't know, really. Canadian Indian, I guess. Was raised in foster homes and never got to know where I was from. Got taken away real young and I don't really remember anything before I was in foster homes." I felt all the shame and nervousness I always felt when I had to explain my history.

"Damn. Sounds like Indians are the niggers now," Truman added, offering me a smoke, which I tucked behind the other ear while they laughed. "You don't know your family?"

"No. No need now, though. I'm old enough to be my own person."

"Shit, man. Everybody be needin' fam'ly!" Lonnie said. "You know, I hearda this guy runnin' around tryin' to tell folks he be Hawaiian? A man can't be his own person if the man don't know himself. Right, Mama?"

"Thass right." Delma reached over and patted my hand. "My kids have all known their fam'ly history ever since they was old enough to listen. No matter what happens to them now, they always gonna be proud of who they are. Always."

"Must be kinda nice to have that. You all seem so together. Like a family's gotta be, I guess. Me, I never had that. You're lucky. Real lucky." I took a long swallow of beer. I wasn't so sure about talking so openly to strangers.

Maddie winked at me and dragged me out of my chair onto the dance floor, where we shuffled around to a song called "Caledonia" that's still one of my favorites to this day. The family whistled and pointed and laughed all the time we were out there, and I remember feelin' like I was welcome and it felt real good.

We danced and laughed and talked all night long. The music got better'n better and by the time it was over we were all kinda drunk and the whole lot of us headed over to Delma's in a cab with more beer and a couple pizzas, singing the blues all out of tune, clapping hands and laughing. Maddie was being real friendly and when I caught her brothers looking us over I felt kinda scared until Truman, who was bigger'n Lonnie by about three inches and thirty pounds, started laughing and pointing our way.

"Lookee here, lookee here," he said, his big head bobbing up and down. "Maddie's 'bout to learn 'bout Indian Affairs!"

"Damn," Lonnie said, "snuck right in there, di'n' he? Gotta watch them Arapahos!"

Hanging around Delma's got to be a usual thing. When my money started running out and finding a job got to be almost impossible, she invited me to stay there. By this time she was calling me her "brown baby" and I started to feel like a part of the family and it sure was a good feeling. I told them about the foster homes and how even though you always had full run of things you never ever felt like people really wanted you around. Talked about being a loner and how it felt better most of the time to be moving around instead of sticking somewhere and settling down like other people. Talked about all the empty Christmases or of being shipped off to another home for a couple weeks while whoever I was staying with went on summer vacation. Talked about how all those things leave little holes in your gut and how eventually they all turn into one great big black hole in the middle of your belly and how on lonely nights it still felt like the wind was blowing and whistling through me. Told them lotsa things I had never told anyone before, and Delma's eyes used to get all shiny and she'd hug me real warm and tight and tell me it was gonna be all right.

Never talked about Indians though. And I never tried to hang around with any. I was taking Lonnie's hint in the pub that first night and was working real hard on becoming black. About six months after I'd met them all I walked into the house with a brand-new sixty buck permed Afro. I had it all picked out and it was like a big curly black halo around my head.

"Sheeee-it!" Truman yelled when he saw me. "My man got hisself a natural. Superfly lookin', downtown brown now!"

"Damn," said Lonnie.

"Shit," said Delma.

Gladdie, Maddie and DeWayne just shook their heads and smiled and everyone started bumping and jiving to a Buddy Guy record while I studied my new look in the mirror. It wasn't too long after that that I started dressing like Lonnie and his brothers, adopting their strut and mannerisms and really feeling like I'd found where I wanted to be in life. The blues was everywhere and I was liking it and my new friends more and more. People in the clubs were talking to me and about me now. I was getting the eyeball from women, and being an Indian was the furthest thing from my mind again. I walked around with a head fulla blues, Motown and soul and feeling like I'd come home.

One day while Lonnie and I were heading for the pool hall two scruffy Indians on a corner asked us for change. They smelled of cheap wine and were already unsteady on their feet. I took a step back and looked away over top of their heads, feeling safer behind my mirrored shades. Lonnie handed them a couple bucks and we headed off with their "thank you, brother" ringing in our ears.

"Gonna have to face it someday, my man," Lonnie said, pointing back over his shoulder with his thumb. "Can't run away from who you really are all your life, y'know."

"Who's runnin', man? I'm doin' what I want with my life, okay? Besides, what have those dudes got to say that would matter to me anyway?"

"Never know till you find out, will ya?"

"Find out what?"

"Shit, man, I don't know. Indian stuff. What it's like out there livin' Indian, man. Maybe the brothers came up the same as you or maybe they know somethin' about it all you ain't ever figured out. I don't know."

"I don't know either, man. All I know is that I've been around this town now about a year and a half which is longer'n I ever stayed anywhere and I don't wanna be anywhere else. I don't wanna be any*where* or any*body* else, okay? You got a problem with that?"

"Ain't never a problem, you know that. I'm just sayin' this 'cause I think you be missin' out on sumpthin' important, thass all, man. Thass all. Don't be goin' all Arapaho on me, brother."

"Fine. That's it then."

"S'it, man."

"Okay."

"Okay."

But it wasn't it really. The more I thought about that conversation the more I started to see the truth in it. Trouble was, I had no idea of how to start up talking to any Indians. There were lots around and I knew the Indian bars but there was no way that I had any clue of how to get to know any people. They still kinda embarrassed me. I was moving a little pot for Lonnie now for extra cash and was wearing some really bad-looking threads as well as always having a few bucks. Didn't wanna be seen talking with or hanging out with scruffy people and I figured Indians were all the same, 'cept for me. I'd found myself and for all I knew then there was no goin' back.

But fate has a way of dealing out the cards with the deck stacked in its favor. Plans and dreams and stuff can really get washed away by one fickle deal, and that's kinda what happened with me. I'd gotten to know a few big-time movers through Lonnie and they all kinda liked me on accounta I knew how to keep my mouth shut. They thought I was kind of a novelty on accounta I was acting more black than most of them and could party down with the best of them. So it wasn't hard to get trusted after a while with important knowledge.

About two years after I'd moved in with Delma, me'n a mover named Curtis were trying to dump an ounce of Curtis's cocaine one Friday night. We were moving from club to club, talking to a lotta people and having a pretty good time running a little business. Around midnight we hit a club on the Yonge Street Strip and Curtis bopped around the tables while I leaned against the bar with a beer. After a while he came back and asked me to hold the coke while he walked outside to talk to a guy.

Didn't wanna take a chance on getting rolled for his dope, I guess.

It wasn't long before a flashy white guy came up and bought me a beer. He was all decked out in a silk three-piecer and acting real friendly with people, so I figured he was cool.

"You holdin'?" he whispered.

"Who's askin'? Somebody knows you, slick?"

"Hey, man," he said with his hands up, "just askin'. I heard you might have some coke is all."

"Yeah, I'm playin'. You wanna score?"

"Sure, man. Make my night. How much you got?"

"How much you want, man?"

"I'll take everything you got, brother."

"Got a little less'n an O.Z. on me. You got long enough green to cover that, slick?"

"Hey, I got better'n that, bro'," he said, whipping out a badge and throwing me up against the bar. "When I said I'll take everything you got I meant I'll take everything you got. You're busted, pal."

There's a rule on the street that you never take anyone down with you when you go, so I never said a thing about Curtis or the fact that the dope wasn't mine. They nailed me with possession with intent to traffic and gave me five years. I was twenty-two. Delma was shocked and cried when the sentence came down and Lonnie just sat there shaking his head and staring at me with tears in his eyes. The rest of the family never came to the trial but they all wrote me while I was away, told me all about their lives and how it was going and tried to keep my spirits up. Keeping the spirits up was a hard go, but I never had a rough time in there really. I managed to get classified as a minimum-security risk and was sent to a work farm outside Peterborough, where I did farm work and walked in the fields a lot. The only bumpy times came when the Native Brotherhood guys started asking about me and where I was from. After a while they just left me alone when I wouldn't talk and I hung with a couple black guys that were in there with me. I read a lot and fell into a quiet loner kinda space and people just let me do my time.

Now if fate's got a way of dealing fickle hands every now and then, well, there's a magic in the universe that has a way of working as well. There I was, doing a five-year stretch, busy being black and planning on getting out and going back to Delma's, finding a job and forgetting all about drugs and penitentiaries and bein' a high roller. Well, that magic was working overtime and one day it arrived all unannounced and funky.

Mail call at the farm was Tuesdays and Thursdays and I was getting used to a letter from Toronto every week or so. I'd done about two years by this time and I was already counting the weeks to my discharge date. By the time I got out I would have served a little less than three years with good behavior. In the pen you count your time by calendars instead of days, so I had a little more'n a whole calendar to go, but that was considered short time by most people in there. Anyway, I was expecting a letter from Lonnie and was glad to hear my name called for mail pickup.

I was handed a heavy brown envelope that had stuff sliding around inside and the postmark said someplace called Kenora, Ontario. When I got back to my bunk and dumped the contents, a thick letter fell out with a whole mess of pictures of people I didn't know. They were all Indians and they were all smiling at the camera with these big goofy grins and looking happier'n hell. A couple of pictures were of a guy who looked an awful lot like me without the Afro and there was something about the country in the background that rang something inside me. Kinda like the effect the blues had on me.

It was from a guy named Stanley Raven and he said he was my brother. He went on and on about how I was taken away when I was a little kid and how my whole family had searched for me through the years but how the Children's Aid wouldn't give them any information. He told me about how he'd gone through school and gotten a degree in social work and went back to our home reserve of White Dog to work and how he managed to talk a sympathetic manager into looking up my old file. He got the address of the last foster home I'd been in and somehow managed to track me down care of the Ontario Attorney General's department.

He told me that I had a whole herd of aunts and uncles, grandparents and cousins that missed me and loved me and wanted me home. He wrote about my brother Jackie and sister Jane, about my mother and how she'd never given up believing all these years that her baby would come home one day and about my father who'd passed away really young but who loved me too even though he never ever saw me again. He told me about the country there, about my language, a little history of our tribe and the White Dog band. And he talked about how he felt lost for years until he'd gotten back home and started living with his people and family again. He said that if I was feeling the same way in my life that maybe going home was a good idea. Then he invited me to write to him and tell him about my life and asked me to come home once I got out.

All the time I was reading about myself and who I was and where I came from the less and less I could feel the cold wind that always been whistling through me. Looking at those people in the photographs, I got a feeling I couldn't label and I felt like crying for the first time in a long time. I must have reread that letter a thousand times over the next few weeks and when Lonnie and Delma came to visit me I told them about it and showed them the pictures of the people who were my family.

"Oh my brown baby," Delma said with her eyes filling up with tears. "Someone got a lotta love for you to track you down after twenty years. You got a home. You got fam'ly. You gotta go there. Much as we want you back with us you gotta go there."

"Yeah, my man," Lonnie said, looking at the pictures and shaking his head. "These definitely you fam'ly. Got the same Sasquatch cheekbones you got. Can't run from this one, brother."

"Yeah, but what do I do when I get there? I don't know anything about no bush country. What do I look like, Nanook of the goddamn north or somethin'?"

"You look like a man needsa home," Delma said. "You always did look that way. Can't be movin' around forever. You gotta find yourself some roots and it's sad to say . . . but they ain't with us. Your roots are callin' you right now and if you run from this you'll be runnin' from ev'rythin' forever'n ever."

"S'right, man," Lonnie said. "I mean, I love you like a brother, man, but you ain't my brother, you dig? This Stanley dude, man, he's your brother. I can't be that for you and you can't pretend that I can now that you got this. You gotta go there, man. You been lookin' a long time tryin' to find your place, man, all that Hawaiian bullshit and all. Now's your time."

"So what do I do?"

"Write the brother, man!" Lonnie said, banging on the table. "Write the brother."

"And what do I say when I do?"

"Tell him the same things you told us," Delma said. "Tell him all about where you been and what you felt like roamin' aroun' lookin' for yourself. He's your brother, he looked for you, you owe him that much, no matter what you decide."

"Okay. I'll try."

"Right on, man. Right on. And we always be your

fam'ly too, man. Ain't nothin' gonna change that. You always got a place with us, man. Always."

Delma said quietly, "You fill up my door anytime, hear?"

"I hear," I said, and I remember thinking that a guy had to be pretty damn lucky to have a family like this and wondering if the Ojibway family I'd just found out about would even come close to this one. "I'll write him and if things work out I'll go there as soon as I get out."

"Way to go, Arapaho," Lonnie said. "Way to go."

Well, it turns out that writing to Stanley was easier said than done. I must have tore up a ton of foolscap trying to introduce myself and not sound like some fool. About a month later I finally got a letter sent away and I gotta tell you I was nervous as hell until the day the reply came back.

Stanley said there was a room being set aside for me at his house and that everyone at White Dog was excited about me coming home. He told me not to worry too much about it because everyone there knew about jail and all, that I didn't speak Ojibway and that I probably needed a lot of time to get used to the place. Then he told me that of all of us kids I was the only one who'd disappeared, that my brothers and sisters had all grown up in the White Dog area and had known my family all their lives. They'd had to go through the foster care system too but had been fortunate enough to stay together and get to know our family. When they were old enough to leave they headed right back to White Dog. I was the only mystery and they were sure looking forward to seeing me again.

He wrote me every month. Long rambling letters about all kindsa things regarding White Dog and the Ojibway life there. The more I read about it the more I got intrigued and I was actually looking forward to the visit by the time my discharge date started rolling up. He knew my date and said if I grabbed the first bus north everyone would be there to meet it when it rolled into Kenora, which was the nearest town with a bus station.

Being free after three long years of even minimum security is sure one hell of a good buzz. There's nothing like having some goon open the door for you and kick your ass out after dreaming about it night after night. It was early summer and the sun was shining and I felt like anything and everything was possible. I was twenty-five. Being in my prime and all and having missed the pleasures of female company for three whole calendars, it was only natural I guess for me to roll into the nearest town for a good night out. Turned out to be about three nights out and in that time I managed to pouff out the Afro a little, score a few clothes and some tunes for the trip and, of course, satisfy the young man's urges.

I also managed to miss my greeting party in Kenora by three whole days.

As the bus piled deeper and deeper into the northern part of Ontario a lot of feelings churned around inside me. I was scared, feeling really outta my element looking out at all the rocks and trees and lakes. I was feeling embarrassed to be meeting a bunch of strangers who knew about me being in jail and I was nervous about fitting in. But more than anything, I remember looking out that window of that bus, watching the landscape flow by and feeling somehow like I knew this country. I'd been raised in southern Ontario around farmland and skyscrapers, but something inside me told me that I knew, really knew this country outside the window. It was spooky and the more I watched it roll by the more that feeling settled into my belly.

Of course, the closer I got to Kenora, the more the older, more familiar attitude started to take control of me again. I was gonna show these backwoods Indians how you could survive in the city. I was a downtown brown, hip, slick and cool, and there was no way they were gonna make me look bad. I'd been out in the world and done some things and that gave me some kinda advantage over these hillbillies right off the hop. By the time that bus started rounding the long curve at the town's east end I was decked out in my finest threads and ready.

The huge greeting I was expecting never happened, me being three days late and all. So I climbed off the bus, walked into the empty terminal located in some alley downtown and stood there feeling like maybe this hadn't been such a hot idea after all. I was glad I had my shades on because people were just gawking away like crazy. Guess they'd never seen a slick downtown guy like me getting off the bus in their town before. I had my Afro all picked out to about three feet around my head, mirrored shades, a balloon-sleeved yellow silk shirt with the long tapered collar, lime green baggy pants with the little cuffs and my hippest pair of platform shoes, all brown with silver spangles, and three gold chains around my neck. I was giving off the odor of fifty-dollar perfume and bopping up and down like there was a Chicago blues band in my head. I just figured they couldn't help themselves, couldn't keep their eyes off me.

I strolled on out to what looked like a taxi stand and rapped on the window to wake up the fat white guy at the wheel.

"Say, my man," I said, all smiley and nice, "I'm lookin' for White Dog. Can you get me there?"

He stared at me all slack-jawed and eyes wide open for about a whole minute before he started stammering away at me, little flecks of spittle flying off his lips.

"Sh-sh-sh-sure. I-I-I-I can get you there right away. L-l-l-l-long trip though. C-c-cost you s-s-sixty dollars."

"Sixty dollars! Look, man, I'll just find me another hack that'll get me there cheaper."

"N-n-n-n-no cheaper. S-s-sixty's f-flat rate, m-m-mister."

"Damn. Ain't gonna be economical bein' no Indian, is it?" I said and hopped into the back.

The cabbie said White Dog was about eighty kilometres outta town and part of the sixty was paying him for coming back empty since not a lotta people had enough cash to hire a ride into town. He kept staring at me in the mirror.

"Look, man," I said. "What? What you lookin' at? Ain't you never seen no Indian before or somethin'?"

"S-s-s-sorry," he said, "b-b-but I ain't seen anybody round here l-l-l-like you."

"Well, get used to it, slick. My name's Raven, man, and I'm just coming home to White Dog for a visit, so you be seein' my brown ass a bit, dig?"

"R-r-raven? Y-you don't look like no R-r-raven."

"What? I ain't black enough for no Raven or somethin'? Shit, man, I said my name's Raven, my name's Raven, all right?"

"H-h-hey, no offense, you just don't look like the r-r-r-resta them, that's all."

"Fine," I said, looking out the window. "Fine, I can live with that. What's with your mouth anyway, man? You're stutterin' aroun' like Porky Pig or somethin'."

"S-s-sorry," he said, giving me one last wide-eyed look before grabbing the wheel with both hands and staring straight ahead at the road. "It's j-just that, well, you're not quite what we're used to seein' from our our Indians, y-you know?"

"Our Indians? What's that supposed to mean? *Our* Indians?"

"No offense. I-I just meant the ones from around here. That's all."

"What are they? Like the Clampetts or somethin'?"

"Well, not like you, that's for sure. Not like you."

"Make you kinda nervous, does it? Seein' an Indian like me?"

"Nothin' I'm used to, that's for sure."

"Well, relax, my man. Maybe if I hang out here long enough you gonna be seein' lotsa brothers lookin' like this. Maybe what this place needs is a good shot of downtown."

He just looked at me one last time in the mirror and then concentrated on the road, which was just beginning to do its twist and turn to White Dog.

I'm used to it now having been back five years but that first day I wondered where the hell I was landing once we approached the reserve. First there was a big sign on the side of the road with about a hundred bullet holes in it that said: YOU ARE ENTERING THE WHITE DOG INDIAN RESERVE. NO ADMITTANCE. VISITORS REPORT TO THE BAND OFFICE. NO ACCESS WITHOUT PERMISSION.

Then about a quarter mile after that was a sign that read: KEEWATIN'S GENERAL STORE! WHERE NO STOCK ISN'T A PROBLEM! GOOD FOOD! GET GAS! NO LINEUPS! BIG ED KEEWATIN PROP.

We rounded the final curve into the townsite and I swear it looked like something outta a foreign documentary. Houses were perched on toppa rocky outcroppings and they all looked about ready to tumble down. There wasn't any siding on a lotta them and it looked like most were just sitting there on the land with no basements, plumbing or furnaces. They were all about a quarter mile apart and there was a lotta dead-looking automobiles parked everywhere. Reminded me of what Lonnie described the Detroit ghettos to be like. There was scruffy kids running around everywhere, shirtless and wearing rolled-down black gumboots, and the occasional old person walking around lookin' tired and glum. Out back of all the houses was a big lake and there were lotsa shaky-lookin' docks around with boats tied up to them. There was a big red brick schoolhouse and a few modern houses all hunched together close by and further away was a buncha aluminum trailers too. First thing I noticed was the missing power and telephone poles, and I saw someone behind one of the houses walking up from the dock with a five-gallon pail with water slopping over the sides. There were outdoor johnnies behind the houses too and I worried about how I was gonna get the slivers outta my ass. It was the only time in my life I ever thought constipation might be a blessing. Everyone looked up as the cab pulled in and by the time we pulled up in front of the store there were about fifty Indians all heading towards us. Kinda reminded me of those movies I used to watch as a kid. One minute they weren't there and the next minute they were everywhere. It was true after all. Indians did just pop outta nowhere.

They were all craning their necks real good trying to get a glimpse of who it was behind the tinted glass, and it gave me a chance to check out the locals and try to see any faces I recognized from the pictures Stanley'd sent. Seeing all those brown faces craning and squinty-eyed reminded me of something you see in National Geographic and I laughed while I handed the cabbie his dough. I could hear them chattering in Ojibway, laughing and rustling around. When I opened the door they all stepped back in one motion like a gumbooted chorus line.

The silence was deafening. As soon as I flung one lime green spangly platform-shoed leg out the door there was a loud gasp all around the cab. And when I stepped out there was about fifty heads all leaning in gazing at my yellow balloon-sleeved shirt and you could hear the sounds of a few dozen sniffers catching a whiff of my fifty-dollar scent. Four or five sets of hands were scrunching up my Afro and I could hear giggles from the kids as everyone was pressing closer and closer towards me. When the cab pulled away in a flurry of gravel, they surrounded me. It was true after all. Indians did love to surround you.

There was another loud gasp when I took off my shades and smiled all around.

"S'app'nin'?" I said, bobbing my head and reaching out for hands to shake.

"Ho-leeee!" someone said.

"Wow!"

"Ever look like Stanley!"

"Ever, eh?"

"Ho-leeee!" said about three together.

Just about then a tall guy with a long ponytail reached through the crowd all excited like and started pushing people back amidst grumbling and something that sounded like cussing. When he made it up to me he stopped and looked at me with shiny eyes and kinda reaching out with his arms then pulling back, reaching out and pulling back. Finally, tears started pouring down his face. Everyone got real quiet all of a sudden and when I looked at this guy it was almost like looking into a mirror except for there being a ponytail where the Afro should have been and a definite absence of funky threads. He stared at me for what seemed like an eternity with all kindsa things working across his face, and when he spoke it was a whisper.

"Garnet," he said. "Garnet. Garnet. Garnet."

He reached out and touched me finally, one soft little grab of the shoulder, and then he collapsed into my arms sobbing like a kid while everyone around us moved in a little closer too.

"Twenty-two years," he said, sobbing. "Twenty-two years, my brother. Twenty-two years."

I was crying by this time too and all the faces around me went kinda outta focus through the tears but I could tell we weren't the only ones breaking down and I remember thinking I wasn't exactly being downtown cool, but right then it didn't really matter. Holding my brother in my arms was unlike anything I'd ever felt, and as we cried I could feel that lifelong feeling of wind whistling through my guts getting quieter and quieter.

He looked up finally, threw his arm around my shoulder and turned to the crowd.

"This is my . . . my . . . my brother," he said, choking up and sniffling. "The one that disappeared. He's home."

People started coming up and shaking my hand and smiling and touching me and there were tears everywhere as I heard the names of aunts and uncles and cousins and just plain White Dog folk for the first time. Stanley stood off to the side looking over at me and smiling, smiling and smiling. After a while they all moved away and started looking me over again.

"Ho-leeee!" said a voice.

"Wow!"

"Sure he's a Raven?" someone asked. "Looks like a walkin' fishin' lure or somethin'!"

"Yeah, that hair's a good reminder to the kids 'bout foolin' round with the electircal!"

"An' what's that smell? Smell like that should have fruit flies all around his head!"

"Damndest-lookin' Indyun I ever saw! Looks kinda like that singer we seen on TV that time. What's 'is name now? James Brown? Yeah. We got us one James Brown-lookin' Indian here!"

"Come on," Stanley said once people started moving away. "There's a buncha people up at my house been feelin' kinda down 'cause they figured you weren't comin'. Seein' you's gonna make 'em all feel a whole lot better. You okay?"

"Yeah," I said. "Least, I think so. It's kinda weird, man."

"Yeah," he said, "I guess so. Wanted to ease you in slow but you weren't on the bus. What happened?"

"Nothin', man," I said. "Don't matter."

"Least you're here now," he said. "That's all we wanted. Took a long time to find you."

"Tell me about it," I said. "Tell me about it."

*They been comin' for our kids long time now. Nothin' new. Not for us. They been comin' on the sly for years. I always thought it was us Indyuns s'posed to do all the sneakin' and creepin' around. But those white people, boy, they got us beat when it come to sneakin' through the bushes. Maybe we taught 'em too much. Heh, heh, heh.*

*The boy's story's not much diff'rent from what we seen around here for a long time. Sure, in them movies us Indyuns are always runnin' off with children and raisin' them up savage. Give 'em funny-soundin' names like Found on the Prairie, Buffalo Dog or somethin'. I always figured they shoulda called 'em Wind in His Pants, Plenty Bingos, Busts Up Laughing or Sneaks Off Necking. Somethin' really Indyun. Heh, heh, heh. But in the real world it's the white people kept on sneakin' off with our kids. Guess they figured they were doin' us a favor. Gonna give them kids the benefit of good white teachin', raise them up proper. Only thing they did was create a whole new kinda Indyun. We used to call them Apples before we really knew what was happenin'. Called 'em Apples on accounta they're red on the outside and white on the inside. It was a cruel joke on accounta it was never their fault. Only those not livin' with respect use that term now.*

*But we lost a generation here. In the beginning it was the missionary schools. Residential schools they called them. Me I was there. They come and got me when I was five and took me and a handful of others. The boy's mother was one of them. They took us and cut off our hair, dressed us in baggy clothes so we all looked the same, told us our way of livin' and prayin' was wrong and evil. Got beat up for speakin' Indyun. If we did that we'd all burn in hell they told us. Me I figured I was already brown why not burn the rest of the way, so I ran away. Came back here. Lots of others stayed though. Lots never ever came back and them that did were real diff'rent. Got the Indyun all scraped off their insides. Like bein' Indyun was a fungus or somethin'. They scraped it all off and never put nothin' there to replace it but a bunch of fear and hurt. Seen lotsa kids walkin' around like old people after a while. Them schools were the beginning of how we started losin' our way as a people.*

*Then they came with their Children's Aid Society. Said our way was wrong and kids weren't gettin' what they needed, so they took 'em away. Put 'em in homes that weren't Indyun. Some got shipped off long ways. Never made it back yet. Disappeared. Got raised up all white but still carryin' brown skin. Hmmpfh. See, us we know you can't make a beaver from a bear. Nature don't work that way. Always gotta be what the Creator made you to be. Biggest right we all got as human bein's is the right to know who we are. Right to be who we are. But them they never see that. Always thinkin' they know what's best for people. But it's not their fault. When you quit lookin' around at nature you quit learnin' the natural way. The world gets to be somethin' you gotta control so you're always fightin' it. Us we never fight the world. We look around lots, find its rhythm, its heartbeat, and learn to walk that way. Concrete ain't got no rhythm, and steel never learned to breathe. You spend time in the bush and on the land, you learn the way of the bush and the way of the land. The natural way. Way of the universe. Spend time surrounded by concrete and steel, you learn their way too, I guess.*

*Back when I was a boy there was still a strong bunch of us livin' the old way. Lot of us crossed over since then and with those of us who's left maybe only a handful still practicin' the old way. Rest are Catholic and some other whiteman way. S'okay though. They're still our people no matter how they pray on accounta prayin's the most important thing anyway. Long as there's some kinda prayer there's some kinda hope. But there's not many of us old traditional people left walkin' around. Not many for the young ones to come to no more. That's why you hear more English than Anishanabe around here. Some other places too. Other tribes, other Indyuns. S'why it's so important for old guys like me to be passin' on what we know. I'm not talkin' about bringin' back the buffalo hunt or goin' back to the wigwam. I'm talkin' about passin' on the* spirit *of all those things. If you got the spirit of the old way in you, well, you can handle most anythin' this new world got to throw around. The spirit of that life's our traditions. Things like respect, honesty, kindness and sharin'. Those are our traditions. Livin' that old tribal way taught people those things. That they needed each other just to survive. Same as now. Lookin' around at nature taught the old ones that. Nature's fulla respect, honesty, kindness and sharin'. S'way of the world, I guess.*

*But lotsa our people think that just learnin' the culture's gonna be their salvation. Gonna make 'em Indyun. Lotsa young ones out there learnin' how to beat the pow-wow drum and sing songs. Learnin' the dances and movin' around on the pow-wow trail ev'ry summer. Lotsa people growin' hair and goin' to see ceremony. Think they're more Indyun that way. S'good to see. But there's still lotsa people out there still drinkin', beatin' each other up, raisin' their kids mean. All kindsa things. That's not our way. So just doin' the culture things don't make you no Indyun. Lotsa white people doin' our culture too now and they're never gonna be Indyun. Always just gonna be lookin' like people that can't dance. Heh, heh, heh.*

*What I'm tryin' to say is tradition gives strength to the culture. Makes it alive. Gotta know why you dance 'steada just how. It's tradition that makes you Indyun. Sing and dance forever but if you're not practicin' tradition day by day you're not really bein' Indyun. Old man told me one time he said, the very last time you got up in the mornin' and said a quiet prayer of thanks for the day you been given was the very last time you were an Indyun. Then he said, the very last time you got handed some food and bowed your head and said a prayer of thanks and asked for the strength you got from that food to be used to help someone around you, well, that was the very last time you were an Indyun too. And he told me he said, the very last time you did somethin' for someone without bein' asked, bein' thanked or tellin' about it was the very last time you were an Indyun. See, it's all respect, kindness, honesty and sharin'. Built right in. Do that all the time and boy, you just dance and sing up a real storm next time. Heh, heh, heh.*

*That's what we gotta pass on. 'Cause tradition'll keep you goin' when you're livin' it. Us we need to remember these things.*

*Keep 'em alive inside me. Live 'em so they stay strong. Lotsa kids comin' back nowadays really need to be shown. Tough thing to do when the kids are forty-four, twenty-five or whatever.*

*Nowadays the whiteman comes in lotsa diff'rent ways. Oh, they still come with their schools and their foster homes, but we got some of our own teachers and social workers now, so kinda gettin' better there. But they still come for the kids. They come with their TV, money, big inventions and ideas. They come with big promises 'bout livin' in the world, with their politics and their welfare. They come with their rap music, break dancin' and funny ways of dressin'. All kinds of shiny things. Kids get all excited, funny in the head 'bout things, wanna go chasin' after all that stuff. Tradition? Ah, it's just borin' stuff for old guys like me can't rap dance. Somethin' you gotta do when you ain't got no other choice. That's how they come nowadays. On the sly. Harder for kids to come back from these things than from them schools or foster homes sometimes.*

*That's why we gotta pass it on. Always gotta be someone around who knows. Always gotta be someone around to catch 'em when they land here all owl-eyed and scared, askin' questions, tryin' to find if they belong here still. If they wanna stick around. Always gotta be someone who knows the kindness built into tradition. Ease 'em back slow. Got the Indyun all scraped offa their insides, carryin' 'round big hurts an' bruises. Poke around too much you hurt 'em an' they run away. So you bring 'em back from the inside out. Nothin' in this world ever grew from the outside in. That's why I help the boy understand. He learned 'bout respect before he ever learned to sing or dance. Learned to be kind and share before he learned to tan a hide or how to hunt. Learned to be honest before I let him be a storyteller. Learned about bein' Indyun, about himself. That way he'll survive anything.*

*He looked funny enough when he got here wearin' all those strange things and havin' a head of hair looked like a cat been through the dryer, smellin' like fruit and talkin' funny. Guess if he could survive walkin' around lookin' and smellin' like that, learnin' to live an' learn off the land was gonna be simple. Heh, heh, heh.*

The first thing most people notice about us Indians is how we're laughing most of the time. It doesn't really matter whether we're all dressed up in traditional finery or in bush jackets and gumboots, seems like a smile and big roaring guffaw is everywhere with us. Used to be that non-Indians thought we were just simple. You know, typical kinda goofy-grinning lackeys riding out to get shot offa our horses by the wagon train folks. Or standing around on a corner in some city bumming smokes an' change but yukking it up anyway. But the more they stick around the more they realize that Indians have a real good sense of humor and it's that humor more than anything that's allowed them to survive all the crap that history threw their way. Keeper says laughin's about as Indian as bannock and lard. Most of the teaching legends are filled with humor on accounta Keeper says when people are laughing they're really listening hard to what you're saying. Guess the old people figured that was the best way to pass on learning.

Once you stop to remember what it was you were laughing at you remember the whole story, and that's how the teachings were passed on. Guess if it was thirty below and I was hunched around some little fire in a wigwam I'd wanna be laughing too instead of listening to some big deep talk.

Teasing's big around here too. You get lotta teasing from people on accounta teasing's really a way of showing affection for someone and like me at first, a lotta people have a hard time figuring that out. Get all insulted and run away. But once you figure that out it's a lotta fun being around a bunch of Indians.

When Stanley and me got to his cabin that first day I was expecting a big warm family kind of scene like on "The Waltons." I figured there'd be a big spread on the table, maybe a little wine, music and a party happening. Instead there was about ten people sitting around drinking tea they were pouring out of a big black old-fashioned metal pot on a pot-bellied stove in the middle of the room. There weren't any decorations or anything unless you can call six or seven pairs of wool socks hung over the stove pipes decorations.

They all looked up as we walked in. The silence was deafening.

"Ho! Whatchu got there, Stanley?" said a big gap-toothed guy with a brushcut. "Not Halloween yet, is it?"

"Ho-wah!" said a large fat woman with gumboots, a kerchief around her head and smoking a pipe. "Thought he was coming from T'rana, not Disneyland!"

"Reee-leee!" said another woman. "Who'd you say adopted him? Liberace?"

"Ahh, he's just dressed fer huntin'," said an old man with so many wrinkles he looked like he was folded up wet and left overnight. "Wanna make sure he don't get mistook fer no deer."

"Deer? Maybe get mistook for the northern lights but sure ain't nobody gonna be thinkin' he's a deer no matter how dark it gets," said a tall spindly woman busy pouring herself another tea.

Stanley eased me into the center of the room with his hand on my shoulder and I could feel the pressure of it getting a little firmer the more nervous I got. Like he wanted to hold me from bolting for the door, which was exactly the thought going through my mind at the time. He smiled at me and waved at a large round woman leaning in the doorway and staring real hard at us both.

"Your sister," was all he said. Or at least I think that's all he said because I got swept up in her big brown arms and disappeared for about five minutes. I could feel her breathing deeper and deeper as she hugged me and when she finally let me surface for air she was crying real quiet and smiling at the same time. She was a lot wider than me, but it's kinda spooky when you look at someone you swear you've never seen before and you can see your own eyes looking back at you. I didn't doubt for a minute that this woman was my sister.

"Hi, bro'," she said. "I'm Jane. Do you remember me at all?"

"No," I said real quiet. "No, I don't think I do."

"S'okay," she said. "S'okay. I remember you real good. Little bigger than before but I remember you, all right."

"Ahh, get the hell outta the way, Jane, and let us meet this boy kept us waitin' three days and twenty years anyway!" said an energetic little guy. "How you doin', T'rana? I'm yer uncle Buddy."

Well, they all lined up and for the next half hour or so I was introduced to my uncles Gilbert, Archie and Joe, aunties Myrna and Ella, Chief Isaac McDonald and wife, Bertha, and the wrinkled-up old guy who said his name was Keeper and who left right away with Buddy.

Two things really got my attention that day. The first was the way they just seemed to treat me like I was someone they'd always known. Like the twenty years didn't matter to them or the way I was dressed, the Afro or anything. It was like I was already a part of their lives and let's get on with it all. The second thing was the absence of my mother and my other brother, Jackie. Of all the things I was scared of, meeting my mother after all that time was the biggest and I wondered why she wasn't there. Anyway, after all the introductions were over everybody just visited with each other and it was like the excitement was over and life was back to normal for them. Me, I was pretty confused.

"Take a walk, Garnet, you, me'n Jane," Stanley said. "Only here's a pair of shoes to wear around till you get some of your own. Those heels'll kill you round here."

I wasn't real surprised when they fit perfectly, Stanley being the same size and all. He waved to everyone as we walked out the door and they all just waved and went back to their conversations. I shook my head and fell in between the two of them.

"Okay, bro'?" Jane asked and put her arm around my shoulders.

The words sounded strange to my ears. I mean, up to then "bro'" was just something you tossed around like pal or chum, buddy or dude. Now all of a sudden it had a whole different meaning. "Yeah. Yeah. I just feel weird about all this."

"S'okay," Stanley said. "S'okay. Ev'ryone's been waitin' for you and they all really want you to stay with us. Me too."

"Me too," said Jane. "Me too."

"I don't know. I don't know whether I can get into all this, man. I mean, I been city all my life, y'know? I guess I'm not too sure I can handle it."

"Nothin' to handle," Stanley said. "Might be hard for you to understand, Garnet, but people been dreamin' 'bout this day for a long time and they held onto you all the time you were away. People been prayin' and makin' offerin's and that old government guy, Cary Stevens, who opened your file is like some kinda local hero around here now. So you don't need to handle yourself around us. Just be here, man."

"S'right," Jane said and held my hand. "Guaranteed you're a funny-lookin' Indyun right now, kinda look more like a parakeet than a Raven, but this is your home, these are your people and your family. I held you when you were just a baby. I watched you learn to crawl'n walk. You belong with us. Settle in for a bit. Let us know you."

"Know me? Hell, I don't even know me."

"S'what I mean," said Stanley. "Here you don't have to be anybody or anything. People gonna be feedin' you and spoilin' you just like you're a little kid for a long time. So be a kid. Look around, learn, let them take care of you."

We stood there awhile in silence. The three of us taking turns glancing at each other before turning our heads to pretend we were studying something in the distance. The day was one of those bright, cloudless, windless days we get around here every once in a while and every day like that these last five years reminds me of that one moment my first day home. We started walking again without comment.

"What're you thinkin', little brother?" Jane asked finally.

"Thinking? Lots at the same time, I guess."

"Me too," Stanley said, stooping to pick up a flat rock. He skimmed it over the lake. "We used to do this."

"What?" I asked.

"This." He picked up another rock. "The four of us. You, me, Jackie'n Jane."

He cupped the rock in his hand and with a spinning sidearm motion hurled it in a high, wide arc over the water. The wild spinning of the rock continued right through its climb and down into its entry into the water. It hit with a dull plop instead of a splash. The sound made me laugh.

They were both grinning at me.

"You always did that," Jane said.

"What?"

"Every time those rocks landed in the water you always giggled just like that. I remember. You always got a big kick out of that sound."

"When was this?"

"You were only about three," Stanley said, sending another rock spinning into the air. "We'd go for walks in the bush and wind up at this little creek had a big beaver pond in it. The four of us. You'd sit on a log and watch as we chucked rocks into that beaver pond. Jackie was the one who first made that sound and when you heard it you laughed just like you did just now. Cracked us all up. We rolled around on the shore of that beaver pond and laughed till our guts were sore. So we got into this kinda contest makin' them sounds to find out who could make you laugh the most."

"Yeah. And Jackie'n Stanley even worked up a scorin' system. Had somethin' to do with height, I think. The higher you could make that rock go spinning up and still get that ploppin' sound, the more points you got. I think I won."

"You never won," Stanley said. "Was me! Losin' your mem'ry in your old age?" He ducked Jane's playful slap.

"Anyway, little bro', you just kinda sat there'n laughed all the time. Useta make us all real happy. Funny how you laugh the same way after all this time," Jane said.

"You guys remember all this like it was yesterday or something," I said quietly.

"Hey-yuh," said Stanley.

"Yes," Jane said, quietly too.

"Wish I could. I don't remember anything. It's weird. I believe you and everything, but there's this part of me that thinks there's some kind of scam going on here and I'm the patsy."

"There's no scam, Garnet," Stanley said. "Nobody here wants anythin' from you. We all want lots *for* you but nothin' *from* you."

"Like what?"

"Well," Jane said, "we all kinda want for you to wanna come home. To be with us again. We all kinda want for you to be happy. And we all kinda want for you to want all that for yourself."

"I don't know what I want, really."

"You wanna be here?" Jane asked.

"I don't know. I'm not sure why I even came here."

"Maybe you're s'posed to stick around and find that out," Stanley said.

"Maybe. Maybe I am." I thought for a bit. "You know how sometimes when you get to the end of a jigsaw puzzle and you think you got it licked. Then you find out that someone lost a couple pieces on you. Pisses you off, eh?"

"Yeah, it does," Stanley agreed, looking at me a little more intensely.

"Well, that's kinda how I felt all my life. Pissed off because someone lost a few pieces of my puzzle—my life. Tried to make other pieces fit but they never did. Pissed me off more. Now I'm here with two pieces of that puzzle right in front of me and I don't even know if I wanna use 'em. Does that make any kind of sense at all?"

"All kinds," Jane said, putting an arm around my shoulder. "All kinds."

"So what do I do?"

"Well," Stanley said, sitting down on a rock, "one of two things, I guess. One, you can split and figger it was never gonna work out anyhow. Or two, you can start all over again at the beginning puttin' it all back together and hope that maybe them pieces'll appear when you get to them. One's easy, other's hard'n takes more time."

"You split, we'll understand," Jane said, sitting beside Stanley. "Only, at least write us and let us know where you are and what you're doin'. But we'd rather that you stayed and let us help you put that puzzle back together."

"You'd do that?"

"Hey, we're always willin' to keep hurlin' them rocks as long as you're willin' to sit there," Stanley said, looking at me with a hard edge to his face.

"Maybe I will . . . Can I have some time to think about it?"

"All the time you need man, all the time you need." Stanley's voice broke a little. "After twenty years we're just happy with any time at all with you."

"Yeah, bro'. And besides, you haven't really lived till you get some a Ma's hamburger soup and bannock into your belly. Me, I like it a little too much!" Jane slapped her belly and laughed.

"Where is my mother, anyway? I thought she'd be right here when I got here. Did she split?"

"Nope," Stanley said. "That's her house up on that hill over there, but she ain't home right now. Her'n Jackie are in Winnipeg till tomorrow mornin'."

I looked up at the house. "She didn't wanna see me?"

Jane sighed and pulled me down beside her on the rock. She held my hands between hers and looked right into my eyes. She didn't say anything for a while and finally looked out over the lake. "Ma's just like you, Garnet. Scared and not knowin' really what to do. She's scared of you. Scared that you hate her for losin' you all those years ago. Scared that you won't like her when you meet her and that you'll turn around and disappear again. Scared that when she lost you she lost the right to be your mother."

"S'right," Stanley said. "But you oughta know that she never gave up believin' that you'd make it back to us. Never quit missin' you either. Talked about you all the time all through the years askin' us what we thought you looked like, what you were doin', what kinda stuff you liked when you were a boy. That kinda thing."

"Yeah, bro'," said Jane. "Us we never knew for sure that you were even alive anymore, but Ma, she just kept right on believin' and when Stanley told her he'd got holda you she cried all night long."

"Wow," I said.

"That ain't the biggest part either," Jane said a little firmer than before. "Ma was with a guy named Joe after our dad died. Went with him a long time, maybe ten years. Anyways, Joe didn't have no Indian status, lost his treaty rights and all and he wanted Ma to marry him. Wanted it real bad. Us we liked him. Wasn't nothin' like our father but we liked him okay. But Ma kept puttin' him off and puttin' him off year after year and Joe finally got pissed off and left her.

"But he showed up here 'bout a year later wantin' to know why. You'da been 'bout sixteen then. Ma told him she couldn't marry him for five more years until she knew that you were twenty-one."

"What!" I said.

"Twenty-one was legal age back then," Stanley said. "You'da got your own treaty status. Your own rights. Ma knew that and she also knew that if she married a non-status Indian back then before you were legal, you'da lost your treaty rights too."

Jane said, "Even though Ma really loved this guy, she loved you more, even though she hadn't seen you in years. So she wouldn't marry Joe until she knew you were old enough not to lose your rights. Law's changing now, s'all gonna be diff'rent, but Ma stuck to her guns back then. Joe, he couldn't understand an' he left, hasn't been back."

I didn't know for sure what all this treaty rights business was all about but it made me feel proud, like I really meant something to someone all these years, like I was special.

"Ma never gave up and she never forgot," Stanley said. "Never got sad 'bout Joe leavin' either on accounta she loved you more and she knew you'd be back."

"But how could she know? I never knew. You never knew. No one knew. Hell, I was gettin' kinda happy livin' where I was livin' and with who I was with. This was never a plan."

"I don't know either, Garnet. I don't know either," Stanley said. "Ma just sorta followed the feelin' she had. Stick around, you'll see lotsa stuff'll kinda make you wonder."

"It still doesn't tell me why she isn't here," I said. "Hell, I'm scared too."

"Of what?" Jane asked.

I thought carefully. "I'm scared that she won't like me because I'm not like you guys. Not Indian. I grew up different. Hell, I've been living black for about five years now and I just got outta the penitentiary! How are you supposed to be proud of a son like that? Non-Indian, ex-con, James Brown–lookin' nowhere kinda guy. That's how I feel right now. And shit, if you want to know the truth, more than anything I'm scared that if my own mother doesn't like me where the hell do I go from here?

If I don't fit in here, where can I? I wish you hadn't found me, Stanley."

They both watched me as all of this tumbled out. Looking at them that day I could see little parts of my face on theirs. My little turned-up grin, squinty kinda eyes, my cheekbones, my chin and a way of holding their heads tilted I first noticed in my mugshot.

"First of all, you've always been an Indian, man," Stanley said, touching me on the shoulder and smiling. "Always have been and always will be. The Creator's the only one can change that and he ain't likely to. Maybe you learned diff'rent than us, maybe you think diff'rent right now, but that's all just influence, man. You spend some time here you get diff'rent influences and maybe somethin'll wake up inside you again. 'Cause it never disappeared. It's just been put to sleep by other stuff's been workin' on your spirit. But if you leave, man, that thing might never wake up. You might never get handed those missin' pieces of your puzzle.

"Second thing is, Ma's got just as many things runnin' through her head right now as you do. A woman don't go through all the things that Ma went through for twenty years and just up and be prepared to face somethin' like this. You got the easy part, pal. You never hadta live with the memory of a baby in your belly or the feelin' of bein' responsible for losin' it."

We sat on that rock until the sun went down. We sat there in silence thinking our own thoughts and catching each other peeking at the others every now and then out of the corner of our eyes. I wanted to cry. Wanted to lay right down on that big flat rock and bawl my eyes out. Wanted to look up into the haunting blue of that evening sky and bawl and bawl and bawl. Wanted to rip the lining off whatever'd been holding my insides in all these years and spill everything.

"Wow," said Jane finally, when those northern lights started wriggling around above us. "Wow."

Later on at Stanley's, Jane, who's the family historian on accounta she's the one likes to gab the most, told me more about my family. My brother's always been one of those "early to bed early to rise" guys and he'd retired just after we'd got back to his cabin. A slow wink, a squeeze on the shoulder and he was gone.

I guess my ma and pa were never married. At least not in the usual whiteman way. There were no rings exchanged or papers signed, but because they were traditional Ojibways both of them had to spend time getting coached by elders. The elders explained to them all about the way Ojibway people behaved in marriage. Talked about the roles of men and women as spiritual, mental, emotional and philosophical equals and how that always had to be remembered and respected. Talked about the sacred manner they had to live with each other. About how their union was made by the Creator and how they always had to respect that too. About caring for each other and the role of honor and respect in Ojibway marriage. When they were all coached they were joined together in simple ceremony by my grampa, Harold Raven, somewhere out on the trapline. It sounded really impressive to me, and my ideas about my own people changed a little right there and then.

Then she told me about the sacred role of children in marriage. How kids represented the spiritual union of male and female spirit and how they were looked on as being on loan from the Creator. Because of that kids were supposed to be treated respectfully and raised to learn the traditional way. They were sacred. She told me how my dad had wanted us kids to have our mother's last name because we came from her body. How he respected women's ability to give life and wanted us to carry the name of the woman who'd brought us into this world. A lot of traditional Ojibway men do that when they've been married in the Indian way instead of the white way. And so we were Ravens.

When we were taken away my parents were devastated. They couldn't believe someone was disrespecting the sacredness of their family circle. They started to think they'd done something wrong along the way and that the Creator was taking us away because of it. They thought they failed and because they didn't understand the system, or even speak English enough to talk to anybody, they didn't know what to do.

Both of them went a little crazy. Both of them started hanging with the drinking crowd in Kenora and Minaki, trying to forget their hurt in the bottle. It was that way for a couple years before my ma decided she'd had enough and came back here and settled into a regular life again.

It was different for my dad though. His name was John Mukwa and he was a bush Indian through and through. He'd been raised in the bush all his life and there's those around even now who talk about how he knew the land better'n anybody ever had. He was a traditional man and his life was lived on the basis of the Indian way. The wounds carved into him by losing his children were deep and festered a long, long time. No amount of drinking would wash them away or even soften the scars so he could be comfortable. Nothing could have cut so cleanly and deeply as the shedding of my father's family.

He ended up living alone in a small shack across the railway bridge from Minaki. He'd come into town to buy a few bottles and head on back to his aloneness. My ma would try and talk to him but by then even she represented his failure and he always waved her away. "Mukwa" is Ojibway for bear, and my father lived like a wounded bear in his tiny shack across the river. There was no approaching and no helping. He just lived with his wounds and bothered no one. People would see him now and then wandering through the bush or sitting looking out over the reservoir to the place where the old trapline camp used to be. He never talked, just wandered through the bush he knew so well but couldn't seem to touch anymore.

They found him one foggy morning on the shore of the Winnipeg River. Most believe he fell off that railway bridge while walking across in the rain with his bottle. No one really knows. Some believe he just had enough, that when they cut into his family they removed a section of his soul and on that foggy, rainy night alone on that bridge he faced the future the only way he could.

"So you see, little bro'," Jane said after a long silence between us, "you were brought into this old world from a lotta love. An' that love ain't died down even though you been gone so long. Still all around you if you want it."

She sat there in her chair, leaning forward, elbows on her knees, hands folded together in front of her, looking straight at me the way she always does.

"All you gotta do is want it, bro'. All you gotta do is want it."

I just stared back, unsure of what to say.

"Guess the thing of it is though," she said, "even if you decide to take off an' go on back to that other life out there, that love's still gonna be here. We're still gonna be holdin' on to those missin' pieces of your puzzle for whenever you wanna pick 'em up an' use 'em. You should know that." She rose and smoothed back her hair.

"Jane?"

"Yeah, bro'?"

"Thanks."

"You're welcome. Only we say meegwetch."

"Say what?"

"Meegwetch. In English it means thank you, but in our language it means more. Means . . . I hold what you've given me with honor. Think about it. Now, we gotta be up early to meet the bus in Kenora. You gonna be okay out here?"

"Yeah. Just wanna sit and think about things awhile."

When she'd gone off to bed I sat there in the darkness of my brother's cabin looking out at the pure velvet of that northern night. I'd remembered nothing of my childhood. It was like blank pages in a photo album. The things I'd seen that day and the things I'd been told about my early life and the lives of my family were new and strange. I felt like someone who'd come back from a coma and had to be reintroduced to his life. The missing years as cold and black as the holes between stars.

As I drifted off into sleep I thought of my father and what he might think of me now. I thought of his last night of this earth and how the wind must have whistled through his gut like it had whistled through mine all those years. About his loss and mine too. About the connection to a childhood that teetered briefly on the edge of darkness, faltered maybe in its misery, reaching back for footing but tumbling nonetheless into that dark, dark cavern of time.

There was a note pinned to the doorjamb when I woke up the next morning. I'd gotten used to being woke up at seven in the pen and I thought that was real early, but Stanley and Jane had already been up and out. Their note said my mother and brother were on the seven-thirty bus and they'd be back with them about nine. There was some thick black tea on the stove, so I grabbed a cup and sat on the steps outside to wake up.

Thinking about my mother being on her way towards me right that very minute was enough to get me anxious and wanting to run again. Maybe it was the fact that it was a long walk to town that held me there, but even more it was the talk me'n Jane had. Operating without a history all those years had made running real easy, but now that I actually had a history I found myself wanting more. I really wanted to see this woman who'd given me life. I'd always wondered what she looked like and I had all these images floating around my mind through the years. In some she was a gorgeous Indian princess with flowing black hair and a killer smile. In others she was old, gray-haired, looking like a queen of the woods.

I was standing inside pouring myself more tea when I heard a car horn from close by and saw Stanley's beat-up old black Mercury pulling up. Jane was peering up from the front seat like she was wondering whether I'd actually stuck around, and I could make out the shapes of two other heads in the back. The teacup started trembling a little in my hand when the doors eased open and people started piling out. I went and stood by the front door waiting for someone to tell me where to go, what to do, what to say.

Stanley was the first one in and he just looked at me with eyes all shiny and walked on into the living room to the teapot. Jane was next, and she just grinned at me and disappeared into the other room too.

A tail, lanky guy with long, long hair and a red bandana, wearing one of them red-checkered hunting jackets, jeans and workboots, clumped into the doorway. He was taller'n me'n Stanley and a little heavier but he had the same kinda face. He stood looking at me for a long time, nodding his head real slow and breathing real deep and long. Finally he reached out and shook my hand real firm, saluted me with a raised fist and walked on into the living room with Jane'n Stanley.

I heard her footsteps on the stairs outside kinda slow and measured. My breathing was getting shallow and I looked down at the floor, the cup shaking in my one hand while the other was opening and closing, opening and closing at my side. Her shadow fell across the floor in front of me and I stared at it for what seemed like an eternity, unable to lift my head and look at her. I heard a sniffle, a sigh and then my name whispered over and over and over.

"Garnet. Garnet. Garnet," she said. "My boy. My boy. My baby boy."

I looked up and saw a short woman with curly black hair that framed a round face that was still young-looking, with eyes all sparkly and wet. They were my eyes. She was built more along the lines of Jane than Stanley'n Jackie'n me and she was dressed in white slacks and a bright pink turtleneck that gave her a kinda glow. Real knockout, actually.

We stood there facing each other, neither one of us knowing whether to move, until she finally reached out and grabbed me and held me close against her. She was strong and her hug was tight. The teacup tumbled from my hand, clanged onto the floor, and I lost myself in that strong, warm hug. I could hear her start to sob and she hugged me even tighter till I thought I was gonna faint.

What happened next is what I've learned to accept as part of the magic my ma talks about all the time.

I'm standing there in that doorway with a sobbing woman in my arms, feeling tears starting to well up inside me. Welling up from someplace far removed from my eyes. Welling up from the edges of that great big hole the wind used to blow through, getting bigger'n bigger until they finally break loose and I find myself sobbing too all loose and uncontrollable. We stood there sobbing away, hugging tighter and tighter still. And then as the tears began to quiet down the magic happened. Our breathing got slower and deeper. Still locked in that hug I started to be able to feel the rhythm of her heartbeat against the empty side of my chest. My attention got focussed on it and I felt its *barrrrumpa, barrrrumpa* echoing through me. And bit by bit as I lost myself in that heartbeat, any doubt I ever had about this woman being my mother began to disappear. My speeding brain got quieter and quieter and I felt more and more relaxed and safe and sheltered and warm until I began to realize that I'd felt this same way somewhere back in my past. I don't know what it was but something somewhere deep inside me recognized that heartbeat. Recognized it from the days way before I ever slid out into this world. Recognized it from when her body kept me safe and sheltered and warm. Recognized it from when she was all vibration, fluid and movement. From when our souls shared the same space and time. My mother.

And I cried deeper and longer than I ever had before or since.

It still took me'n Ma a while to get around to actually speaking to each other. We roamed around the house all that day peeking over at each other while everyone else gabbed on and on. Every now and again we'd meet up at the teapot and I'd kinda reach out and touch her sleeve or she'd touch my shoulder and we'd just smile all shy and quiet at each other. Me, I didn't know what the hell to say and I guess Ma was in the same boat. Stanley'n Jackie'n Jane just shook their heads and grinned whenever Ma'n me would pass each other by.

I conked out for a nap sometime in the early evening and when I woke up the house was empty. Walking around looking out windows, I saw Ma sitting out back of her house up on the hill beside a small fire. She looked all small and alone so I decided I'd head on up there and keep her company. I could still feel the effects of that long hug in the doorway.

She saw me coming from a ways off and by the time I got there she had a fresh pot of tea brewing on the fire and an extra cup set beside a camp chair. I watched her watching me as I approached.

"Ahnee, my boy," she said and smiled. "Nuhmutabin. Sit here. Tea?"

"Sure," I said, settling into the chair and looking around. "Nice view up here."

"Hey-yuh," she said. "Me, I come out here lots. Winter even too sometimes."

Something in the way these people talked was kinda soothing and it felt real familiar already. The soft roll of Ojibway was gentle on the ears. As if she were reading my thoughts she smiled over at me.

"Don't speak Indyun, eh?" she asked.

"No. Never learned."

"Ah, s'easy. What I said to you there, nuhmutabin, means sit. Try it."

"Me? Nah. I'll never learn."

"Never know 'less you try. G'wan."

"Well, okay. How's that again? Nuh . . . mut . . . bin?"

"Nuh . . . mut . . . AH . . . bin," she said, a little slower and smiling. "Nuh . . . mut . . . ah . . . bin."

I tried it out while she smiled and nodded. The words felt good rolling offa my tongue and I giggled to think I'd just said something in Ojibway for the first time.

"Nuhmutabin!" I yelled and waved at a small group of people goin' by in a boat on the lake below us. They gave me a weird look then waved back.

My ma laughed and I watched as her face all crinkled up with it, the fire starting to throw small shadows on it.

It was getting darker by now and the air had that crisp northern edge.

"Yeah, me I come out here lots," she said. "Drink tea, think, look around. S'good."

"Yeah. It's nice. Good to be out."

"Was it tough in there?"

I'd only meant it was good to be outside. "Kinda," I said. "You learn to just keep to yourself and no one bugs you."

"I'm sorry you had to go there."

"Yeah, me too. Me too. It's over though."

"Hey-yuh. S'over."

We looked at each other just then and with that fire kinda crackling and the wind picking up and whistling it reminded me of something but I couldn't recall what. Again it was like she was reading my mind.

"We used to sit like this, the buncha us, way over there. See that place where the lake cuts in there, way down? That's where we used to have a camp when you were just small. The buncha us would sit there in the evenin's round the fire like this. You useta really like that, watch the fire all the time."

"I, uh, I . . . don't remember. Not really anyway."

"S'okay," she said and grinned at me, "s'okay. Us we remember for you."

"You remember all about everything, don't you?"

"Hey-yuh. I remember all 'bout ev'rythin'. Ev'rythin'. All them years. Ev'rythin'."

"I don't blame you, you know. About me going to foster homes, I mean. I don't."

She smiled, and her eyes were wet with tears. She started poking the fire with a long stick sending embers flying up in the breeze that I had to duck from. She stared into the fire for a long time before she spoke again.

"Me, I did. Your dad, him too. He was good man that John Mukwa. Good man.

"We di'n' know what to do. We come home that day an' your granny was runnin' around all crazy lookin' for you kids. We searched the bush and called for you all that night. Was round noon next day when they came with their letter'n tol' us what was goin' on. We di'n' understand. Your dad, he never did. We di'n' know nothin' 'bout their system then, di'n' know we coulda fought it. We jus' thought we failed you all.

"Two years after that your sister found me in Minaki. She run away from that home and come lookin' for us. Us we were drinkin' it up all over. Lucky she found us. Tol' me 'bout the other two boys bein' okay an' then she tol' me you were gone, she di'n' know where. We cried together in that bush that day me'n Jane.

"Pretty soon I sobered up. Started askin' for visitin' rights and got 'em after a while. Saw those kids regular all through the years till they come home on their own. Stayed together in those homes, all three of 'em.

"Your dad, he never forgot or forgave 'em for what they done. Couldn't. They hurt him real bad. I tried bringin' him home one time an' he stayed here 'bout a week, pacin' round, takin' long walks in the bush, hardly talkin' and you could tell he was fallin' apart inside. One day I woke up he was gone. Died 'bout three months after that. He was a good man, John Mukwa. You look like him, you know?"

"Really? Do you think . . . do you think he woulda liked me?"

She smiled all soft across the fire at me and a little tear skied down one cheek. She nodded real slow and then looked off across the lake, breathing deep and long.

"Oh yes," she said really quietly, "oh yes. Useta come an' talk to you while you were still in my belly. Tol' you things, like my name, his name, all 'bout your fam'ly, even sang you songs at night. Sometimes he'd be singin' so soft an' low that me, I'd fall asleep. Wake up after and him, he'd be sleepin' too with his head on my belly, one hand kinda lay across it. I remember thinkin' that me, I had two little boys in my belly those times. Oh yes, he'd liked you, my boy, he'd liked you."

I gazed out cross that lake, watching that eternal blue edging into darkness and thinking about this man that was my father. John Mukwa. The name had something to it now and I got the feeling that it would always mean quiet nights and fires, songs sung low in Ojibway and sleeping deep and long, safe and sheltered and warm. My father. As I watched that night be born, I saw a tiny little star wink into view and I named that star the Bear Star right then and there. And I knew that whenever I felt lost or lonely that I could wander out when the night was being born and wait for that tiny little star to wink into view and talk to my father, tell him about my life and maybe even sing him a song in Ojibway all soft and low.

We sat by that fire most of that night, Ma'n me. We didn't talk too much but we shared that time together and it felt right. Just before she got up to head on in to sleep she looked over at me and smiled.

"M-m-m-Ma?"

"Yes, my boy?"

"I . . . I know my father's name. But . . . but . . . I don't know what your name is."

One wrinkled brown hand went to her throat for just a second and she sniffled slightly. When she spoke it was very soft.

"Alice. My name is Alice Raven. But all I ever wanted you to call me was Ma. That's all, my boy, just Ma. 'Kay?"

"Okay, M . . . m . . . Ma."

"Wanna know why I like to come here so much, my boy, winter too even?"

"Yeah. I wanna know that."

"Well, us Indyuns, we sing songs all the time. Songs are 'bout as important as prayer. We sing them songs to the spirits of our ancestors who are part of them northern lights now. Sing songs for the animals we hunt, songs for the Creator, thank him for life, all kindsa songs.

"When I d'in' know where you were no more, I wanted to sing a song for you wherever you were. Maybe protect you out there, keep you safe. Maybe even bring you home to me sometime. Wanted it to be a special song, wanted it to be your song forever.

"But I couldn't find no words. Came out here night after night tryin' to sing you somethin' but couldn't find no words. Too much tumblin' round inside me to find what I wanted to sing most. After a while though a song was born and I been singin' it almost ev'ry night for 'bout fifteen years now. Wanna hear it?"

Of course I wanted to hear it. She closed her eyes real tight and her foot started beating on the ground, one two, one two, one two. A heartbeat rhythm. The rhythm of the drum. The rhythm of prayersongs. Her head started bobbing to the ancient rhythm and her tears glistened in the firelight and brought a few to my eyes too just then. Finally she started to sing, soft and low.

"Bih'kee-yan, bih'kee-yan, bih'kee-yan," she sang, her voice breaking over the words. "Bih'kee-yan, bih'kee-yan, bih'kee-yan."

That's all. Just one word over and over and over again for about five minutes, with her foot still tapping that rhythm, her head still bobbing in time, tears flowing like a river down her face and her body swaying and swaying with her arms hugged around herself.

"Bih'kee-yan," she sang, "bih'kee-yan, bih'kee-yan."

When she finished she looked over at me and smiled, rose up, walked to me and grabbed me up into a great big hug and held on for a long, long time.

"What does it mean, Ma?" I mumbled through tears and her hair. "My song, what does it mean?"

She breathed really deeply one more time and said, "It means, come home. Come home, come home, come home."

She hugged me again and headed into the cabin, looking over her shoulder one last time to ask, "You wanna come stay with me, my boy, make this your home now? Come home? Be with me? With us? You take that empty room 'side mine, okay?"

"Yeah, Ma, yeah," I said. "I'll be in soon."

"'Kay then," she said and waved.

"'Kay then," I said.

I sat by that fire and thought for a long, long time. The sounds of loons and wolves in the distance, the wind, the water lapping up softly on the dock down below, everything seemed to punctuate my thoughts that night. I thought about this James Brown Indian coming home, about these strange-talking, strange-looking people who opened up their reserve and their hearts to me, about my ma, my dad, my brothers, my sister and the sound of the wind that was breezing by my ears instead of ripping through my guts that night. Thought about all them years spent moving, running, searching, trying to find who held the missing pieces of that puzzle. And I thought about an old Ojibway woman beside a small fire on a lonely winter's night, staring out across the land and the universe towards someone, somewhere in a place far away, singing soft and low, over and over and over . . . bih'kee-yan, bih'kee-yan, bih'kee-yan.

BOOK TWO

# BEEDAHBUN

First of all, you've got to realize that the lake is like a reflector, okay? What I mean is that on those long, calm nights we get around here, a voice can carry for miles. We used to eavesdrop on conversations whenever we'd see Myron Fisher and Mabel Copenace heading out on the bay in her auntie's canoe. They'd be talking all lovey-dovey across the bay and we'd catch every line. Old Myron would be mad as hell and chase us all around the townsite whenever we'd repeat what we figured were the sweetest lines of the evening. Myron and Mabel have been married for about three years now, got themselves a boy named Theodore and are living in a house at the east end of the townsite. Maybe all the teasing helped, I don't know. Anyway, the lake is like a reflector that can take a whisper clean across.

Now according to Mabel's auntie—not the one with the canoe, the other that's older and has a face like a fresh-scraped deer hide once the wet's all squeezed out—there was a time on this reserve when the lake was the only way to get a hold of someone on the other side. People would just wander on down to the dock and yell across.

Actually, White Dog's not the only reserve up here's got their own open-lake telephone. This northern part of Ontario's full of lakes and we Ojibways always seem to be finding ourselves settling down on the shores of one. Once you've seen one of our long summer sunsets from across a northern lake, well, you start to get a better idea of why the old people would settle down there.

Anyway, I'd been back here about four months. My ma had cut my Afro off about three days after I was home and around about that time I was one scruffy-looking Indian. Funny how fate turns things around, eh? I told Ma about the old Pancho Santilla gaffe I used to run on people before I became a black man and she just looked at me and laughed.

"Good thing you don' try that now, my boy," she said. "People see you like this with no hair now they be callin' you one a them Mexican hairlesses!"

Funny lady, that Ma.

Making White Dog my home wasn't as easy as maybe I make it sound. For days on end I still wanted to hightail it back to familiar streets. I felt like a very big fish out of water for the longest time and to tell the truth, it was scary. But the White Dog folks and the feeling that was seeping into me from this land all started getting me to feeling more and more comfortable the longer I hung around. In fact, I don't remember ever making the decision to stay. It was more like one day I was walking around and it was already made. Nobody was coaxing the answer out of me all that time either. I took to feeling like I'd just been a part of the place forever and like Stanley had told me those first few days, everyone just seemed to want to treat me like a little kid. The little kid they'd never got a chance to know. Pretty hard to think of leaving a place when everyone's feeding you, giving you things and making you feel all special all the time. Anyway, I fell into the idea of being home long before I even knew that's where I was. Took some getting used to though.

See, there wasn't much to do except hang out with my brothers and their friends and try to fit in and not stick out all at the same time. Which is kinda hard when you don't speak the language, never done any of the things people like to do around here like hunt and fish and all and you're running around with a heada hair looks like a bad scalping job by a near-sighted Cree. But I was slowly getting comfortable. Most folks knew who I was, where I'd been, some of the things I'd done out there, and were pretty hip to the fact that I hadn't been around my own people for a long, long time. They'd kid me about it but generally they tried to help me get feeling I was home again. It happened over the course of that first summer, but slowly. Living with Ma helped the most.

Anyway, there was a big bunch of us sitting around on the other side of the bay one evening. We had a fire going and were listening to Wally Red Sky singing all his favorite country-and-western songs. Wally's okay, I suppose, but I always figured someone should have told him back then that there was a few good tunes written after 1952. See, Wally's always been the big dreamer around here. His family goes back a long way in the local history. What with his great-grandfather being one a the main signers of Treaty Three back in the 1870s and every Red Sky after that somehow getting into the politics, making big plans has been a Red Sky mainstay for as long as most can remember according to Ma. He'd got hold of his daddy's guitar when he was eight and ever since then has dreamed of being the biggest Indian country singer ever. Trouble is, his high notes sound like what you hear in the bush during rutting season and his low notes sound like a moose four hours after a feeding frenzy on skunk cabbage. But a nicer guy can't be found. He was right in the middle of some sappy ballad about some long-haired gal named Sal who lived in the middle of the wide open spaces when we heard it.

See, the open-lake telephone system can be kind of spooky when you're not ready for it. Voices have a habit of floating up at you outta nowhere. My cousin Connie

Otter just about jumped right outta her skin when we heard this voice go, "Hoo!" That's all, just "Hoo!"

Whenever Ma'n me head out blueberry picking she's always hooing away when I pick my way outta her sight. One good hoo can carry a long way by itself even without the benefit of a reflecting lake. Ma says it's the way the old people used to locate each other in the bush.

So we hear this hoo and all the rest got lost in the roar of laughing that erupted when Connie Otter hightailed it into the bush so fast she ran clear out of her gumboots. We could hear her crashing through the timber and someone finally had the sense to yell back over, "Hoo!"

Now it generally takes a while for a good hoo to travel across so it was a moment or two before we got a reply.

"GAR ... NET ... RA ... VEN ... THERE?"

"YEAH ... I'M ... HERE!"

"'KAY THEN ... KEE ... PER ... WANTS ... YOU!"

"WHAT? ... KEE ... PER ... WANTS ... ME?"

"YEAH ... KEE ... PER!"

"'KAY THEN ... BE ... O ... VER ... SOOOOON!"

"'KAY THEN."

Wally Red Sky bumped against me in the darkness. I could tell it was Wally because no one else on this reserve still uses Brylcreem. Or at least they don't use as much of it as Wally Red Sky.

"Keeper? Wonder what that old fart wants with you?"

"Don't know, Wally, maybe he needs help finding one a his bottles."

This got quite a laugh because Keeper'd been the local drunk around here for a long time. Well, there used to be a lot of local drunks but old Keeper'd been the one most people talked about most of the time. One of the things you could count on from Keeper was to find him stumbling around in the mornings turning over rocks'n logs and stuff trying to remember where he'd hid his bottle. I remember wondering how anybody could be called Keeper when they couldn't seem to keep anything.

Anyway, he surprised everyone when he went away. Guess he just one day up and walked in and asked chief and council to send him off to the Smith Clinic in Thunder Bay to dry out. This was about three weeks after I got here and no one expected him to really go, so it was an even bigger surprise for folks when old Keeper asked to stay an extra coupla weeks because he figured he needed it.

His best drinking buddies had been wandering around pretty confused about all of it. My uncle Buddy wasn't buying any of it.

"Ah, that old fart's just restin' up," he said. "Been drunk as long as me'n Keeper been drunk, you stay that way!"

He was the one to know. Uncle Buddy used to say that when he's "whistled over" as he calls it, they won't have to waste any money on embalming fluid on accounta he's drunk enough in one lifetime to keep him pickled forever. And there's those around who agree.

Anyway, there was a lotta differing opinion on whether old Keeper meant what he said about having enough. I thought about this all across the lake. Keeper was one of the people who were there in Stanley's cabin to meet me that first day. I hadn't seen too much of him after that, being so busy getting to know folks and visiting around like I was then. I remember carrying him outta the bush once when he'd passed out in there and was getting rained on real good and I remember catching his eye one night on the shoreline staring out across the lake while I was sitting there doing the same, but we weren't exactly buddies or anything. Still, one of the things you learn around here first is that you gotta respect what the old folks either tell you or ask you to do. It's part of the way we are. So I headed over to find out what the old guy wanted.

I stopped by home to grab a warmer jacket and found my ma sitting at the table. Ma's one a the best moccasin makers in the area and she was hard at it again that night. She was trying to teach me how to do things like beadwork and stuff but my fingers never went the way they were supposed to and I was always leaving little piles of half-done things lying around for her to fix up. Anyway, she was sitting there sewing away like her hands don't need help from her eyes and she was smiling.

"Ah-ha. Got holda you, eh? Keeper's lookin' for you."

"What for? That old guy doesn't even hardly know me."

"Well, that ol' guy's got somethin' he wantsta tell you. Might help you find your way around."

"You talk to him?"

"Hey-yuh," she said. "We been friends long time, Keeper'n me. We were in the residential school together for a while and we even been drunk a few times too."

"Oh, I get it. Maybe now that he's all sobered up and got his memory back he wants to tell me some juicy stories about him and you!"

"Hmmpfh," Ma said, but smiling all the while. "Ain't no juicy stories! Even if there were, that old guy couldn't do any real good stories proper justice anyhow!"

"So where is he?"

"'Member the old cabin we showed you round the bay?"

"Where my grampa lived?"

"Hey-yuh. He's stayin' there now."

"'Kay then. I'll be back soon."

"''Kay then. Careful walkin' through that bush."

"'Kay then."

My grampa was the oldest person on this reserve when he died. He'd have been about ninety-eight and passed on about three years before I made it home. He'd never ever learned English and from what my ma and other people told me, he was the last of the real traditional Ojibway around here. He had a sweat lodge near the cabin where I was headed, made tobacco offerings, tried to help people and held pipe ceremonies at his place now and again. Real traditional man. I never knew anything about all that when I went out to meet Keeper that night and frankly all the talk I'd heard about it freaked me out.

Sometimes it was hard to shake those old images of my people out of my head, and when I heard talk about spirits and ceremonies and stuff I always envisioned big fires with drums going crazy, people dancing around in strange get-ups, war whoops and planning a raid on the unsuspecting settlers. It was spooky on accounta life around here was nothing like that.

It was always the hidden parts of my people that worried me the most. It was fine to wander around the reserve learning bits of the language and how to hunt and stuff, but all the talk of ceremony and ritual bothered me. I remember watching my uncle Gilbert praying and sprinkling tobacco by the base of a big pine tree when he took me out deer hunting one day. Gilbert said it was what we were supposed to do before we went out. Making that offering of tobacco showed respect for the animal we were gonna take and was also a prayer for our hunt to be good. My ma was always singing and praying and covering herself with the smoke from smoldering cedar, moss and something called sweetgrass, but she never tried to force me into doing any of it.

I was never a religious guy. I'd been forced to go to Sunday school in some of the homes I was in and I liked some of the stories about Jesus and how he always looked after kids on accounta I wasn't getting to much looking after as a kid. But I never followed it up. I got old enough to not go to Sunday school anymore. A couple of times me'n Delma went to the church she attended occasionally and I really dug that on accounta the choir was really funky and alive but I didn't really listen to the preacher at all. Praying and church-going were just something you did when you had to and I didn't see what it had to do with being Indian. Besides, all the ritual I saw around me was far different from what I was used to seeing from people who were supposed to be praying. It all struck me as being pretty close to voodoo.

But Grampa was a big believer. He belonged to a society that called themselves Midewewin. Some of our people called them medicine men and when I heard that I really wanted no part of it. To me medicine men were large painted-up guys with the scary faces shaking rattles and small dead animals around people's heads and sending them off on the warpath. I remember thinking that if I had to go and see one just to stick around White Dog it was gonna be back to black for me.

Stanley tried to explain it all to me one night but it got to be so complicated that I just shut him off in my mind. I figured all I really needed to do to be an Indian was learn to do what everyone else was doing and I'd be okay. I didn't see anybody doing any big ceremonies so I figured it was okay for me to leave it alone. But heading through the dark bush towards the cabin where my grampa lived out his last days got me to thinking about him and his beliefs and the amount of stuff I had to learn about my own people and my own history still.

I could see the lights of the cabin from a long way off. It's a heavy darkness around here. It almost seems like the rocks and trees and even the water sometimes all soak up whatever light there might be. It kind of explains why the Ojibway got to be such a superstitious bunch and why their legends are filled with all kinds of monsters and spirits.

He was sitting in the doorway smoking his pipe when I walked up.

"Ahnee, Garnet," he said, "ahnee" being the way we Ojibways greet each other, means howdy and all that.

"Ahnee, Keeper. Boy, you sure look good!"

"Oh, meegwetch, meegwetch," he said and stuck his hand out. "Feel pretty good now too!"

I watched as he paused to relight his pipe and noticed how his hands didn't shake like I remembered.

"Pretty steady, eh? First thing people notice 'bout us ex-drunks."

"Must feel good."

"Hey-yuh. Haven't felt like this in a long, long time."

Around here the old people, even the women, take to smoking pipes and you have to wait a long time sometimes before they seem to recall they're talking with you and get around to it again. What with smoking their pipes and staring away across the sky like they do, there's always huge holes in the line of talk. Not like black people who keep up the patter nonstop. Indians stare at the sky lots between words. Waiting for the words to fall, I guess. So I waited awhile before he got around to talking again.

"Used to spend lotsa time here once. Old man an' I did lotsa talkin' here."

"Old man? My grampa you mean?"

"Hey-yuh. Harold. Your grampa. Knew him a long time. Since I was a small boy. He was the lasta the people round here really knew about Midewewin. You heard about that?"

"Not lots. Heard they were medicine men, did lots of ceremonies, stuff like that."

He laughed just then. It was good to hear. It came from somewhere deep inside him and echoed across the bay.

"Stuff like that. Stuff like that. Well, Midewewin were the people's guardians. All kindsa people gotta have someone lookin' out over the world for 'em, teach em how to walk around in it, show 'em where they gotta go, how to get there. Midewewin did that. Other Indyuns got their teachers an' protectors too, but us, we had Midewewin.

"They used their ceremonies an' rituals to keep the people healthy. Knew all about plants and animals, all the teachin's that come from there. Knew the world. Knew the universe. Knew about everything an' did lotsa prayin' for the people.

"Had a real natchrel way. Made stories an' legends for the people to learn from. Made rules for behavin' meant to keep the people together through anything. Used the pipe, sweat lodge an' prayer. Lotsa prayer."

"What happened to them?"

"Hmmpfh," Keeper said, and stared away across the lake for a while before he continued. "Times changed.

Times changed an' the people changed too. When the whiteman came here with all his shiny things the people got distracted. Started lookin' more at the whiteman's world than their own. Pretty soon work an' money an' gettin' those shiny things got to mean more than prayer an' ceremony. See, you look too long at the shiny an' your eyes go funny. Can't see the world like you used to. People didn't see that the ones who carried the knowledge were startin' to die. No one was coming around to ask an' learn. Pretty soon the old ones were all gone and mosta what they knew went with 'em. Works that way sometimes in this world. Gotta starve awhile before you learn to recognize your hunger. People are just now startin' to get the idea they're missin' something. The old ones who knew are gone from here though. There's still teachers around other places though. Still someone to go see."

He paused to thump his pipe against the cabin wall, and it echoed across the lake like someone beating a small drum way off in the darkness.

"You mean there's no one around here anymore who knows those things?"

There was another long silence. I could hear him breathing deep and long and he started nodding his head up and down.

"Almost no one." He got up slowly and went into the cabin. I could hear things being moved around and finally the first faint glow of the fire flickered through the door as he opened it and gestured to me.

"Peen-dig-en. Peen-dig-en. Come in. Got somethin' to show you."

We sat by the fire and he reached down to cradle a large hand drum in his arms. A hand drum is just what the name says. A drum you hold in your hand to play. Ours are made of rounded wood frames from the trunk of a tree and covered with deer hide or moose hide stretched across it and tied all together on the underneath side. Most of the ones I'd seen were plain but the one Keeper held was painted with a bright, intricate design.

"This was your grampa's. Before that it was his grampa's. Been around long time this drum. Maybe three, four hundred years."

"Where'd you get it?" I asked respectfully, nervous that if he dropped it it might just shatter.

"Harold. He passed it on to me. But it don't belong to me."

"Who's it belong to?"

"Drum like this always belongs to the people. Same as the songs you sing with it. Old man taught me some of those songs, told me about their meanin'. When he died he left a message with your mother that I was responsible for the drum. Learnin' those things meant I had a responsibility. See, the drum's always gotta have a keeper. Called a drum keeper really."

"Is that why everyone calls you Keeper?"

"Well, yes, but that's not really why."

He took his time reloading his pipe and I watched as his face got softer and softer in the flickering light of the fire. It reminded me of the look on my ma's face when she told me about my dad. He looked over at me for a while before he started to explain.

"Harold, your grampa, was my teacher. Picked me outta all the boys on the reserve. Said I had smarts and courage. I run away from the residential school they sent me to and came back here. I was about ten. He liked it that I wouldn't let them take me away from here. He was a young man then. 'Bout maybe forty-five. So he'd bring me out here on nights like this, make tea an' we'd sit by this fire an' he'd tell me all about the old Midewewin. Talk about the old ways. Told me stories, legends, all kindsa things I never heard before.

"Daytime he took me for walks. Showed me plants and animals. Told me their old names an' what kinda things they could do for the people. Introduced me to all of it for the first time. The world, I mean. While the other boys were out playin', huntin' and fishin' I was out in the bush with the old man. Learned about bear medicine, deer medicine, all the songs for all the animals. He was my friend."

"Did he teach you to be a Midewewin?"

"No," Keeper said a little sadly, "no. I walked away. I walked away. Felt like I was missin' out on somethin' big not bein' with my friends so I walked away. Didn't learn enough to be a real teacher.

"But all that knowledge was inside me. Ev'rythin' he gave me, all the things he taught me, ev'rythin' he put inside me stayed right there. Didn't go away. All the time

I was runnin' around with my friends it didn't go away. I'd be looking at somethin' an' remember what it was called by the old people and what it was used for. Wanted it all to go away but it didn't.

"Got older. Still wouldn't go away. I learned too much too deep. Every time I'd see him around I'd try'n go the other way. But him he always had a waya meetin' my eyes. Never said nothin' all that time but his eyes spoke lots. Drilled right into me. I knew what he was tryin' to tell me but me, I didn't wanna hear it. All I wanted was my friends. All the parties, the adventures, all the stories. When he died I was drinkin' it up with your uncle Buddy. When we heard we got even drunker. Least, I did. Was your ma finally told me about me bein' the drum keeper. I knew some of it. Learned it before I walked away on accounta I think he was trainin' me for it but I didn't know the whole thing.

"In our way we believe that the drum holds the heartbeat of the people. The songs you sing with it are very sacred. Nothin' to be played around with. When you sing you're joinin' the heartbeat of the people with the heartbeat of the universe. It's a blessing. You're blessing the land and the water and the air with the pure, clear spirit of the people. In return you're gettin' big blessings from the land. Food, shelter, water. It's a big thing you do when you sing with the drum. The keeper of the drum's one who's learned the prayer songs like the old man taught me. Knows how to give blessings. So the keeper's gotta be one who lives life in a good way. Pure, clean way.

Keep the drum pure, heartbeat of the people pure and strong, and me I knew this.

"Pretty soon I was feelin' real guilty. Like a traitor. Knew there was no way I could shake off responsibility for the drum an' I knew how important it was for the people but I felt too guilty over walkin' away an' not learnin' the rest of it. Didn't think I was worthy no more and bein' drunk started to feel better.

"Reason they all started to callin' me Keeper was on accounta I'd be all drunk an' cryin' about your grampa an' I'd try an' tell 'em I was the keeper of the drum. They just laughed. Don't blame 'em, really, but it still felt like a big knife in the belly. They laughed and started callin' me Keeper as a big joke.

"Couldn't sober up 'cause I figured it was too late. Thought I was unworthy an' after a long time I was too guilty, too scared an' then just too damn drunk to care. Too damn drunk to care.

"But one day I got tired. Tired of the guilt, tired of bein' drunk, sick, bein' all dried up inside. So I went an' talked with your ma and went away.

"Thought about you when I got back. Remembered you coming here that first day, lookin' all strange, smelly kinda. Watched you tryin' to move around here. Tryin' to find yourself. Saw you tryin' real hard to be Indyun. Kinda reminded me of me. Not as cute maybe, but me anyway."

He looked away, a distant, vacant stare that he held for a long time, beating his pipe against his leg slow and regular like the drum he was holding in his lap. We could hear the loons calling out to each other across the lake, and when he looked over at me again he was smiling.

"Let's go back out," he said, getting up slowly and lifting an old sweater from a hook by the door. "Sure were a funny-lookin' thing when you stepped into your brother's cabin that day. Heh, heh, heh."

We settled ourselves on a rough-hewn bench by the door. Both of us gazed upward almost automatically at the stars that were shining like little chips of ice and a big orange moon that was just starting to rise in the east.

"Hey-yuh. Funniest-lookin' thing I seen in years. But, important thing is you're home. Gone long time, you. Learned diff'rent ways. Ways that stick on you, make you move an' behave diff'rent, look diff'rent even though you're one of us. A Raven. Anishanabe. White Dog Indyun. But you, you need a guide right now. Someone to help you find your way around. Help you learn to see things Indyun instead of white . . . or black even. Heh, heh heh. An' me, well, I need someone to help me too."

"Help you? Help you what?"

"Hmmpfh. Been gone long time myself. Could use a good guide too. See, you'n me got a lot in common. Lotsa things the same. You, you're tryin' to learn to fit in, tryin' to be at home here, tryin' to win back all them years got stolen on you. Me, same thing. Got a lotta years to win back.

"Takes lotta courage to come back here. Brave boy, you. An' I can tell you got smarts by the way you're always watchin' things go on around you. Never say nothin', just watchin'. Learnin'. Tryin' to see with dif-f'rent eyes. S'good. Lot of us we try 'n tell each other how much we know about things, how much Indyun we are, but all the time we're scared inside on accounta we know we don't know much. So we use our mouth to hide our real feelin's, our lacka knowin'. Not you. Learned lots already by bein' silent. S'good.

"Kinda like me when your grampa took me up here. Said I had courage an' smarts too. And we're the same now as men. Both of us lookin' to find our way back, both tryin' to win back some time got taken away. You, you need someone to teach you about your own people. An' me, me I kinda need to pay back a debt. Need to give back what the old man gave me. Need to become the drum keeper he wanted me to be. Find another teacher around to keep on learnin' and need to pass on whatever I learn.

"So I wanna spend time with you. Nothin' big. Just walkin' round talkin', lookin' at things. You got questions you ask an' I'll try an' answer. That way we both help each other find ourselves. Kinda be each other's guides. Sound good?"

Now it was my turn to stare away across the bay and up towards the sky. That was the first time I ever realized why those old Indian people did that so much. Staring away across the universe like that started all kinds of things tumbling through my mind. Things like that sandbox and a little red truck with one wheel missing and all the times I'd heard someone tell me "You can call me Mom" or "This is your home now" and wondering which one of the dozen or so really was or if home or Mom was something I'd ever really have. The feeling of searching for something but never knowing what and the anger that smolders away so deep inside you that you never really think it's there but that keeps you moving and searching anyway. I thought about being tourists in this life and how an old man, a moon across the water, the sound of loons and the smell of trees can suddenly feel like something you've worn around forever like an old pair of moccasins, all loose and comfortable.

"Yeah," I said finally with Keeper smiling away at me with his eyes. "Yeah. That sounds good. Real good. When can we start?"

"Soon as that moon goes down behind them trees over there an' we see the first light in the east. It's called Beedahbun. First light. We'll burn some cedar, smudge ourselves with the smoke, say a little prayer. Then I'll sing the morning song the old man taught me on this drum. After that we walk back to the townsite an' you make the old man breakfast, ham'n eggs, old style, lotsa bread with lard, tea. Good way to start."

We sat in silence the rest of that long night. An old man and me. Keeper'n me. Watching that moon working its way across the sky, watching its reflection in the water, both of us thinking about the mystery of things and wondering where that mystery might lead us. It was a deep, comfortable silence.

"Ever slow, that moon, eh?" he said finally, and we laughed.

*Talk about sweetgrass or smokin' the pipe to some people and they think us Indyuns are gettin' high all the time. Heh, heh, heh. Don't know why that is. Seen this show on TV one time in Winnipeg had this priest walkin' down the aisle in church wavin' a big smokin' pot on a chain. Wavin' it all around. Smoke ev'rywhere. Garnet said that partic'lar church was into the incense. Hmmpfh. Me I thought incense was somethin' bad you done with your own fam'ly. Glad the boy straightened me out there. Heh, heh, heh.*

*Anyway, what I was meanin' to say is, them missionaries when they came here saw all these Indyuns ev'rywhere prayin' real strange. Strange to them anyway. Had big pipes they were passin' aroun' and sittin' there passin' smoke over themselves offa burnin' grass, moss and partsa trees. Some were goin' into sweat lodges. Prob'ly looked like little smokin' tents to them missionaries. Guess they couldn't figure out what was goin' on so they decided we all needed helpin' in a big way. Called us savages, heathens, pagans. Said we needed direction. Said our way of prayin' was wrong.*

*See, them they came ashore with what they called The Great Book of Truth. Us we never knew truth to be somethin' had to be spelled out. Always figured was somethin' we each carried around inside. True human bein's got that. Truth inside. You see it in the way they move around the world. Always kind, respectful, honest. That kinda way. You learn that from watchin' nature. The world'll teach you everything if you look long enough. Natchrel laws true for everything. Anyways, they come here with their Great Book, lookin' strange at our ways, not takin' time to learn about it, not askin' for a guide, judgin'. Guess when your truth's all spelled out for you you got no need to learn no more. I don't know.*

*But they seen all these Indyuns prayin' and singin' strange. Had pity on us. Hmmpfh. We pray lots. Least the ones who still try to follow the teachin's pray lots. Lots don't but its the same with ev'ryone, not just Indyuns I guess. Go anywhere you see it. Lotsa people come around to our pow-wows and them they always start with a prayer. Takes long time. Gotta be grateful for lotsa things, thank the Creator for all of it. Gotta ask for strength an' direction to learn howta live through lotsa things. Takes long time. Them they get all shifty-footed, embarrassed. Guess they figure anyone gotta pray so long needs lotsa help. Same with them missionaries. So they brought out The Great Book of Truth, told us that all we hadta do was believe in the Great Book and all the problems of the world would disappear.*

*Get on your knees an' pray, they said. So those Indyuns back then they got on their knees outta respect for their visitors' ways. Us we do that. And they prayed and they prayed and they prayed. Prayed long time with their heads all bowed down to this strange higher power lived in a book. Prayed an' prayed an' prayed. Wanted all their problems to disappear. When they looked up from all that prayin' they discovered all their land was gone. Up to then us Indyuns never figured the land was a problem but accordin' to the Great Book it musta been on accounta it was the first thing to disappear. Salvation and real estate been workin' hand in hand ever since that time. Heh,*

*heh, heh. Sorry. Don't mind me. Get goin' kinda always wanna throw in a funny. Heh, heh, heh.*

*But's true. Seen us prayin' strange and got fulla fear about it. Not their fault. Us we're all the same, us humans. See somethin' we don't understand we get scared. Fear. If you fear somethin' long enough you get to feelin' you gotta control it, destroy it, change it. Better in the long run to take time to understand but don't work that way in the world lots. Fear done lots to make up hist'ry. Other people's fear pretty much made up us Indyuns' hist'ry anyway.*

*Never was nothin' to be scareda. Us we always wanna share our way with those that want it. Welcome everyone. Even pow-wows got them inter-tribunal dances meant for ev'ryone. Ev'ryone from every tribe of man. Dance together, celebrate the power of the Earth, heal each other, dance and make up one big circle. Like the universe. So if they had asked us, we woulda told 'em what we were doin'. And all we were doin' was prayin'. Prayin's a good thing. People who pray are gonna be happy and happy people, well, they ain't likely to hurt each other.*

*That smoke I was talkin' about is where our truth is. We light up our prayer things every day on accounta our truth is gonna be different each day. So we smudge ourselves in smoke each day to help us face that day's truth an' to remind us of the one great truth same for ev'ryone. That us we need help. Us humans, Indyun or not. So we pray an' ask for help. And the smoke carries our earthly thoughts to the spirit world. Watch smoke sometime. Curls around an' around and pretty soon disappears right in fronta your eyes. Like prayer. It's real while you do it but when you're done . . . it's gone. Into that place we can't see. But when you smudge you go walk around your world an' get a whiffa that smoke sometime through the day, kinda reminds you that you prayed, asked for help. Keeps you thinkin' an' behavin' in a good way. That's what we were doin', givin' ourselves a reminder that it's not our world an' we gotta follow the rules. Be good to each other. Help each other. Thass all. You walk into someone's house who's smudgin' an' getta whiffa that smoke an' you feel good all of a sudden. Comfortable, safe, happy. 'Cause it hits you in your center, your spirit, connects you to everything again.*

*Me'n the boy burned cedar that first mornin'. He di'n' know what to thinka it all. Could see the doubt in his eyes, way his hands shook around some. Us we take that cedar, the leafy part from the branches, kinda roll it together in a little pile and light it with a wooden match. Outside we use the end of a burnin' stick or log an' put the cedar on there to get it goin'. Anyways, once it gets to smoldering we pass some of that smoke over our head, heart and body. It's a purifyin' thing. Meant to purify our body, heart and mind on accounta it's the place the Creator gave us to live. His temple, I guess you could say. So we use that smoke to purify that temple. Make us ready to live the right way, think the right way, feel the right way. That's what it's about. When I told him all what I just said he started to understand more. Felt like he was more a parta us here after. Found a big parta himself that was gone a long time. I know how that feels. See, when you're prayin' you're comin' outta your center. And when you're done and you're walkin' around in the world you're operatin' from that center still. From that truth. Man who faces his own truth each day is gonna be humble, kind, respectful, on accounta he knows he hadta ask for help just to get through the day.*

*When I was out there drinkin' I wasn't operatin' from no center. Anything that takes you away from your center is your enemy. Booze, even negative thinkin' an' behavin', takes you away from it, the place where your truth lives. Robs your spirit from you. Starts you livin' opposite to yourself. Livin' pretty soon outta your head insteada your heart. Old man told me one time he said, the head got no answers and the heart got no questions. Human bein' livin' by the heart's gonna live a good way. One livin' by the head's gonna come lookin' for a guide before too long lead 'em back where they oughta be. Good man, that Harold.*

*Spent lotta years out there lost and wanderin' around. Just like the boy. That's why I like him so much. Gotta lotta me in him and me, I got lotsa him too. Burnin' that cedar joined me up to my center again. Got started in the clinic I went to. Was hard. Hardest thing I ever done. I was real sick for about three weeks on accounta all the booze from all those years was comin' outta me. Kinda snakes outta you in sweat an' fear and tremblin'. But the sickness went away after a while an' there was just this big hollow feelin' in my belly. Mind kinda cleared up too but that hollow feelin' wouldn't go away. Made me afraid. Made me wanna run, go have a drink, feel that burnin' in my belly insteada hollow. Told one of them counselors one day an' she took me into her office, put a blanket on the floor, laid out a bowl and cedar. Lit it up an' said a prayer for both of us on accounta I was too ashamed an' scared to say one for myself. Then she smudged me with that cedar. The smell hit something deep inside me I hadn't felt in a long, long time an' I cried real deep an' long. Cried for Harold, cried for my shame, my fear, all them years. When I was done that hollow feelin' was gone. Counselor told me it was on accounta I was back in my center an' the hollow feelin' was the big empty that happens when we decide not to live outta there no more. It's a natchrel thing for us humans to wanna be livin' outta there an' when we're not it's a natchrel thing to have a yearnin' for it. But us drunks we learn to think that booze gonna not make us feel that yearnin', that ache, that hollowness. It does for a while but comes a time when even the booze turns its back on you an' won't make it go away. Then you drink to just disappear an' me I disappeared for a long, long time. Was cedar brought me back.*

*Had to fight though. All them years of drinkin' make you pretty stubborn inside and that big empty come back day after day. But me, I started to remember what that old man gave me an' I kept on smudgin' an' smudgin', prayin' an' prayin' and pretty soon one day I was goin' to sleep an' I realized I never felt that hollow all day. Slept good. Dreamed lots an' remembered 'em next day. Stayed extra time at the clinic on accounta I didn't wanna go back to the bottle an' I wanted to be strong enough to come home an' stay that way. Pretty good. Bin five years now, so me'n the boy been home about same time, really. Home with ourselves, I mean.*

*So when you see us Indyuns passin' that smoke over ourselves it's not gettin' high, it's gettin' deep.*

According to Keeper, that first light of morning's been a big part of the Indian way around here since anyone can remember. The aid people called it Beedahbun. First light. They used to gather for sunrise ceremonies and offer prayers for guidance through the day. It was a grateful time for everyone. Sleeping's not really called sleeping around here. Oh sure, it's definitely called sleeping by those that stay in the sack until noon or so but it's referred to by the traditional people as "the half-death" on accounta you just check right outta the regular world and head on into the land of dreams for the night. Laying there you don't even know where you are. You're in a different reality. See, us we pay a lot of attention to dreams and you can get a lotta understanding from them once you learn how to remember them and talk to the elders about them. Our brains miss a lotta what's going on around us and dreaming's the way we can catch up on what passed us by that day. The first thing most people feel in the morning's a sense of gratitude for being alive. At least most people who are trying to live in a good way feel that. So the old people would gather for special ceremonies and express their gratitude and ask for help to be good people. That's where the name came from. Anishanabe. Means the good people and it came around on accounta that's all we're supposed to pray for every morning. Learn how to be good people that day and us we always believe our prayers are being answered.

So naturally having Keeper around once I got home and settled meant that I'd have to be springing up outta that old half-death sometime just before sunrise every day. I'll tell you, winter mornings when it's minus thirty around here and windy makes you kinda almost wish you'd gone the other half of the way. There's nothing better than a cold slab of cabin floor on the bare tootsies to get a guy up and hopping around. But I'm up early, before Ma even, grab a fast cup of tea and head on over to Keeper's for a sunrise ceremony. That's where we smudge ourselves with cedar, sing a couple songs with the drum, smoke the pipe and pray. Then I gotta cook breakfast while I listen to the old man talk about whatever's on his mind that day. With Keeper that could be almost anything and we're usually laughing pretty good by the time we eat.

Ma said all along that it's good for me. One of the biggest parts of being Indian is living with respect. Young people learn respect real early and for me, being young at being Indian, it was important that I get into thinking that way right off. Having to get up and walk over to Keeper's to pray and make him breakfast was a good way of learning a respectful way real quick, she said. Sure, I grumbled like hell, but looking back I sure learned a lot awful fast by doing it. Pretty soon it got to be as natural as could be and I was waking up long before the alarm clock. Keeper says I was finally learning the real meaning of "Indian time." So I've been making that morning trek every day since I hooked up with that old guy and it's still one of my favorite things in the world. Peaceful. When you spend a lotta your life shopping for it, a little peace every day gets to feeling like a real bargain once you find it. Anyway, it's quiet come morning and making that walk really gets me in tune with things. You walk out the door and walk down this little trail to the dirt road that winds through the townsite. Going down that rocky little hill gives you a pretty good scan of the area, and I always stop for a moment and have a good look. Still amazing sometimes to me that I'm here. Five years later it still has the same effect on me it had that first morning. Standing there on that rock looking over a world that most people wouldn't think existed in their own country. I love it. Small cabins kinda peering through the trees with a bunch of old cars and trucks parked around the front. There's trails leading off into the bush, out past the johnnie or down to the dock dependin' on which side of the dirt road they're on. Got the usual corduroy-ribbed dogs hanging around that slink out as you pass for a quick lick at the hand or to offer a hesitant kinda bark like they're trying to convince even themselves they're dogs. The kids leave their bikes'n stuff laying around everywhere and here and there behind cabins you can see where there's hides being stretched for scraping, fish-smoking set-ups, cast-off furniture sitting beside firepits like Ma's where people sit in the evenings, some rusted swing sets or just tires hung from trees, maybe some old moose antlers and a clothesline that somehow has always got someone's frozen wool longjohns bobbing up and down in the winter breeze like a big headless puppet.

Down further where the hydro lines end it's different. Around Chief Isaac's house there's a new satellite dish and a couple of newer trucks. Some of the band councillors live beside him and they've got shinier pickups too and you notice right away there's no trails leading past the johnnies. They've got indoor plumbing down there and lotsa folks around here figure it's a big treat to wander over and have their morning constitutional at one of their houses or else at the band office or community hall. Big joke around here has to do with Chief Isaac visiting over at Len and Clarice Bird's one night and having to go to their outdoor john. He spent a whole lotta time out there I guess and the joke is that the reason he took so long was on accounta he couldn't figure out how to flush the thing. But things do look different down where the hydro is and the ones who live down there kinda act different too.

There's a cluster of modern buildings where the schoolteachers live. They come and go about every year with the occasional one sticking around for two years but mosta them get kinda lonesome for the city after a while and head on outta here when their year's up. They've got these little townhouse units all brick and siding with big picture windows that never have the shades up and wouldn't look too outta place in most cities. Some of the ones that were here a few years back put up little wire fences to try'n keep the kids'n dogs outta what they call a yard, but they don't work. Indians and especially the kids just grow up believing that the land's their yard and a fence is just another something to jump over or play with. So mosta them are about half up and half down with no sign of anyone trying to fix them up. The school, which is really only a five-room brick building with a small gym out back, sits right next door to the teachers' units.

Doc and Mrs. Tacknyk are the only ones making an attempt to live like the rest of us. They've got one of them log cabins with the varnished coating that sits right at the edge of the modern area. Got a veranda where they sit at nights when Doc plays his clarinet and Mrs. Doc sews or knits. They're okay. Came here about ten years before I did, liked it and settled right in. They get invited over to lotsa places for supper and fires on accounta Doc's got a lotta pretty funny stories about his years as a medic in Korea and Mrs. Doc gets along good with the ladies. They don't try'n get folks to behave different like the schoolteachers all seem to wanna do and they've even been seen to dance the inter-tribunals at our annual pow-wow. Folks like them even if they do refer to Doc behind his back as Cool Hand Luke, or even Dr. Coldfinger. No need to tell you why, I guess. Only guy I know gets about half a dozen of them pocket hand warmers every Christmas. Never ever had any kids of their own, but they sure do treat ours good. Always seeing kids pouring outta the medical unit with some treat even if they didn't have an appointment. Doc and the Mrs. are part of White Dog and probably always will be.

There's the community hall beside the hockey rink and ball diamond that's just a long low building all done up with cedar shakes and heavy-gauge wire over all the windows. Too many slapshots or foul balls busting up the glass over the years. Us Ojibways are big on hockey and baseball so it's a pretty busy area year round. Nights they got games and movies sometimes or else people just drop by to talk and listen to radio static that passes as hockey games or music on Bert Otter's big portable. Bert's one of my uncles on my father's side and acts as the community development officer and lives in one of them modern houses near the chief. He's in charge of programs down at the hall and for setting up the house league baseball and hockey leagues each year. Funny kinda guy, real serious for an Indian, reads lots and talks like one of them mad scientists on those old movies he shows. Nice guy though.

All that first summer I was being introduced to people who were my relatives. One of the things about small isolated little communities like this is that everyone knows each other and is somehow related to each other. No one moves in or out much so the community stays pretty stable. I met aunts, uncles, cousins, nephews and nieces from both sides of my family. They were all a little shy around me at first and vice versa but the more time I spent here the warmer things got. That's the nice thing about White Dog, everywhere you go there's a friendly face to meet you, greet you or feed you. I liked that last part best for a while there.

The Ontario Provincial Police got a trailer they use for an office whenever they drop by here set up beside the hall. Them OPP have a hell of a time with us White Dog Indians. All the English disappears soon as they come around and even Chief Isaac gets into the act with them. Tells them things like you're never supposed to look an Indian in the eye when you're talking to them on accounta it's an insult. Or moving your hands around a lot when you speak is good, makes us comfortable, wanna trust you. So you always see them OPPs looking down at their feet and waving their hands around whenever they're talking to someone and meanwhile we're making funny faces at them. That and teaching them how to speak Indian all wrong gets a lotta laughs and they never ever figure out how come we're laughing all the time they're around. Most of them are real young and just new to the job, sincere and unspoiled by too much job pressure so everyone gets along fine. Whenever there ever is any trouble around here they just sorta sit back and let us iron it out between ourselves before they'll step in and deal with it. Us we appreciate that. Looking after our own's a big source of pride with us and it's good they understand that. Our Indian leaders are all calling it self-government these days and making big noise about how they're gonna bring it to the people. Us we always had it.

The band office is right across the road from that. That's where all the regular business of White Dog is taken care of or where Chief Isaac goes to get away from Mrs. Isaac whenever he's shy of a good excuse. It's a modern building with a lotta glass up front and varnished cedar shakes covering the walls. Most people don't go there except on cheque day when everyone's up real early and waiting for their monthly money. Funny thing about welfare is it doesn't really seem so insulting a thing when everyone around you is using the same thing to live. Me, I found it tough adjusting and sure was glad to get some work when it happened, but folks around here have gotten used to the promises of the government about working being empty words and just wait patiently for the fishing and hunting seasons when they make big money off the tourists. Lotsa families make a couple hundred a day easy when the Americans arrive, more if their guests catch their limit or bag their moose, bear or deer. But it's the "bait the tourist" game that's the highlight of fishing and hunting season. See, Americans always wanna be knowing all about Indians. Especially us bush Indians. Get them out in a boat or around a fire deep in the bush and they start asking questions. Course, the first thing they wanna know is the cuss words. Wanna be going home and cussing out the boss, the wife or the dog in Indian. Get a big charge outta that. Anyway, they ask about everything and we get a lotta laughs outta teaching them wrong and then watching them trying to do what we told them. Talk around the fires gets real hilarious when the fishing and hunting seasons are in full swing and people work real hard at coming up with the best bait job.

The best one for years was my uncle Gilbert's. He got a real hangdog kinda face and he can put on the serious real good. You start believing him right away on accounta the I-just-lost-my-dog expression. Them tourists they get caught right up in it. Anyway, Gilbert's getting ready to take a big party out for pickerel early one morning and just kinda minding his own business loading up the boat. One of them Americans sidles up alongside him and asks him if there's a special Indian ceremony that we use to ensure good fishing. Well, Gilbert's been a guide for years and he can spot a fish coming better'n most. Both the in-the-water kind and the outta-water kind. So he gets that look going and says that there is but it's so sacred that not a lotta people can know about it. Two big words around here that get tourists' noses to twitching and eyes to bulging are "tradition" and "sacred." Lay those out and they just swarm for the bait. So Gilbert had this guy hooked and landed before he even knew what was happening.

"Ain't s'posed to be tellin' no one who's not initiated into the ceremony. 'Gainst my religion," Gilbert told him.

"Aw, come on. I'll make it worth your while," the tourist said, reaching back for the wallet they all carry no matter how deep in the woods you go or how far out on the lake.

"Well, I could use some new paddles for the canoe, I guess, but hey, don't you be tellin' no one I told you this," my uncle told him, reeling him in slow and gentle.

"Okay! Okay! Here!" he said and handed Gilbert over a brand-new U.S. fifty.

And as he's telling us this around the fire at Kenny Keewatin's one night, Gilbert's reeling us into the tale too. People take great pride in being able to tell a good story and my uncle Gilbert's one of the best when he knows he's got a captive audience. Telling this one was one of the high points of his summer that year and he was playing it to the top.

Guess old Gilbert walked this guy down to the end of the dock with his arm draped over his shoulder all buddy-buddy. When they got there he took a good slow look around the area, squinting his eyes real hard and cupping a hand to his one ear like he was listening for something. The tourist's watching this with the look old Keeper calls "all owl-eyed." Then Gilbert pulled him closer and started whispering in his ear.

"Here's what you gotta say. But you gotta say it real slow, real serious, like a prayer, you know. Won't work unless you get real serious, 'kay?" And the guy's edging even closer and closer to catch what Gilbert's telling him.

"Now repeat after me, real slow. It's three words but each one's real important. Get it wrong you'll curse this trip. We might not even make it back alive today, so you listen good!"

And the tourist's just nodding his head fast and excited, breathing all shallow and fast.

"'Kay. First you say . . . an' say it slow an' serious now . . . you say . . . O-wah. Got it? O-wah."

"Yeah, yeah. I got it, I got it. O-wah. That's easy. O-wah. What's next?"

"'Kay, that's good," Gilbert said, patting him on the back and taking another long slow scan of the area with his eyebrows all pushed up secretive like.

"Second part's like this . . . you go . . . Tah-goo. Get that? Tah-goo. That's all, just . . . Tah-goo. Real slow, real serious."

"Got it. I got it. Tah-goo. Like that?"

"Yeah, yeah, only put same stress on each part. Gotta sound real serious. Heavy kinda."

"Okay okay okay. I got it. Stress each word, yeah, yeah. What's the last part?"

"'Kay. Listen close. Most sacred parta all. Real sacred word. Don't you be throwin' this around after this, 'kay?"

"Yeah yeah yeah. What is it?"

"'Kay. The word is . . . real sacred, 'member . . . gotta get it right! Word is . . . Fye-am. Fye-am, got it?"

"Yeah yeah yeah. Fye-am. Fye-am. Got it."

"Good," said Gilbert, giving him another buddy-buddy on the shoulder. "You keep practicin' that while we cross the lake to the spot. An' when you get there you gotta lean out over the boat, spread your hands out, palms down over the water where you're gonna fish, make big wide circles over the water an' you say them words over an' over real slow, serious an' loud. 'Kay then?"

"Right! Got it! Thanks! Boy, those other guys are sure gonna be surprised when I bless the water with a real sacred traditional Indian thing!" the tourist said, just shivering with delight.

All the way across the lake Gilbert could see the guy mumbling them words over and over and over with his head down, not looking around at the rest of them. Really getting into it. When they got to the little inlet where Gilbert just knew there was gonna be fish, the whole boat got busy rigging up for the first cast, except for Gilbert's student, who sat there looking back at my uncle all nervous and shaky.

"Get . . . it . . . right!" Gilbert mouthed real slow to him, and the tourist nodded his head.

"Guys? Guys?" he said finally to the rest of the boat, who all looked at him kinda aggravated on accounta they all wanted to have the first line in the water. "My friend here, our Ojibway Indian guide, has just taught me a very sacred Ojibway Indian blessing that's guaranteed to get us a successful day's fishing. Now, before we get all excited and just start fishing, I'd like to honor this trip, this boat, all of us and of course honor our Ojibway Indian hosts, by offering this blessing now."

Well, I guess everyone was more than a little surprised and they all held up their casts while the guy leans out over the side of the boat with his hands palms down out over the water and his head leaned back with his eyes all scrunched together tight. Had his hands going in big wide sweeping circles real slow and meaningful for about a minute before he started to talk. His voice was real slow, real deep and real loud.

"O-WAH! TAH-GOO! FYE-AM!" he said, his voice echoing back off the shoreline and spooking a couple deer a hundred yards away. "O-WAH! TAH-GOO! FYE-AM! O-WAH! TAH-GOO! FYE-AM!"

By about the fifth time through, everyone was laughing so hard the boat was rocking and water was sloshing up into it. The guy suddenly realized what he was really saying and looked at his hands still stretched out in front of him palms down over the water, and stared and stared and stared while the rest of them, including Gilbert, just busted up laughing. After a while his shoulders started to shake and tears started rolling down his face as he busted up laughing too. They laughed and laughed for about ten minutes before anyone could breathe well enough to speak.

"Attaboy, Mitchum! Those pickerel are gonna be real hungry after a good laugh like that!" one of the others said through tears of laughter.

All through that day someone would suddenly start to smirking and choking back the laughter and the whole boat would erupt all over again. The guy was real good about it and told Gilbert to keep the fifty and they even tipped him another fifty when they all caught their limit that day. Even threw back lots, Gilbert said.

Needless to say, everyone around Kenny Keewatin's fire that night roared long and loud too.

Great story. You hear lotsa great stories around here. See, one of the things I caught onto real quick was the humor. Reason no one minds the welfare so much, or the government's empty promises, or the lack of lots of things, is on accounta they always find some funny way of looking at it. They find a way to laugh about it. Keeper says that it's the way they've survived everything and still remained a culture. Lotsa Indian ways changed when the whiteman got here, lotsa people suffered, but they stayed alive on accounta they learned to deal with things by not taking them so damn serious all the time. Go anywhere where there's Indians and chances are you'll find them cracking up laughing over something. Humor's a big thing with Indians.

Another place other than the fires where they get together to tell stories is leaning on the railing down at Big Ed Keewatin's store. It's the very last building down where the hydro is, right across from the Doc's, and people are there night and day. Big Ed's called Big Ed on accounta he's about six foot three and three hundred pounds. Real gentle though and lets everyone have whatever they need on credit until cheque day comes. He's got about five kids and his family's real popular around here because they're all real kind and gentle. Anyway, the store is the big hangout and that's why there was so many people around the day the taxi let me off there. You could almost call it the center of White Dog life, and the Keewatins are pretty much always the first to know things when they happen around here.

So looking around on that rock each morning reconnects me to the life of this place and walking through it all alone helps me see it a whole lot different than I did that first day. Then, I figured I was on another planet. Now, this is the only place that makes sense. It took a long time though. Keeper says all of us just get to a point where we're ready to really start seeing. For me I guess it started that night I met him at the cabin and my vision's been getting better and better ever since. I would have called the stuff lying around out here clutter and junk on accounta that's the way my eyes worked before I came here. But now I see it all as evidence of people living the way they wanna live. It all spells out home to me now and I'd miss every bit of it if I had to go away. Sure changed me lots. Like those people living down where the hydro is, I acted like parts of the outside world were pasted to me. It took hanging with Keeper and working into the rhythm of the people to peel it off.

According to Keeper there's two kinds of silences us men like to use more than anything sometimes. There's the smoldering, angry kind we use instead of our fists and there's the big, open embarrassed kind we fall into when our mouths can't move through the motions our hearts are going through. Learning how to work through both of them's likely the biggest struggle us men have, Indian or not. Keeper says the real warriors in our circles are the ones who never surrender to silence. Says the only stone-faced Indians doing any good out there are statues. Funny guy, that Keeper.

Anyway, I never gave that kinda thinking much attention until that first summer I was here. Learning how to fit in wasn't just a matter of landing here and being embraced into the community. No, sir. Us Indians we learned through the years that not everyone that comes along is gonna be real trustworthy. People's history has a good way of teaching you that, especially when your history's full of broken promises and "government fooh-fah" as Chief Isaac puts it. Fooh-fah's not an Ojibway word but it should be, I figure. Anyway, our people can be pretty suspicious at times, especially when it comes to Indians walking around acting white—like me when I got here. Most people who knew about me were kind and good about it all but there were some who really wrestled with wondering whether I really belonged here and if I was still carrying around an Indian heart after all I'd been through.

Having an Indian heart's a pretty important thing. See, because nowadays not everyone's walking around wearing braids and buckskin. Us we got a lotta different looks and lifestyles on accounta the modern world has been creeping into our camps quieter'n your average Cree. So meeting an Indian's not as cut and dried as it used to be. Chief Isaac got a brushcut he's had for years and years. My brother Stanley wears his hair in a ponytail or braids now and again and the women have perms, braids, short hair or whatever. No one dresses a particular way either, from the chief's double-knit leisure suits to the old ladies' shawls and print dresses and gumboots. Go to the city and you'll find lotsa different-looking Indians walking around. We got punk rock Indians now, lawyer-looking brothers and sisters, cowboy Indians and the traditional-looking kind with braids and beaded hide jackets. See them all at pow-wows when you go. Don't much matter what you look like nowadays but's still important to carry an Indian heart inside you. Lots don't. Lots surrender to the influence of the outside world and get thinking "pretty mainstream" as Stanley says. That's about when he launches into the philosophical rambles he likes to go on and starts explaining that "what you think is how you'll act, how you act is how you'll feel, an' how you feel is what you are" kinda fooh-fah. Not his fault. It's all that social work stuff he had to learn in school. Me, I'd rather listen to Keeper, but I love my brother and listen anyway.

Anyway, lotsa Indians nowadays get swallowed up in the influence of the outside and look like all-around brown but not carrying a brown heart anymore. Our people have a hard time accepting that and so have a hard time accepting those kinda people.

Keeper says there's a bunch of reasons why people go that way. Some, like me, got taken away and put into a whole different world and learned a whole different way. Others were put into the residential schools and learned how to be ashamed of their heritage on accounta the priests and nuns taught them from day one that they were dirty, stupid and helpless as Indians. Still others got kinda beat up around home on accounta their families were getting away from the traditional approach to being family and just walked away hurt and angry. Lots more got caught up in the booze and drugs and it sorta washed away all the Indian from their insides. Others started out pretty strong as Indians but started gradually easing over to the mainstream by going through school, marrying non-Indians, working in non-Indian places, hanging out with other kindsa people, joining some kinda church and learning how to grab onto things other than smudge, pow-wow and prayer. Lotsa city Indians are like that now and it happens so gradual they aren't even aware it's happening until someone points it out to them. Keeper says the ones like me and the ones that changed gradual are the easiest to bring back, but the others all gotta work through their hurt, shame and anger before they really get back home to themselves. That's what's important really, Keeper says. Learning how to be what the Creator created you to be. Face your truth. Do that he says and three big things happen in your life. First, you learn how to be a good human being. Second, you learn how to be a good person, and in the process of learning that you learn how to be a good Indian. Can't happen the other way around on accounta you'd be so busy trying to be the ultimate Indian you'd kinda miss out on just being happy being a person. Going through the process is what gives you an Indian heart. Your insides in tune with your outside. Get that way and you can pretty much be anything you wanna be, live anywhere you wanna live, look any way you wanna look and you're still gonna have a true heart. An Indian heart. Funny guy, that Keeper.

Anyway, that's what scares people the most I guess. Walking around without a true heart makes you kinda untrustworthy. On accounta history us Indians don't mix well with untrustworthy people. So I had my share of folks on White Dog and in the area looking at me with a kinda suspicious eye for a while. Some people used the language against me. They'd start talking away in Ojibway whenever I'd come along and be laughing away pretty good together. Me I'd always feel like it was me they were laughing at. Pretty soon though my ma got me to talking bits of Ojibway and that helped. She'd ask me for tea or something in Ojibway and point to what she wanted. Little things like that and it wasn't too long before I could hold small conversations. Jane would walk around with me and drill me on the names of things all the time, so that it wasn't too long either when I knew what people were referring to around me and I'd kinda get the drift of the talk. Soon as I started busting in on conversations people started to change.

Others just used silence and that probably hurt the most. Hard to figure where you stand with people when they won't recognize you in any way. I didn't mind the name calling I'd get every now and then, especially from the younger crowd, on accounta I'd grown up with that and kinda learned to ignore it. And I didn't mind the teasing I got when I didn't know how to do things that even the little tykes knew, like cleaning fish or starting up a fire right off. Once I learned or even showed some desire to ask someone to show me things all the teasing went away.

Got used to all of it and learned how to deal with lotsa different reactions from people. By the time that first summer was over I'd come a long way towards being comfortable with being here and being a White Dog Indian and most folks had gotten comfortable with me. There was a lotta laughing going on about something I'd done or tried to do, something I'd said all wrong or some way of behaving and even now those stories bring a lot of laughter.

That's why the stony silence coming from my brother Jackie was so hard to figure out. While the rest of my family just swallowed me up and took me in, Jackie sat on the edges of it all aloof and distant. He was bigger'n me and Stanley and it made me uneasy having him around on accounta he'd just stare at me most of the time and not say anything. He had a big, brooding silence whenever we were around together. After a while I think we just gave up trying to get through and we settled into that awkward kind of silence that can make strangers outta brothers.

We were sitting around the fire outside Ma's one night, Keeper'n me, Ma, Stanley, Jane, Jackie and my uncle Gilbert and auntie Mavis. Gilbert was showing us the new hand drum he'd made and Keeper decided he should show me how to sing a song with the thing.

"Yeah, Keeper," Gilbert said with a laugh. "Time he learned our way of singin'. Gotta learn that we got a few good tunes of our own, us Indyuns."

"I seen him dancin' around to that music he plays all the time an' kinda looks like he's got some Indian rhythm in him, all right," Jane said, giving my bum a little tweak. "Moves them skinny little buns around pretty good."

"Hey-yuh," said Ma. "One of these days gonna teach him how to do a real dance. All boys gotta know how to do a jig, you know. You like fiddle, my boy?"

"I seen him eyeing up the Keewatin girls the other day," Stanley said. "Kinda looked like he had fiddlin' around on his mind then, all right!"

Keeper laughed. "Wanna win a girl over you gotta know a good love song on the drum. These days our women want a sensitive man around. Drum's good for teachin' sensitive."

"Hmmpfh." Ma looked over at Keeper out of the corner of her eye. "Lot you know about it. When's last time you ever paid a woman any mind? Old fart."

"Be surprised what some old guys can do," Keeper said, grinning back across the fire.

"Promises, promises, promises," Ma said, and we all laughed.

Keeper started a slow, steady rhythm on the drum and we all got quiet and listened. It was the kinda rhythm we use in our round dances. Round dances are the big get-together dances lotsa Indians use. You join hands and move around in a big circle, moving your feet in rhythm with the drum and kinda moving in and out from the center every now and then, coming nose to nose with each other then moving back out. It's a lot of fun, and the songs are lighter than other kindsa singing.

"Ah-ho my girl I love you so
Give ev'rythin' I got to you
My home, my heart, my love you know
My truck, my dog, my money too."

We all laughed again. Keeper kept on singing and drumming away so we all got up to shuffle around the fire while he went on and on.

"Your hair so black your eyes so brown
I want to lay you on the groun'
To make papoose just you an' me
A big Ojibway family."

We all laughed and sat back down for more tea and the fried bread Ma'd made for the occasion. Jackie was the only one who hadn't danced. He just sat there staring into the fire while the rest of us had carried on. Once we'd settled in Keeper handed Gilbert's drum over to me.

"S'a good drum, Gilbert, s'a good drum," he said. "Give it a try there, boy!"

It was the first time I'd held one and it felt light but clumsy in my hands. The beater was just a foot-long piece of clothes hanger all wrapped up with hockey tape and a big knob at the one end. I didn't know what to do with it.

"Just copy what Keeper did," Jane said. "It's okay. Try it."

They were all watching me now, even Jackie. I tried to remember the rhythm I'd gotten used to at Keeper's in the mornings and then tried to tap it out on the drum. Lightly at first, then a little stronger and stronger. It sounded okay to me, but when I started to sing one of the songs I heard Keeper singing in the mornings I lost the rhythm. The beat got all scattered and the song fell apart on its own.

Jackie stood up and just kinda stared at me. "Real Indyuns got a feel for the drum. Got that rhythm right here!" he said, thumping his chest real hard. "Shouldn't be bangin' that city crap on no hand drum! All of you should quit encouraging him. Tryin' to dance, tryin' to speak the language, tryin' to drum an' sing. He ain't no Indyun. Got more white an' black in him than he does us. Gotta be able to see that. I sure do!" He stalked off into the darkness.

No one said a word, just stared at the empty space in the darkness he disappeared into. I handed the drum back to Gilbert. I could feel everyone's eyes on me as I stared into the fire. My ma put her arm around my shoulders and when I looked up I could see Keeper watching me from across that fire, his eyes glowing from the reflection and tears as he nodded his head slowly, slowly.

"I don't know, man," Stanley was saying a few days later while we were walking through the bush. "Jackie's always been a little more intense than the resta us, even when we were kids. Maybe things just hit him more than the resta us."

Me'n Stanley spend a lot time wandering through the bush together. Even now. He just stops by Ma's and we head off without even saying anything to each other or Ma about where we're going or what we're gonna do. It's one of those unspoken brother things that kinda grew up on its own soon after I was home. Stanley takes a lotta pride in the fact that he got through social work school, got a degree and came right back home. He says lot more people gotta do that on accounta it's the only way our reserves and communities are really gonna benefit from the outside world. Him he calls it stealing horses.

"They always used to call us Indians horse thieves way back when, might as well be that now," he'd always say in that social worker kinda educated voice he uses when he's thought about something lots. "Only now we gotta steal diff'rent kinda horses, brother. We gotta steal all the whiteman's horses to make our circles strong again."

I've learned through the years to just nod my head and listen when he gets going like this on accounta Stanley can really get on a roll and it's pretty near impossible to squeeze even a grunt in between his words when he's rolling.

"Diff'rent kinda horses. Education, technology, business, politics, communication, employment an' health care. All of 'em, we gotta steal all of 'em if we're gonna be competitive an' stay alive as people."

One of these days my big brother's gonna find his way into politics and I just know he's gonna be doing a good job for the people. He's sure got a way with words, and I learned a whole lotta stuff about our people from just walking through the bush with him and letting him ramble on. Better than any history course and lots funnier too.

Anyway, we're walking through the bush that day and Stanley's not saying a lot. Jackie's behavior at the fire that night had everyone wondering and worrying some too. I guess outbursts like that have been a mainstay of my brother's life for as long as anyone can remember.

"He was always kinda wild inside," Stanley said finally. "Always kinda wild. Hung out with our grampa lots when we lived on the trapline an' was the only one of us that really ever went an' stayed with our father before he died. He was really connected to the men an' when they died he took it hard both times.

"Sometimes I think the wilderness he was born in kinda stuck to him, you know. Always had that untamed thing about him. He's always gonna be a strong Indian, that Jackie. Never let anybody roll over him, not even when we were kids.

"You know, that day they came and took us away, he punched that guy right in the face when he was droppin' us off at the foster home. Just reached up an' gave him a good one right in the teeth. He was only six. Hurt his hand but I kinda think he hurt the social worker more. Once he realized we were being kidnapped he got real mean. Come to think of it, we had our problems too when he found out I was gonna go off an' study. Didn't really settle down about it until I told him I was comin' right back here. Can't stand social workers even to this day, that Jackie."

Something in the big brooding silence I saw coming outta Jackie made all of this easy to believe. He was a big, strong man. I seen a lotta guys that looked like that in the pen and I knew that my brother was one of the those guys you really didn't wanna cross too hard. Kinda give them their territory and let them be was the best advice. I'm no slouch when it comes to a good go, but I know my limits and teeing off with my brother wasn't within them.

"I remember comin' out to the barn one day in that foster home," Stanley was saying. "You were already gone about three weeks an' all of us were hurtin' pretty bad about it. I'm goin' out to the barn to start chores an' I see Jackie leanin' out the hay mow window, way up on the one side lookin' out towards the road. I watched him. Pretty soon I saw him lift a rifle to his shoulder. That farmer guy always let us bigger kids use the .22 to shoot woodchucks, an' Jackie had it with him in the barn. Anyway, pretty soon I heard a car comin' an' Jackie heard it too. Was the farmer. Mr. Wright, his name was. He turns into the long lane an' Jackie's pointin' that gun at him all the way up the lane. Followed him with that gun even after he got outta the truck an' walked into the house. He never put that gun down for about a minute after Mr. Wright went inside. After that I watched him each day after school an' ev'ry day he was up in that hay mow trackin' Mr. Wright with that .22. Ev'ry day. Never ever let him know that I saw him. Figured it was his little secret. But it was sure spooky, boy. That's how wild he was, even then. Was only seven then. He really hated the place an' he hated them for lettin' you be taken away, an' sometimes these days, little brother, I think he kinda hated himself for not bein' able to stop it. I don't know. I don't know."

We walked through the bush that day for a few more hours, me'n Stanley. Both kinda lost in our memories of childhood, thinking about our big brother and where he might be at inside himself. Until this conversation I figured I was the only one who ever really had a hard time because of my being taken away. But from what Stanley was saying and from what I could see, there was a different kind of pain seeping outta my brother Jackie. A throbbing kinda ache in the bones. The kind heroes must get when they realize all of a sudden that they can't save everybody. The losing overshadowing the saving.

Me'n Jane were thumbing through her photo album a few weeks later. I can't believe the memory that woman's got for even the smallest details. Like she soaks up everything around her all the time and all you gotta do is give her memory a little squeeze sometime and it all drips out, every detail. She loves talking about it all too and her eyes get that big shiny look you see in the eyes of kids on Christmas or birthdays. I like seeing her like that and even now I'll ask about something just to see her light up again. A walking, talking Raven encyclopedia, that one.

We're going through the pages and she's introducing me to people I haven't met yet when we come to a bunch of pictures of her'n Jackie and big bunches of other people in different places. Everybody's got long hair and wearing red bandanas or red armbands in each picture.

"You guys had a club goin'?" I asked.

She smiled at me the way she still does sometimes when I ask about things that she figures I oughta have known about.

"Yeah. Yeah, bro'. It was a club, all right. A war club was what it was. Ever hearda AIM?"

"Yeah. It's a toothpaste takes the danger outta getting close!"

She likes it when I'm being funny or jiving around to my music at Ma's. She says that's when she feels like she's around the little kid got taken away from her. Kinda like living the childhood we never had together. Funny lady, that Jane sometimes.

"No, this AIM was no toothpaste. Stands for the American Indian Movement. Me'n Jackie got involved with 'em back in the early seventies. AIM was a really strong Indian organization. Tried to change the way government an' even our own people were dealin' with our problems. Lotsa young people got into it. Lotta angry young people. Me'n Jackie fit right in, 'specially him.

"Around here we got into this thing called the Ojibway Warriors Society, which was tied right up with what AIM was tryin' to do. We didn't figure our leadership was doin' much in the way of stoppin' our land bein' taken away. Didn't figure they were doin' much about anythin' really. We figured us young people had more power an' more answers, so we got together an' started pushin'.

"Lotta us didn't take no shit from anybody. Real strong in our Indian beliefs. The Ojibway Warriors an' AIM were our way of sayin' we wanted the best for our people. Wanted the treaties honored, promises kept, wanted a future. Jackie got to be a real leader. Ev'rybody listened when he spoke an' he spoke good. Real hardline. You know, you seen it."

"Yeah," I said. "Seen it. But I still don't know why he's pissed at me."

She took my hands in hers and looked at me in that soft sister way she has. "It's not you he's mad at, Garnet. You're just an innocent bystander really. Jackie's a lot like our dad."

"How so?"

"Well, they did spend some time together before he died. Jackie'd go an' sleep over at Dad's cabin and they'd talk an' stuff. Not lots but a few times. He knew more about our pa than anybody and he's like him lots. Dad'd take him out on the trapline when he was just small on accounta Jackie learned things real fast and could do things that most kids can't do till they're maybe thirteen, fourteen. Him'n the bush are pretty tied up together. Just like Pa.

"Our dad was real strong on the fam'ly. That's why what happened hurt him so much. Fam'ly an' keepin' it together was all that mattered. He'da fought anythin' that threatened it. Bear, wolverine, anythin'. But the system was somethin' he didn't understand an' when you can't understand somethin' you don't know how to fight it. Dad figured he lost. Figured he was weak. He died thinkin' that. Jackie inherited that fam'ly waya thinkin' from him an' he was always angry at what happened to us. Turned into a big broodin' angry wounded bear kinda guy just like our dad was in the end. Gotta lotta the bear in him, that Jackie. Gotta lotta the bear in him."

"So what's this gotta do with me? Why won't he talk to me? And why the hell does he seem so pissed at me?"

"AIM was Jackie's way of gettin' back. He didn't know how to fight the system either, an' when the Ojibway Warriors an' AIM came along he found his way of fightin' it. Not only fightin' it but gettin' back at it. Also found a way of gettin' all that anger out.

"Spent a lotta time with the traditional elders we got to lead our actions. Us young people back then really saw the strength in the old ways an' we didn't do nothin' without consultin' the elders, smokin' the pipe, doin' sweats an' prayin'. Used the slogan "In the spirit of Crazy Horse" on accounta that's exactly how Crazy Horse prepared himself for battle. Traditional way. Prayer. Pray for the enemy as well as yourself. Pray for the people. Jackie was one of the most eager.

"In '74 the government was tryin' to take away a big chunka land belonged to one of the reserves outside Kenora. Turned it into a park an' called it Anishanabe Park like that was enough to keep us happy. Makin' money offa that park but never gave no money to the people. So we went in there an' took it over one summer. Took it over an' demanded that they honor the treaty that said it was Indian land. We had guns an' lotsa support from AIM after a while. Had the OPP, the army an' even had some FBI wanderin' around once it all got into full swing.

"Jackie was the spokesman. Good speaker. Made it all make sense for them reporters who never understood anythin' about Indians before. Made them cops an' army guys back right off too. All that anger was right up front with him an' it served the people well that time.

"We stayed in the park all that summer an' when we fin'lly got a promise that the people would be compensated we came out. Never fired a shot but got what we wanted. Jackie an' three others got arrested but no one went to jail. Too much newspaper coverage by then.

"Mosta us just went back into our lives but Jackie kept on goin'. He went to the States an' hooked up with AIM an' traveled all around doin' things with them. When he came back here he didn't talk too much about it but he was even stronger in pushin' for

Indian ways in ev'rythin'. AIM kinda died out after a while, but Jackie's still got all that stuff inside him. Strong Indian. So seein' you around here again reminds him of all that, all the hurt he felt, all the stuff that never got resolved despite AIM, all the personal stuff, an' I think it gets all that anger stirrin' around in him again. Only this time there's no place to put it an' I think that scares him some."

"Sure don't seem all too scared to me," I said, wondering how the hell I coulda missed out on hearing about this when it was happening.

"Gotta lotta the bear in him, like I said. Bear's a good warrior. Doesn't show fear. But the bear learns how to live with it though, an' that's what Jackie never learned. How to live with it."

Summer turned over slowly into autumn and before we knew it we could feel the chill of that winter easing into our mornings. Around here the seasons changing are so gradual you gotta learn to feel them before you ever see them. The grass gets a different texture when you're walking on it and the lake gets itself a slightly sharper edge when it sloshes up on your hands as you're filling up that lard pail with the day's water. The air doesn't move so much and you start to hear things a whole lot better, especially in the early mornings. Keeper says the winter months are special on accounta that's when the old stories are told. Once those "long snow moons" arrive the elders in those old tribal days would gather the people around a fire and tell them stories long into the night sometimes.

Keeper says there's two reasons why stories are told only in the winter months. One was on accounta the spirits of the world get kinda sleepy then too and some of them drop right off into slumberland. So if someone was telling a story about bad spirits, they wouldn't overhear and maybe get offended and want some revenge or something. The other reason was on accounta the people. See, winter being such a brutal time in this country, all cold and windy for about six months, sometimes getting down to thirty below for weeks at a time, there wasn't lots for the people to do. Couldn't hunt real good and too cold for the kids to play, so they could give all their attention to the stories. Elders knew that trying to get our people to listen to stories and the teachings within them was next to impossible in the summers when there was all kindsa other distractions. See, the important thing about our stories isn't so much the listening, it's the time you spend thinking about them. There's lots of traditional thinking buried deep within each story and the longer you spend thinking about it the more you learn about yourself, your people and the Indian way.

Anyway, winter slid in pretty easy that first year. Ma'n me got a lotta meat from people on accounta I was no screaming hell at hunting yet, and we got Big Ed to freeze most of it in the big locker he kept at the back of his store. Stanley, Jane'n me and our uncles went picking wild rice and got enough for the winter for everybody. All around the reserve people were getting ready for the long snow moons that were looming up big and cold and powerful on the other side of the horizon.

I was over visiting Keeper one day just after the first snow flew and he was asking me whether things had gotten any better between Jackie'n me.

"Not really," I said. "He don't come around Ma's so much and never tries to talk to me."

"Hmmpfh," Keeper said, lighting up his pipe. "Hmmpfh. Gotta lotta the bear in him, that Jackie. Gotta lotta the bear in him. So I guess you kinda need to use a little of the bear to get his attention back. Sounds like a bear thing to me."

"Whaddaya mean, bear thing? Jane said that too. What do you want me to do, hibernate with him?" I get a little irked at the way Indians will lay something out there like this "bear thing" and then not explain. I've learned since that it's just the way they get your attention when they wanna lay something important on you, but it still irked me some.

Keeper banged the ash from his pipe into the garbage can. "Us humans, we're not born with the same kinda gifts the animals got. Sure, us we got lotsa things they don't too but they come out ahead in a big way. See, animals got a better deal on accounta they're born knowin' exactly who an' what they are. Us we gotta search for that. Bear comes out into the world jus' knowin' it's a bear. Fox same thing. Rabbit same thing. I been around a long time an' never seen no erotic bear."

"Erotic?"

"Yeah, you know, confused like."

"No, no, no, no," I said, laughing and putting my hand on his shoulder. "Neurotic. Erotic means horny all the time. Neurotic means confused."

"Oh," Keeper said, laughing pretty good too now. "In that case I have seen a few erotic bears! Fact, I guess I been kinda new-rotic 'bout bein' erotic too a few times! Heh, heh, heh."

It took a while for us to settle down.

"See," he finally continued, "animals right off know who an' what they are. So the old people knew this an' started watchin' the animal people to learn from 'em. That's where big parta the Indyun way comes from. From the animal people. Another big part comes from the plant people an' rock people but that's another story. Us we get to know we're human bein's after a while. Know pretty soon we're boys or girls, maybe even know lots 'bout our fam'ly tree. Still, takes us long time before we find the truth about who we are. You know this good already on accounta comin' back here an' all. But us we all gotta search out our own truth an' find our own life.

"Someday you watch bears. Never no trouble gettin' along in the bear fam'ly. Wrassle lots, growl around too, but always close an' lovin' with each other. Mother bear teaches them young ones an' they learn. No big fuss, jus' bear learnin'. You gotta be same way now. Gotta be like bears an' play."

"Play? *Play?*"

"Bears they play lots. You watch 'em, you'll see. Play lots. Mama bear knows that gettin' the attention of them cubs gonna be tough. So when she wants to teach 'em how bears should be she makes up a game. You watch how she teaches 'em to hunt. She'll take 'em to a big meadow an' start to gallopin' around after mice. When she catches one she'll give it to the cubs an' run off to gallop around some more, really playin' up the fun of it. Well, pretty soon them cubs get to likin' the taste of mice an' bein' cubs they take natchrel to all the runnin' an' gallopin' around. Pretty soon they're out there chasin' them mice an' not even knowin' that they just learned somethin' that'll keep 'em alive forever.

"Same way with you an' that brother of yours that's got a lotta the bear in him. It's gonna take playin' to get through."

"Okay, but play what?" I was thinking maybe this was just another Indian riddle.

"You gotta figure out what to play. Reason you gotta play with each other is on accounta you never had no chance to do that ever. Maybe if you be kids awhile you'll learn more about bein' men. It's a bear thing really."

I walked back to Ma's that day through that first real staying-on-the-ground snow of the year wondering about this bear thing, wondering what to play, wondering how to get Jackie to play it anyway and wondering if what we were gonna learn in the process would keep us alive forever.

Funny how things work out sometimes. I must have spent about three weeks trying to figure it out. Every morning I'd catch him peering over at me with a twinkle in his eye on accounta he could tell I was still trying to work it out. He wouldn't say anything though and pretty soon I just kinda surrendered to the problem and asked for a little help to learn to see my way through when we prayed in the morning. Funny how it works out sometimes.

Hockey season got started in a big way and the White Dog Flyers were starting to look around for players. I played every winter in the pen for the farm team and I've always had pretty good wheels. I like passing more than scoring and I had a lotta pride in my play making and skating ability. Never was the scrapping type on accounta I figured I could finesse my way through anything. So naturally I wanted to try out for the team.

Around here hockey's the next biggest thing to bingo. My uncle Gilbert's known as the best talent to come outta this area and once got to scrimmage with the Chicago Blackhawks back in the days when Bobby Hull was just a rookie. So around here Raven's to hockey what Red Sky is to country singing. Both Stanley'n Jackie were regulars on the Flyers and had been for years, with Stanley being a stay-at-home defenseman type and Jackie more of a power forward who kinda likes the rough stuff in the corners. What with my uncles Joe and Charlie still skating and Gilbert kinda part-timing through the seasons you'd almost think we should have been called the White Dog Ravens. Anyway, I was looking forward to playing. Both to relieve the boredom and to get some exercise.

"Gonna make an Indyun hockey player outta your baby boy," Uncle Joe told my ma one night when we were down at the community hall watching Bert Otter flood the rink. "Gotta be tough to play Indyun hockey, Garnet, not like them city leagues an' lot tougher'n your jail playin'. Lot tougher."

"That's right," Stanley said. "Around here when they ask you how hard your slap is, they're not talkin' about your shot!"

Jackie walked in about then and nodded to all of us and turned to watch the flooding. I was kinda glad I was gonna be playing on his side on accounta he's so big regular he was gonna be huge with pads on. I shivered imagining him lining somebody up for a big bodycheck. Glad it wasn't gonna be me.

"Garnet's comin' out for the Flyers, Jack," Stanley said. "Gonna be a full five of Ravens out there this year. Says he's some kinda slick passin' center, make your game better."

Jackie shook his head and looked over at the rest of us. He sized me up and shook his head again before he spoke to Stanley.

"He's gonna get killed out there. This is Indyun hockey. Gotta be an Indyun to take it. Prob'ly spend mosta my time peelin' him offa the blueline."

"Don't worry about me," I said to everyone and Jackie in particular. "Can't hit what you can't catch!" And I started jiving around the room like Muhammad Ali.

They laughed. I caught Jackie's eye and could have sworn I saw a little flash of warmth. But it was gone pretty quick.

"Jus' what the Flyers need this year," he said, walking back out into the night. "Some city-slick center gonna look like a bagga antlers in a uniform. Hmmpfh. Indyun hockey player."

"Man, does that guy ever lighten up?" I asked Stanley.

"Yeah, actually hockey's kinda the way he gets a lotta steam off. Plays on the team but comes out ev'ry mornin' by himself to skate around, work on his shot an' stuff. Keeps the ice clean every day for everyone else. Kinda mellows out ev'ry winter, except when there's a game. Then watch out."

"Every mornin', eh? Hmmpfh." I went and joined Ma to set out for home. "Every morning."

I wasn't sure how it was gonna turn out but I found myself lacing up my skates one morning about nine o'clock. Bert had done a great job on the ice and it was smooth and fast. I was just picking up my stick when I heard Jackie's voice from a ways off.

"Hey, bagga antlers! Good time to be out here for

you, no one to get in your way or see your wobbly style!"

"Don't mind me," I said, leaning on my stick in my best Ken Dryden impression. "That swishing sound you'll be hearing for the next little while's gonna be me blowing by you."

"Yeah, right," he said with a sneer. "Hope you got an extra blade on your ass 'cause that's what you'll be skatin' on when you blow by me!"

He hopped over the boards and set to lacing up his blades while I skated around warming up. He started skating around at the other end of the ice and for the next little while we both concentrated on getting loose and not really paying the other any mind except for the occasional glance to check out each other's skating.

I heard the net being hauled over the boards and went off to drag mine over too. Pretty soon you could hear the solid whack of sticks on pucks and the occasional thump of a puck hitting the boards. There's no glass at the ends of these outdoor rinks, just heavy-gauge wire, or sometimes chicken wire on the poorer reserves, so when I started trying to nail the upper corners of the net with slapshots there was a lotta pinging of pucks off of wire. It took me a while to hear the silence coming from the other end of the rink.

"Only count when they go *in* the net!" Jackie yelled. "Gotta drop your bottom hand more on your stick, lean into it more. Golf season don't start till spring."

"Yeah, well why don't you show me how it's done, then, hotshot." I passed the puck the length of the ice. "I heard your slapshot looks like a butterfly heading towards the net. Got more wobble than a wounded duck, I heard."

"Heard wrong, Downtown," Jackie said and skated up to my end. He stopped just short of the blueline. "Heard wrong."

He nailed the top right corner with a shot I just barely saw. I picked the puck up outta the net and passed it back while I retrieved mine from the corner. He nailed the top left with another sizzler and then just stood there smiling at me.

"That's how it's done, son. That's how it's done."

We started firing away at the net and pretty soon we were both retrieving pucks and passing them around. We started skating around more and making passes between us. It got faster'n faster the more we warmed up and pretty soon we were flying around that ice making two-way passing plays that ended up with a wrist shot or a big slapper from the blueline.

"Oooooo-hoo-hoo-hoo!" we'd yell. "Nice shot!"

"Great little pass," he'd say. "Right on the tape! Didn't even think you saw me."

"Good speed," I'd say. "More good for a big guy."

"Fastest bagga antlers I ever saw," he said and whipped in to steal the puck off my stick, giving me a little elbow at the same time. "But not fast enough!"

Around here we call an elbow in the chaps like that a nudge, and I skated up to swipe the puck back an' gave him a little nudge myself before skating away. He shook it off and turned to chase me up the ice. It had become a one-puck game pretty quick and we chased each other around and around, getting faster'n faster, neither one of us wanting to slow up or show the other we couldn't take it. It went on like that for what seemed like hours, both of us trying to outdo the other.

Finally, just as I was making my famous loop-de-loop at the blueline, he reached out and bear-hugged me to the ice. The force made us slide into the corner with our arms wrapped around each other, sticks sprawled at the blueline and the puck forgotten. We were laughing real hard and almost choking from lack of breathing. We lay on the ice for a long time like that, laughing and getting our wind back slowly. Pretty soon we started to notice that we were still bear-hugging each other and there got be a kinda embarrassed feeling but we never let go.

"I missed you, man," Jackie said, laying his forehead on my shoulder. "All them years? I missed you.

"I remember when you were small. Little guy just learnin' to run around. Had my gumboots on one day, runnin' around in them. No clothes on an' them gumboots were way too big for you, kept runnin' right outta them. But you kept on puttin' 'em back on an' runnin' around some more, just laughing and laughing. I remember. That's where I started calling you little bagga antlers on accounta you were such a bony little kid.

"You used to come over in the middle of the night an' crawl in with me. I remember how you used to fall asleep holdin' on real tight to my hair. Wouldn't go to sleep unless I let you do that. Slept with me lots back them. 'Member?"

"No," I said, feeling kinda trembly inside all of a sudden, "I don't remember any of that, man."

"Well I do, man, I do." Tears were coming down his face. "I wanted to shoot these motherfuckers when they took you away! Wanted to shoot all of 'em. Wasn't a year went by for a long time I didn't think about you, man, where you were, what you were doin', what you looked like. Not one year. Then I guess I gave up. Just gave up and tried to forget you. Was easier that way. Pretended I never had no baby brother. Pretended I didn't have a lotta things."

"You got a brother, man. I ain't no baby no more but I'm your brother. I just can't understand why you act like you don't want me around, why you don't talk to me." I could feel the melting ice seeping through my jeans, but I didn't want to let go either.

"Don't know how, I guess. I spent all my life hatin' them motherfuckers. Hatin' them for takin' you away, hatin' them for killin' my father, hatin' them for makin' our people suffer, for lyin' to us, makin' promises they never fill, for keepin' us down, for all the kids that die ev'ry year on accounta they can't get what they need to live, ev'ry one of our people that drink themselves to death, ev'ry beaten-up wife, ev'ry welfare cheque, and hatin' every damn social worker, cop, shrink, politician, judge, doctor making money off our people's suffering. Hated them for all of it, man, all of it. After a while I just hated anything havin' to do with white.

"Then you show up here, all white, black, anything but Indyun, and I found myself hatin' you. Hatin' you, man! Knowin' that it ain't your fault on accounta they kidnapped you and you didn't have no choice. Kidnapped you and turned you into that thing that crawled outta that cab that day. Knowing all of that but hatin' you anyway on accounta you're walking around here tryin' to be some kinda instant Indyun. Knowin' you're just trying to get back but hatin' you because of the whiteness I can see all over you. My own brother! My baby brother I used to sleep with an' hold onto when he was a little guy! Hatin' you for the white that ain't your fault. An' I'm afraid, man! Afraid that if I talk to you or spend a lotta time with you then that hate'll spill over onto to you and you'll go away again an' I'll never see you. And I'm afraid that if I don't you'll go away anyway. That's why, man, that's why."

We were both sobbing away now lying there on that ice. Two grown men, water seeping through their jeans, breath coming out in clouds and still not wanting to move away. It didn't matter right then if anyone walked by and seen us there. Didn't matter that it was cold and we were gonna catch a real good fever before too long. All that mattered was that big, warm bear hug that neither of us wanted to break and the tears. Took me a while before I noticed I was holding his long ponytail with one hand.

"Keeper's teachin' you good, isn't he?" Jackie asked after a long while as we untangled ourselves from each other. "Learnin' lots, eh?"

"Hey-yuh," I said. "Learnin' to see things lot different than when I got here, that's for sure, man."

"Musta been hard, comin' back here. Hard to believe after all them years, eh?"

"Yeah. I never figgered on bein' no Indian, man. I was kinda happy being black. But not as happy as right now."

He smiled at me and I could see different light in there. "You listen to what he tells you. He knows good things. Got 'em from our grampa, you know. You'll be drummin' an' singin' right after a while. Sorry about that shit back then, man. I was screwed up."

"It's okay, it's okay. I understand." I told him how all these years I hated the motherfuckers too a lot of the time only I was always too scared to do anything about it. "Most of the time I didn't even know I was angry. Too lost, really. And I know I got lots to learn, but I don't feel so lost anymore. I feel I really *am* home. For the first time ever. But I need your help too, brother, on accounta you're a big part of who I am."

He looked up at the sky. "Guess I need your help too, man. Maybe helpin' to wash that white offa you gonna help me understand *them* a little more. Never really tried that.

"Hey." He slapped me on the back. "Let's go to Ma's and get warm and dry. She'll like that."

"Won't get an argument from me, man."

"Last one there's gotta chop wood for the other for a week!" He scrambled for the boards to get out of his skates.

"Sure as hell ain't gonna be me, pal!" I said and started to scramble too.

We got out of our gear in record time that day and ran through that ankle-deep snow all the way down that dirt road through the townsite with people grinning out their windows and waving to us as we laughed and ran and tackled each other to the ground. Stanley'n Jane were standing out on his porch when we roiled by and we could see them smiling away and nodding their heads slowly up and down. By the time we got to Ma's we were covered in snow.

We were kicking the snow off our boots and getting ready to go inside, when Jackie looked at me for a long moment.

"You know, I had them walls up pretty good. Took a lot of guts to get out there to play shinny."

"It's a bear thing really," I said with a little grin. "It's a bear thing."

The Raven family really came together after that. Ma's became the gathering place and pretty much every night of the week there was a big fire going out back right through that first winter. The White Dog Flyers became the best native hockey team in the area and we won our fair share of tournaments with the big line of Garnet, Jackie and Gilbert Raven the scourge of the league. Had Stanley'n my uncle Joe on the blueline with us, and in a way, playing hockey as a unit really helped us men come together as family too. Jackie gave me a

White Dog Flyers jersey with the name Bagga Antlers on the back instead of Raven and I've been wearing that thing every year since then. Keeper kinda became a combination assistant coach and mascot and Jane became our main cheerleader. We played a lotta games, and by the time spring started to break through we'd melted away a lot of those lost years.

Those nights are just like the nights we share now, the six of us sitting around my ma's living room with a good fire blazing in that pot-bellied stove, each with our cup of tea. Keeper'n me got our feet propped up on the pipe coming out the back, Stanley's reading something or other, Jackie's cleaning a rifle while Ma'n Jane are playing checkers or working up moccasins or something. Sometime around nine or so there'll be a knock on the door and a whole flock of Ravens will fly in. More tea'll be made and we'll all head out to stand around the fire. Uncle Joe'll start sawing on his fiddle and Ma'll have me up there trying to get through the "Red River Jig" while the rest are grabbing their bellies in laughter. Nights haven't changed much since that first winter, really. Those nights were real family nights and they huddle up in my memory the same way, not much difference between any of them.

What sticks with me most and what still gets me through the rough times these days is Keeper'n me one morning in February, standing in knee-deep snow watching that first light breaking over the horizon. It was a deep, deep February cold and the air was hardly moving at all. We could hear the trees snapping like they do when it gets real cold and every little motion of our clothing seemed amplified in that still morning air. There's real magic at that time of day. When the light starts creeping in and the world gets all purple around you and the air's as still as it was that day, it's like everything's vibrating with energy. Like it all has to work real hard just to hold itself together instead of erupting in a big celebration. It's a strong sense of magic. And when the colors start to break, all the pinks and blues and gold and orange and all them other colors they have no name for in English, well, it's like you can hear them sizzle deep inside you and you start to feel a part of yourself start to sizzle too. Something deep, deep inside that takes mornings like that and opening yourself up to them to get to and feel.

"Feel that?" Keeper asked real soft that morning as we stood in that snow and watched that day break open.

"Yeah," I said, real quiet too. "Yeah, what is that?"

"S'Beedahbun," he said. "S'Beedahbun."

"First light?"

"Life," he said, very soft now and respectful. "Life. That's what you feel. Beedahbun's life. When that light breaks on that horizon, you stand here, be part of it, you feel life comin' back. All around you, life comin' back. Rides in on that light. Whole universe shruggin' its shoulders, wakin' up together. That's what you feel. The wakin' up inside.

"You come here. Become part of it. Walk around the rest of the day bein' part of it too. Never get lost. No one ever got lost bein' part of somethin'. Only when they're not. Beedahbun connects you to life. Them colors become a part of you, them trees a part of you, rocks a part of you, water a part of you, animals a part of you, everything. And you . . . you . . . you're a part of all of it too. It's Beedahbun. That first light comes through your eyes, moves through you, all of you, fillin' you with light. The lighta life, all around you and part of you forever. Beedahbun."

BOOK THREE

# SOO-WANEE-QUAY

*The drum's the heartbeat of Mother Earth. Mornin's when the boy'n me sing those old songs, we use the drum to join us up to that heartbeat. It's always there, but us humans we get too busy sometimes to listen. Wanna jump outta bed, dress like the firemen an' run out into our life. The only heartbeat we hear when we do that's the one that's goin' like crazy in our chest all day. So us, we start our days out joining up to the universal heartbeat. Makin' ourselves parta it. The reason's easy to understand. See, when we're little babies rollin' around inside our mothers all we can hear is her heartbeat. Boom-boom boom-boom all around us when we're in there. Nothin' like a noisy womb-mate, I always say. Heh, heh, heh. Sorry. Was there, had to use it, you know?*

*Anyways, when I was meanin' to say was that we hear that heartbeat goin' on all around us in the darkness. Boom-boom. Boom-boom. It's all we can hear. We're floatin' around an' we feel all warm an' safe an' that heartbeat drumming away in the background makes us feel even more safe an' protected. Reason we cry when we get sent out into the world's on accounta that sound gets cut off and we get scared. All we hear's the world then, all noisy'n loud. Scary soundin' when you're used to the dark an' that boom-boom all the time. The more we hang around in the world the more we forget the sound of that heartbeat an' how we felt when we could hear it all around us. Get kinda used to the sound of things out here. Sometimes we hear the birds or water or somethin' nice around us an' it makes us feel good. Peaceful. Quiet inside, on accounta we all move through our lives with the echo of that heartbeat inside us an' them nice things remind us of it. Come close sometimes but not really. Our ears forget what that heartbeat sounds like, but our insides never forget. Them nice things ring awful close to it on accounta it's the heartbeat of Mother Earth we feel around us.*

*Then one day, us Indyuns, we hear that drum, hand drum or pow-wow drum, an' right away we feel good. Kinda all safe an' warm again. Boom-boom boom-boom. All the time we're around it we feel good. Reason is, it reminds us of that first drum we ever heard. That heartbeat in the darkness. Boom-boom boom-boom. Always wanna be around it. That's why there's so many Indyuns at pow-wows. Some'll try'n tell you it's on accounta they wanna dance or sing or visit, but it's really on accounta that drum makes 'em feel the way they felt when they were parta their mothers.*

*That's why we use the drum in the morning. We hear it an' get reminded of how we felt hearin' it in the darkness when we were little. Reminds us too that we gotta stay joined up with Mother Earth an' that we can feel all safe an' protected that way too. Reminds us to stop an' listen for that heartbeat goin' on all around us even now. That's why we use it. Not for our ears, for our insides. Us we gotta learn to live from the inside out. The drum teaches us that when we know what it's for.*

*Lots don't. The boy brung me this book by some white guy gettin' men to use drums. Called* Iron John. *Me I thought it had to do with a better way to build an outhouse. Heh, heh, heh.* Iron John *says drummin's the way for men to get back to their tribal nature. Their wildness. Kinda get rid of womanish things. Be a real man. Guess there's lots buyin' into it but they're missin' the real teaching of the drum. Beatin' away on them drums, gettin' wild, but missin' out on teachin's that'll keep 'em alive forever.*

*See, the drum's about motherhood. It's about the woman power all around us. Woman's only one got power to give life. That's why we call this land our Mother. Land gives life to Indyuns. Get all we need to survive from our Mother. The drum reminds us to treat her with respect. But drum's also about the spirit power of the female.*

*Women got more power than men on accounta they can give life. More power. Spirit power. The old people taught that women were more holy than us men an' us we had to treat them with the most respect we had inside us. Mother Earth, birth mothers, mothers of our children, treat them all the same. That's why the drum's round, like the womb an' like the universe too.*

*Like life. You watch sometime. Us men get around our drums get real respectful all of a sudden. Those of us followin' the Indyun way don't go near the drum when we're drinkin' or acting in bad ways. Smudge ourselves real good with sweetgrass or cedar first. Get cleansed so we can approach it with respect. The drum teaches respect. Reason pow-wow singers put tobacco on the toppa their drums when they sing's on accounta they know that their songs are another offering to the power of the earth, universe too. Female power. Power of life.*

*Those wildmen they're missin' that. They're missin' too about the female part of themselves thass never gonna go away. Beat that drum all they want but female part's never gonna go away. Us we known that long, long time.*

*See, when we get sent out into the world we come here carryin' two sets of gifts. The gifts of the father an' gifts of the mother. The two human bein's that made our life. We came here carryin' those two sets of gifts, each one equal to the other. But sometimes the world gets hold of us and makes us see diff'rent way. We get told as men that we gotta be strong, gotta be fearless. Lotta us kinda start ignorin' the gifts of our mother. Go through life just usin' gifts of the father. Bein' tough, makin' our own plans, livin' in the head. But if you do that you can't be whole on accounta you gotta use both of them equal setsa gifts to live right, to fill out the circle of your own life. Be complete. Gotta use the mother's gifts too. Like gentleness an' nurturin', livin' in the heart. That's where the female power comes from. Livin' in the heart. Them that's tryin' to chase the female outta themselves an' their world are chasing out half of who they are. Busy bein' incomplete. That's not our way. That's not what the drum's about. Drum's a tool to help us remember the power of the female, in the world and in us all. The balance we gotta have inside. Both sets of gifts. Using them in everything we do. And that female power, that female side's always gonna be there. Never goes away.*

*Drum's the heartbeat. Heartbeat of our Mother. Heartbeat of the land. Heartbeat of our culture. Power of the female to give life to ev'rything. Land, culture, us too. So you gotta respect that power everywhere you find it. That's why the boy'n me do what we do ev'ry mornin'. Outta respect. Man livin' with respect can't do nobody no harm. Reason behind that's on accounta respect's big center of it all. Give respect, you give kindness, honesty, openness, gentleness, good thoughts, good actions. Simple, eh?*

*That's what it's all about the Indyun way. Simplicity.*

*Us we always believed that keepin' things simple makes it easier to remember. Easy to be yourself. Easy to remember what gave you life. Never seen no confused tree all my life, an' I been around. Heh, heh, heh.*

*The reason us Indyuns survived everythin' that happened to us these last five hunnerd years is on accounta we never lost that simplicity. Like faith. Faith's gotta be simple to work. Sure, lotsa us gettin' caught up in that big shiny world, chasin' them complicated kindsa livin', but there's always believers around to catch them when they fall, kinda help 'em back to simplicity again. You can have all that too, don't get me wrong, it's okay to have all that, as long as you got a simple faith workin' in your life. If you don't you're gonna need the elders. Ones who lived lots. Lived in a good way. Lived simple. That's why we use the drum. Kinda remind us. Remind us that simplicity kept us Indyuns alive through everythin'. Kinda help us live in balance with the whole world.*

Around here there's two ways of doing things. There's the slow methodical Ojibway method and there's the slow non-methodical Ojibway method. Either way seems to work out for most folks but for someone used to the fast pace of downtown living it sure took a lotta getting used to. Things move slow here. They seem to just kinda develop at their own speed. Indian time. Keeper says it's on accounta the simple way our people are used to living.

In my old life I was used to things happening quick. Once you made a decision you got into it. That downtown lifestyle was built on speed, the kind you feel in the bones when the party's going, people are bopping, chicks be checking you out and life feels kinda on the wild side. Lonnie called it livin' large. Livin' large meant you had things going. Lotta money, lotta flashy clothes, lotta plans, lotta friends—big living. There wasn't no small, regular or medium. It all had to be large.

White Dog living was far from large. There were times in that first year when I thought I'd scream from boredom. I even toyed with the idea of going back to Toronto. Kinda got to writing Lonnie regular and telling him how it was going and he was hip enough to start sending some good blues and R&B tapes after a while. That helped some, but still I thought I'd burst.

People put up with me and there's some who kinda adopted my music. In fact, the rumor around here now is that the Miracles are actually an Indian group on accounta they got such good rhythm. The way it's told is, they got their name misspelled on their album covers. It's really the Maracles, like Chief Dan Maracle and his family from Shoal Lake. Anyway, the music helped, but not lots.

I'd wandered around a long time wondering if Garnet really existed at all and now it felt like two. There was this innocent side that was waking up to my Ojibway background and really beginning to understand something about it and myself. That side could wander along the shore of the lake and get blown away by the beauty of the land and the simplicity of these people. The side that got real turned on by those morning ceremonies and was feeling some faint stirrings of faith inside. A wide-open guy with a new family and a new history to provide the anchor I'd needed all my life.

And then there was the side of me that was going rapidly stir crazy. The one hungry for all the flash and motion of the world I'd walked away from. The downtown side that still believed that he needed all that flash and motion to be alive. The scared side.

As usual, of course, it was the least likely thing to get things rolling. See, Wilbert Fish and his buddies are really into hockey. Not playing, betting on games that come in on the radio. The fact that no one's got any money around here doesn't stop those boys. Usually the bets work out to be a cord of wood being chopped and delivered, a moose hide tanned, a ride into town on demand, a good feed of pickerel. Guess when there's actually work involved instead of money the betting gets real intense. Spring was rolling in pretty good that year and folks were busy getting ready for the big break-up on the lake. Once the pickerel start their spawning run in the creeks and rivers, well, it gets real hectic around here. Which is more than fine these days except back then it wasn't really the kinda action I was looking for. Anyway, there was energy in the air but I was missing it on accounta my downtown daydreaming.

Springtime also means that the NHL playoffs start up and that means Wilbert and the boys would be huddled around Bert Otter's shortwave radio in the community hall almost every night for a month.

In a remote little place like this, an everyday thing like radio gets to be important to folks. Chief Isaac with his satellite dish has the only clear connection to the outside. The others, like Doc and the Mrs. or Big Ed, have TVs too but their pictures are all snowed over so you're never really sure what you're watching. Most folks don't even bother trying to watch anymore. Same with radio. This country's got so many big tree-covered hills that them radio signals just get kinda eaten up by it all. Only thing that makes it up this far is the CBC. I've heard the CBC manages to make it everywhere. Why, I've heard of people moving into the furthest part of the north just to get away from it and then finding it's the only thing they can pick up.

Every once in a while, usually when the nights are really clear, them radio signals manage to get through. Then it's a big wrestling match for picking stations. See, a few years back Bert Otter had somehow talked Chief and council into giving him a big bunch of money for one of them old shortwave radios. Being the community development officer and in charge of activities down at the community hall, Bert set that old radio up on a little wooden table just inside his office. Bert's reason for getting the radio was so he could keep an ear to the world and "expand my vision" in order to be a better community development guy. Everyone knew the truth though, and the truth was that as Wally Red Sky's nextdoor neighbor, Bert was getting real tired of hearing nothing but mournful renditions of sappy country ballads cranked out over Wally's big old tube amplifier every night. That radio was gonna be old Bert's saving grace.

But when them radio signals were getting through people would just kinda reach around and turn the tuning knob till they found something they liked. Once in a while we'll get crystal-clear reception from stations all the way down in Chicago or Detroit or even country music stations from Tennessee. Some of the older people like to hear that old-time music and the younger ones wanna hear the new music. The jock guys like Wilbert want the hockey. So that old radio at the community hall sure was a popular thing sometimes. I say "was" because Bert had to get himself another shortwave on accounta that old one got trashed by Wilbert one night, and that's really how this whole story started.

On that particular night, Wilbert and company were trying to tune in a hockey game from Winnipeg. The Jets were challenging the Calgary Flames in the first round of the playoffs and the betting was heavier than usual. Wilbert had the Jets and them being the underdogs meant if he won he stood to win a bundle—a bundle by White Dog standards anyway. Midway through the third period with the score tied and Wilbert within sniffing distance of winning a hindquarter of moose, the signal suddenly vanished. All you could hear was the whistle and grunt of static and the occasional blurt of announcers calling the game.

The boys kept on getting closer and closer. They were shoulder to shoulder and face to face, the six of them, like maybe their bodies could help bring the signal in better. Their faces were screwed up in all kindsa strange expressions and their fists were clenching and unclenching while the whistle and grunt of static went on and on. Nothin' was helping. That signal was coming in and out, in and out so you really couldn't hear anything at all.

With the situation nearing desperate and the game down to the last frantic minute, Wilbert lost all patience and flung the radio clear across the hall where it smashed into a hundred state-of-the-art pieces against the empty Government of Canada job board.

"Damn thing never works when you need it!" Wilbert yelled to no one in particular. "Tell that Bert to send me the bill. I'll pay him off in pickerel!"

Keeper'n me were down at the hall that night playing a few games of checkers and I had half a mind to say what a good idea it was for a Fish to be paying up in fish but about then I didn't figure old Wilbert was in the mood for a funny. Keeper just kinda grinned and proceeded to crown another man.

"Good thing he's not one of them Shoal Lake Skunks. Sure would be a stink 'bout payin' up then!" he said.

Once word got out that Wilbert had trashed the radio, folks were kinda depressed. It's a big wild world out there sometimes and I kinda think hearing about all them strange goings-on helps White Dog folks stay grateful for the simplicity of their lives. It was real quiet around the community hall at night and not many people drifted down there. Wilbert and the boys weren't saying a lot and Bert Otter was wandering around looking like he'd lost his dog. He'd come running in as soon as he'd heard about the radio being flung across the room. He spent about an hour kneeling on the floor with little black pieces of radio in his hands and sighing and sighing. For a while there you'd catch him walking around staring at his hands like he couldn't get the memory of a hundred state-of-the-art pieces off them. Around the fire at Ma's those nights we could hear the distant sounds of Wally Red Sky crooning away in his bedroom with his amplifier turned up way too loud. When you hear that kinda thing late at night you'd wish for a radio too, believe me. Even with the CBC.

I wasn't the only one starting to suffer. Us Indians we believe that everything moves in a circle. The sun makes a big circle when it travels through the sky, our drums are round and life itself is a circle according to Keeper. The way he sees it, we start off with a kinda innocence when we're born and by the time we work our way around the circle of our lives, as long as we live right, we wind up with a kinda childlike innocence again. But an innocence built on wisdom, he says. And humility too, he says. Anyway, the circle that Wilbert started by trashing the radio started to become noticed pretty quick around here.

Him and his pals got real cranky not being able to hear the playoffs. Naturally they got cranky with their families. Pretty soon their wives and kids were being cranky with their friends and their friends were getting cranky with theirs until finally White Dog was one big cranky place to be.

Being kinda outta sorts over this radio thing meant they'd listen more to whining and complaining than they normally do. Around here whining's something reserved for the politicians. Most folks just kinda accept things when they happen. So whiners usually have to be happy with whining all alone. Right then though, whining was fast becoming a new traditional thing. Which suited me just fine since folks started to listen when I talked about how White Dog needed some twentieth-century entertainment.

Turned out one of the most eager to listen to me was Wally Red Sky.

"Holee," he said one day while we were walking by the lake. "Ever lotsa cranky people, eh?"

"Really," I said. "Ever."

"Kinda gettin' hard to talk to people. Yesterday even Doc was snappin' around an' him he never goes that way."

"Well, Wally, it's like I've been saying, too much stone age around here has gotta make you nuts."

"Guess. Never woulda thought losin' that radio was gonna make ev'ryone as crazy as they are, though. Not even like White Dog anymore."

"I'll tell you, it only takes one good DJ to bring people around, Wally. I've heard some guys on those big downtown radio stations just make people happy to be alive. Got their rap down real good, play mean tunes, get everybody tuned in, you know?"

"Really? Don't get that kinda radio on CBC."

"The CBC ain't radio, man! Way before there was TV, radio was getting people motivated. Where do you think Hank Williams woulda been without radio playing his tunes?"

"Hank woulda been a star no matter what. Radio or no radio, Garnet. His music set the world on fire. We'da hearda him anyway."

"Maybe so, maybe so. But radio connected up the

world. Got ideas happening fast. Changed the way people thought. Got them to see the light, like Hank would say. Got the world moving, man, moving. And that's why people are so grouchy, Wally. When you get a little bit of the real world happening around here, people like it. When it's gone they start to see how slow things really are on White Dog."

"White Dog's in the real world too, ain' it?"

"Sure, in a way. But, Wally, man, there's such a big thing out there beyond that fence it'd make you crazy if you and me spent even one weekend together in T.O. Chicks, parties, nightclubs. Yeah, nightclubs, man. There's even hip, happening country places that would make you die, Wally."

"Yeah? Really? What're they like?"

"All sortsa cool downtown cowboys and cowchicks and the best country singers you'd ever wanna hear. Kinda like that *Urban Cowboy* movie Bert showed at the hall last month, 'member?"

"Yeah, that was cool. What about them singers?"

"Just like you hear on the radio when the signals come in from Tennessee. The best. You'd learn lots there, Wally. Learn lots."

"Hmmpfh. Don't know that I could learn more'n I know now. But tell me more about this radio thing. Think we could ever get a radio station up here?"

"Hell, I wish. It's a hard thing, though. Need lotsa cash. But, man, you'd really get this place going full tilt if you had one. Full tilt."

"Hmmpfh. Hard, eh? Think anyone would listen if we had one?"

"Listen? No one'd be outside at night except to be dancing around and living it up. Get a good DJ playing good tunes and look out! A good DJ can be the hero for a lotta people, man. Real hero."

"Hero, eh?"

"Like everyone knows Wolfman Jack, you know? Get talking, tellin' them things they might not have heard, jokes, all kindsa things. If there's one thing this place really needs it's a big dose of the outside. If we brought them big ideas in here maybe we'd feel more with it. Maybe we'd start getting better ideas about how to change things around here real fast instead of slow like they move now. Maybe a big dose of the outside would get everything moving together, get some more hydro, plumbing and lots of good things."

"Figure radio'd really help this place that much?"

"Man, a radio station would bring this place to life. People'd hear about things they never heard of before and maybe start making bigger plans, dream bigger dreams, maybe get some nightlife going on around here. Things'd change, all right. For the better. Get some of the world into White Dog."

"Bring the world to White Dog. I like that."

"Get everyone right up to speed with things."

"Up to speed. I like that too. Got a nice ring to it."

"I'd die for a slice of modern pie right now, Wally."

"Slice of modern pie. Wow."

Wally slapped me up alongside the shoulders and headed off towards his dad's house, and kept on walking around the lake. It was early evening and the sun was just going down. Usually that time of day makes me feel real good, but right around then I was awful anxious and wanting some distraction. I never knew what was coming until it happened.

Them Red Skys have been big movers and shakers around here for as long as most can remember. There was Red Skys around when they signed the treaty back in the 1870s and ever since there's been a Red Sky or two right up front in local politics. Kinda the big dreamers, I guess, and Wally, well, he was a bigger dreamer than most.

Folks around here still like to talk about Wally when he was around ten years old. See, his family's one of the hydro Indians. They moved away from the old skills like tanning hides, netting fish or any of the bush things my family still knows and does regularly, and they got used to being comfortable and thinking different. As a kid Wally was used to playing with a whole different set of toys than even his cousins who lived beyond the power line. Electric stuff, you know?

One year for Christmas Wally's grandfather was coming from Winnipeg. Mrs. Red Sky's one of those White Dog people whose family took off a long time back and moved into town. She only came back after Wally Senior fell in love with her and they got married.

Her daddy was coming back to White Dog for the first time in a long, long time. Wally was all excited and I guess really wanted to impress the old guy with how much of a bush Indian he was.

So what happened was, he found a picture of some snowshoes in a catalogue and figured he'd make his grampa a pair lust like the old traditional people used to make. Ojibway snowshoes are real famous for being the best of the bunch, and Wally figured if he made up a pair, his grampa would really know that his grandson was a big bush kind of Indian.

Trouble was, Wally never asked anybody for help. He just cut out the picture and went to work. He walked out into the bush one day and came back with two long skinny branches of jack pine. He stripped all the rough stuff off them and bent them around in a circle and tied them off with a couple of tough moosehide thongs. Then he got some more thongs and made big sloppy criss-crosses across both of those bent-around pieces of jack pine. Had a couple straps to tie around the feet and I guess in a way they looked like snowshoes but not really.

When the old man arrived Wally was excited as hell. Told his friends at school all about how his grampa was gonna really be proud of him on accounta he was a real bush Indian making them snowshoes.

Well, Christmas morning came along and Wally waited until everything else had been handed around. Then he brought his snowshoes out for the old man.

That was one surprised old Ojibway the way Wally's ma tells it. The old man turned them snowshoes over and over before he finally figured out what they were supposed to be. Then he strapped them onto his feet and started tramping around the house kinda getting the feel of them while Wally followed behind all proud.

Those moose-hide thongs just snapped all of a sudden. Snapped and sprang back straight again breaking all the thonging Wally'd criss-crossed across the frame. His grampa was left standing in the middle of the kitchen with two sticks strapped to his feet. Being a grampa he was real good about it and congratulated Wally on being the first Ojibway to figure out how to make collapsible snowshoes. Wally was real sad about it and it took most of the day for his grampa to convince him that he was still gonna be an Ojibway even though his first snowshoes didn't work out. They still talk about them snowshoes to this day and laugh about it in a good way.

So Wally's always been the big dreamer around here and everyone's kinda got their favorite Wally Red Sky story. Despite his wild singing and big dreams everyone likes him. Little backwards maybe, but a nicer guy can't be found.

About a week later the first signs appeared. Big orange banners, hung up at the community hall, the school, the band office and even stretched across the front of Big Ed's store. Big black lettering that announced the impending arrival of "The White Dog One Radio Network." This was followed by finer print that said we had only a mere two weeks before the "radio beacon of the north" came into all our homes to "obliterate the vast silence of the tundra" with the "back-porch ambiance of traditional country music for the masses."

There was an accompanying handout that laid out the ground rules. For a mere five dollars a month we "sub-scribers" could sign up for four hours a night of crystal-clear, no-drift reception while we enjoyed the "cheerful stay-at-home charm of our aboriginal rusticity" aided and improved upon by the White Dog One Radio Network. Further information would follow, it said.

Naturally this announcement got a lotta people talkin'. The idea of someone bringin' radio right into the reserve was big news but strange news. Good news too for a lotta folks who were really missing old Bert's radio down at the hall.

"Maybe we'll have our own blackout bingo games here now," said Velma Crow, whose monthly bingo migrations to Winnipeg were well known and envied.

"Yeah, an' we can have one of them request lines like they got on the radio in town. Here's 'Forever an' Ever Amen' goin' out to Delilah Runnin' Rabbit from Cameron Keewatin," said Cameron Keewatin all dreamy-eyed, Cameron being on the path for Delilah's affections since they were kids.

"Ah, that's jus' some hare-brained idea somebody woke up with'll never happen!" my ma figured and strolled off to finish up a pair of moccasins she was making for Chief Isaac's nephew.

"Hockey!" said Wilbert Fish. "Hockey!" And wandered off to give the boys the news of radio coming to White Dog.

"Hmmpfh," Keeper said, while we were loading up with supplies for his place that day. Wonder how anyone'd come up with that kinda thinkin' round here." He gave me the once over and smirked.

"Who knows? Good idea though," I said, turning real quick to fetch some lard.

"Sounds kinda like another snowshoe episode to me," Keeper said with a wink. "Gonna be some learnin' in this for lotsa us, I think."

He didn't say anything more about it and didn't act the least surprised a week later when the notice went up at the community hall urging all of us to show up the next night for the unveiling of the White Dog One Network.

"Hmmpfh," was all he said. "Hmmpfh."

People were real anxious and neither Keeper or me were real surprised to find the hall jam-packed the next night. One of them big orange banners was stretched across the front of the room and there was a microphone on a stand in front of it. Someone had borrowed Wally's old tube amp and there was a big tablecloth covering something on the table behind the microphone. People were craning their necks to get a look at the setup and we were all right owly about the delay when Wally Red Sky walked up to the microphone carrying a big bunch of papers. He gave me a huge wink when he passed Keeper'n me.

"Hmmpfh," Keeper said, giving me that once over again.

The groan went up immediately. Wally just put his pile of papers down and waved with his hands to get people to quiet down. Clearing his throat into the microphone and smoothing back his Brylcreem-shiny hair, he went into his special radio announcer's voice.

"Ladies an' gentlemen, boys an' girls, this is the moment you've been all waitin' for."

"Bring on them radio guys!" interrupted Wilbert Fish, eager to hear if hockey was gonna be parta the programming.

"Yeah, Wally, get offa there! We wanna hear about the radio!" yelled Velma Crow.

"This ain't no talent night, for god's sake, Wally!" screamed Wally's dad."Get off an' let the radio guys on!"

Wally grinned and shocked everyone but Keeper'n me when he announced that it was he, Wally Red Sky, who was part, parcel and head honcho of the White Dog One Radio Network. When the groans died down and people started piling on their coats to leave, Wally's voice got suddenly louder.

"For a mere five dollars a month you can have this kinda sound in your own home!" he yelled as Hank Williams singing "Lovesick Blues" filled the room. People stopped and turned around to figure out how Wally managed to get such good sound happening. Most looked pretty impressed with it. Turned out that the tablecloth was covering a pair of record players hooked up to Wally's amp, which was turned up good and loud.

"All you need to do is sign your name on these sheets of paper here agreein' that when I come around the first of ev'ry month you'll pay me five bucks for more radio. I'll be around in the next week to install your own radio unit in your home.

"Then one week from tonight, an' from six to ten ev'ry single night after that, the Red Sky One Radio Network comes into your home! An' the thing of it is . . . an' here's the best part . . . you don' even need electricity an' you'll never haveta buy another battery!"

This was met with murmurs of delight, shock and polite disbelief. Keeper was grinning like I never seen him grin before and I think he was kinda proud of Wally for standing there and pressing his case.

Well, needless to say there was a big rush for the sign-up sheets and no one even stopped to ask about what they could expect from the radio. Five dollars seemed like a hell of a deal for four hours a night of crystal-clear radio, and Wally's enthusiasm pretty much caught on with everybody. There was even people dancing around together while old Hank kept singing away in the background. One week started to feel like an awful long time to wait for lotsa folks.

"Hmmpfh," Keeper said. "Hmmpfh."

"You watch what happens now that this radio's comin' to White Dog," Keeper told me a few days later when we were heading out to gather cedar. "People gonna change. Prob'ly real fast too. Them outside things move fast make people move fast too. You watch."

"You don't like it? Think it's a bad idea?"

"Not a bad idea. More like bad timin'. Things like this gotta come slow, give people time to find balance with it. It's an important thing havin' balance."

"What's balance gotta do with it?"

"Balance is a big thing in the Indyun way. Somethin' you gotta have. Kinda like carryin' a load too big'n awkward for you. Make you walk all funny underneath it, maybe fall, hurt yourself. But you take time to find a balance, that load's easier to travel with. See?"

"Well, yeah, maybe but not really."

"It's like this. You see them eagle feathers hangin' up at my place there?"

"Yeah. So?"

"Eagle feather's good tool for teachin' 'bout balance. Help us remember one o' the biggest teachin's comes from the eagle. See, bird gotta have balance to soar around like he does. Us we like seein' him up there. Looks real free to us. Make us wanna be like that. Trick is, though, we gotta have that same kinda balance. That's why we admire the eagle so much. Somethin' inside us wants to be able to soar around our world like that too.

"But that eagle took a long time to learn about balance. Soarin's just the result of a lotta effort. Lotta work an' learnin' to see an' feel."

"See and feel?"

"That bird's soarin' on air. Air's movin' all the time. When he's floatin' around up there so graceful he's floatin' on moving air. That bird knows when that movin's right for soarin' an' when it's not. Eagles don't soar all the time. Sometimes gotta work hard to stay up there.

"When he's learnin' to fly he's learnin' to see the way the clouds are movin' or if it's clear he's learnin' to see how the treetops are movin' in the air. Gets to know what's what up there. And he's learnin' to feel the air against his body. Learns when it's gentle enough to soar or wild enough to make soaring dangerous. Takes a lotta time for him to learn but he learns. Learns to see and feel so he can know when he can balance against the air an' float around like we always see him do.

"You watch sometimes. See a real young eagle tryin' to soar when that wind's really blowin'. Flies right up into the face of it. Spread his wings like he wants to soar but that wind just pushes him around. Tries again and again. Same thing. Keeps on gettin' pushed around till he learns that that kinda wind's no good for soaring. Gets real tired from the effort. So he learns to sit through it and wait.

"Us we only see the freedom, we don't see the work that went into it. We see the balance in the sky but not the time it took to get it. It's slow coming, that balance. Same for us."

"But what are we balancing?"

"Living mostly. Living. Us we gotta learn to see and feel in order to live good. See what's good around us and feel what's not. Kinda weed out the things that make us uncomfortable. Pick out the bad air from the good air so we can soar. Takes time. That's why we give feathers sometimes. Recognize someone for takin' time to learn balance an' put it into the way they live their life."

"Hmmpfh. So how does that fit what's happening with Wally's radio?"

"It's not just Wally. Got more to do with you really."

"Me?"

"You're feelin' lost here again. I can tell you're wantin' some of that fast livin' again. Way you walk, way you talk sometimes, way you look at things. I figure you were talkin' it up to Wally and tellin' him all about how fast'n shiny that world can be. Kinda got him thinkin' about this radio. Right?"

"Well, yeah, we talked, but I never figured he'd start up a radio station."

"Lotsa people around here like you on accounta you seen the world. Know more about it than them. Makes you kinda special. They listen when you talk about it. Wally just kinda took off on his own after that."

"So what's this balance thing got to do with me?"

"You'll learn about that from what's comin'. See and feel. Find a way to balance this world you live in now with the other one you came from. Big lesson for you. Big lesson. Gonna need it all your life."

"Do you know what's gonna happen?'

"Not really. But people are gonna bump up against the outside world through this an' have to find their own balance with it. Wally. You. Me. Everybody. Can't stop it now. Keep our eyes open. You'll see something for yourself through this."

"Hmmpfh," I said. "Hmmpfh."

Three days later Wally's plan swung into action. Him and his brother Frankie were out bright and early in Roy Cameron's old orange pickup dropping off big bundles of wire around the townsite and even carrying some off into the bush a ways. Looked to be about five miles of wire lying out there by the time they were done.

Turned out that Wally's uncle Charlie, who's been on the band council for about a hundred years, had okayed a loan of seven hundred dollars for Wally's use. That news really had Bert Otter steamed since Bert had applied for some money to replace the old shortwave outfit Wilbert had trashed. Anyway, Charlie told me down at the store one day that Wally'd gone to town and spent it all at the Radio Shack. He'd borrowed Roy Cameron's truck and come back with a big load of wire, connectors and speakers. It sure didn't sound like any radio set-up I'd ever heard of and I was wondering how old Wally was gonna get all set up with a transmitter, antenna and studio in the three days left before the big kickoff.

"Gonna haveta wait like ev'rybody else, Garnet," Wally said when I pushed him on the issue. "Can't be givin' my secret radio formula out to just anyone, you know. This radio's one highly competitive business an' you never know who's listenin'." He said all this while squinting around real fast and cupping a hand to one ear for emphasis.

He was busy in his bedroom scribbling song titles in a brand-new three-ring binder and having a bit of a tough time on accounta the Brylcreem was dripping off his sweaty brow and making slimy little puddles on the paper. He looked like a real executive at work.

"Final phase shifts into gear tomorrow," he said, not looking up and scribbling away like Chief Isaac on a fiscal funding deadline. "People gonna know by then what it's like when the world comes to White Dog, by golly!"

Well, what happened the next day is this. Wally and Frankie, who by now was referring to himself as the Senior Vice President of Subscriptions and Membership, dropped by everyone's house delivering small black speakers, which they wired up, dropping the end of the cable through the bottom of the nearest window. Next, with Wally directing, the senior vice-president began unrolling all those big bundles of wire between pretty near every house on White Dog. They connected the cables hanging out the windows to the one main cable hanging out of Wally's bedroom window. Took them right up into the night to get it all done and folks were pretty puzzled by it all.

When the big day for the official kickoff of the White Dog One Radio Network arrived, excitement was at an all-time high. No one could talk about anything else and big plans were being made for how to spend the money folks were thinking of winning in those big radio contests they'd all heard about. Or some were planning on where they'd take the big cruise vacations they just knew were gonna be given away too. They were talking about the big blackout bingo games to come and of course the latest in country music, since Wally's singing was getting a bit much for most everyone.

By the time six o'clock came on opening day there wasn't a soul out and about on the whole reserve. Even Uncle Buddy and his pals were huddled up around somebody's radio speaker. The whole reserve was quiet as a ceremony.

Wally hadn't been seen since they'd connected the houses an' we all naturally assumed that the final preparations for bringing the world to White Dog were taking up all his time. Frankie wasn't saying anything and told us all to be patient and be sitting by the speakers when "this damn place blasts off into the twentieth century!"

At six o'clock nothing happened. By six-twenty nothing was coming over and by six-thirty people were starting to get a little shifty-butted in their chairs. Even Ma, who's the most patient person I ever met, was starting to think a little less kindly of Wally.

"Coulda used that five bucks for beads or somethin' insteada sittin' aroun' waitin' for that Wally. Boy, when I see him I'm gonna—" Ma's ramble was cut short by a sudden blurt from the speaker.

It wasn't much at first. Sounded like someone shuffling papers, moving the microphone around, sniffling and cussing at the same time. Then there was a long silence. Finally the sound of a scratchy record playing that old fiddle tune "Maple Sugar." Them old fiddle tunes are big favorites around here and whenever my uncle Joe pulls out his fiddle and starts playing on his porch people appear from everywhere for dancing and clapping along.

Well, Ma broke into a great big smile and started tapping her toes along to the music and even I had to agree that even though the record was scratchy it was a lot better sound than anything we'd heard in a long time. Except for Ma's old tape player we used for the blues and stuff. Anyway, when I listened out the front door I could hear the Copenaces next door hootin' and hollering and I could see shadows dancing by the windows. Next door is like a quarter mile out here but the sounds of clappin' and hootin' and hollerin' were plain as day. Seemed like Wally's big dream was off to a rip-roaring start.

Then the music stopped. The final strains of the song died down and I think everyone was just like me, kinda leaning in towards the speaker eager to hear what came next.

"You're listenin' to the White Dog One Radio Network and this is your host and special musical guest Wally Red Sky sayin' hello and welcome to White Dog's own radio station!"

Wild cheering could be heard all over.

"Yes indeed, the Red Sky One Radio Network . . . where we play the tunes you wanna croon. The only radio station that plays music . . . by reservation only! And the only place where you can hear the vocal talents of that gifted Ojibway singer, yours truly, Wally Red Sky, between each and every record we play!"

Well, the groans could be heard from all over too. Me, I just laughed and headed on over to Keeper's to finish listening to this big night in radio history just as Wally launched into his version of "Lovesick Blues."

But I wasn't the only one out and about. People were scrambling from their houses in herds and headed in the direction of the White Dog One studios at top speed. There was Indians pouring outta the bushes faster'n you see in them corny Westerns, and for people with a language that doesn't have any cuss words they were doing pretty well with the English ones that night.

By the time I reached Wally's there was a huge crowd all piled into his room and Wally was pressed up against the wall with a microphone in his hand begging someone out there in radioland to call 911. There was a big smear of Brylcreem across the wall where he'd slid along and people were slipping and sliding around on the drops that had fell to the floor in their frenzy at wanting to get ahold of Wally.

It was Keeper who finally saved him.

Somehow the old guy managed to get heard over top of all the pushing, shoving and shouting around.

"Quiet!" he yelled. "Quiiiiii-et!"

The noise died down to the level of one big mass grumble.

"Means no hockey, I guess," said Wilbert Fish.

"An' no big-money bingo either," said Velma Crow.

"An' no special request lines," moaned Cameron Keewatin.

"An' no way to turn off Wally once he launches into those tunes of his!" said Wally Senior, looking more than a bit disgusted.

"The boy tried," Keeper said. "Maybe not so good as you all think it could be, but us we gotta look at what's not here insteada what is.

"Lotta them old records you like and no one's sayin' you can't get a bingo started, Velma. And think how easy it's gonna be to get hold of someone clear across the reserve now that we're all connected up. An' me, I think even Wally's gonna get tired of singin' for four hours ev'ry night and maybe we can all pitch in to get him more records to play.

"Who knows, maybe even we can get a real radio station in here once the government sees how much we done on our own."

The room was suddenly full of nodding heads and hopeful grins. "Hey, I can set up a bingo real easy. Maybe make some money for the kids' sports aroun' here," Wilbert Fish said, although everyone kinda knew there'd be a gambling side of this to be sorted out later.

"An' maybe I can get on for a few minutes ev'ry night kinda let you all know what's goin' on with reserve business," Chief Isaac said to a few more groans around the room.

"Be easy hookin' a ride to town now too," said my uncle Buddy with a little gleam in his eye thinking about his bootlegger pal Al in Minaki.

Well, people calmed down pretty soon and started talking about plans for improving the White Dog One Network and Wally was allowed to slide off the wall and relax in his chair beside the record player. I had to admit it was a slick-looking little operation. Wally had all his dad's old records piled up on a shelf above a table that held a pair of old turntables. The record players and Wally's guitar and microphone were all plugged into his old tube amplifier, which in turn fed the main line out onto the reserve. Clever.

People started heading home and Wally popped an old Patsy Cline record on and slumped down in the chair in relief.

And that's how radio came to White Dog. After a while it got to be a big part of the community and even though we changed a lotta things in these last five years lotsa people still use Wally's old set-up to communicate.

Velma Crow started a weekly bingo with proceeds going to kids' programs, my ma started a babysitting bulletin board for folks going to town. Chief Isaac talked about politics, known affectionately around here as the White Dog Siesta Show, and people started telling each other where the fish were sitting and whenever there was a good sale somewhere in town. The

White Dog One Radio Network turned out to be a big success and even Wally was starting to sound better with all the practice.

Like Keeper said, people kinda found a balance with it all. Started using it as a tool for the community and it really didn't change things all that fast. The slow methodical Ojibway method worked real good with the radio.

Me I started looking at things different soon after. Kinda started to slow down in the head and feel better about being here. I even go on there even now and play some blues and old R&B late at night, more for myself than anyone else but folks seem to like it.

But I slowed down. This balance thing Keeper was talking about worked real good when you thought about it. For me that outside world was always moving a bit too fast for me to keep up with. Too much to do too quick and when you spend as much time as I used to worrying about falling behind and looking stupid, well, there's a lotta stress there. I started to see that around here you could still live large. Only here it works out to be big family, big country, big dreams and lotsa big laughs. Lotsa big laughs. I'm telling you that on accounta that radio was the start of one of the funniest things ever seen around here, and if I didn't tell you about that I wouldn't be much of a storyteller.

*Heh, heh, heh. Sure was fun that night. Gotta admit I was lookin' forward to seein' what was comin'. Me I known Wally since he was born an' seen a lotta big ideas of his but nothin' as big as this. In his own way I suppose Wally did kinda bring the world to White Dog. Not all flashy like he wanted but he brung it in anyway. Was time I guess to. Us we bin sittin' out here on the edges for a long time just kinda watchin' what was goin' on out there and protecting what we got. Comes a time though when people just gotta join up to it. Both for themselves and for them that ain't born yet.*

*Don't needta bring all the world in though. But enough. The parts that'll help us without drownin' us. See, that's always been the thing. Us Indyuns we seen big changes goin' on all around. Seen the land change from bein' free and open to bein' all closed off an' cut up. Seen our people go the same way. Never learned about being in balance with everythin'. Lots figured they had to be one way or the other and lots just walked away and disappeared. Hmmpfh. No one ever just disappears. Change real big inside but never disappear. Old man used to say, soon's you get somewhere there you are. Never really made sense to me until I sobered up but now it's big parta the way I think. Soon's you get somewhere, there you are. Means you can't disappear. Always gonna take yourself with you so you might as well get used to it. Find balance with things. Yourself. The world. Everything, on accounta change is the biggest law of nature. Fight change you fight yourself. Even these rocks around here are changin'. Hands of the wind are invisible hands but they're workin' on the face of them rocks right now. Changin' them, shapin' them. They look the same to use every day on accounta that change is happening slow, but it's there. Hmmpfh. Good man, that Harold Raven.*

*But when you got no simple faith workin' in your circles, well, change is a scary thing. Always be thinkin' you're gonna lose what you got. Always thinkin' you're gonna lose yourself. Gonna lose ev'rythin'. So you get real protective. Don't let nothin' near. Nothin' different, new or strange. Kinda start losin' your own sense of adventure too. Stop your own growin' on accounta you're usin' all your strength to fight something you can't see. Them invisible hands. Always gonna be there them. How do those young ones put it when they're tryin' out their romantic moves on each other? Don't fight it, baby, it's bigger than both of us? Heh, heh, heh.*

*But us Indyuns, well, history kinda taught us to be afraida change. So we are. Afraid of losin' ourselves. Indyuns got a lotta pride and always wanna be walkin' around bein' Indyun. Don't wanna think they're walkin' around bein' anything else. So lotta times they only do what they think are Indyun things. Hang around with only other Indyuns, only go where other Indyuns go, only do things other Indyuns do. Watch sometime you see it good. It's okay on accounta you get kinda strong that way, but's weakening us too lotta the time. Get all closed in on yourself. It's like a private club like the white people got out there. The only difference is, you always gotta be payin' to join. Ev'ry day you gotta pay to join. Gotta pay up in all kindsa lost opportunity and last chances. Tryin' to stay one way means you're robbing yourself of things might even make you stronger. Me I seen lotsa Indyuns thinkin' that way and all the time robbing themselves and their kids of big things that will help 'em live forever as Indyuns.*

*It's like the boy's brother says all the time. Comes down to stealin' horses again. Stealin' horses was a thing to be honored on accounta a couple things. First, when you took a man's horse you took away his movin' around. Made him less of a threat. Couldn't fight the good fight when he couldn't move around. Second, when you took a horse you gave yourself the power to move faster'n better. Could fight better yourself. Stay alive longer. Hunt better, keep your family strong. So stealin' horses was a good thing and us we were good at it. Well, not so much us Anishanabe on accounta us we're bush Indyuns that never had no horses, but it's true for them prairie Indyuns. Me I'm only borrowin' the story to make a point.*

*But Stanley says we gotta be stealin' horses nowadays too. Gotta look at the kinda horses them outsiders ride nowadays. Need them now to fight the good fight, stay alive, keep our families strong. We gotta steal them horses and use them to get us movin' again. Can't be hidin' behind our Indyun ways all the time now. Gotta find balance between two worlds to survive. And that's what this radio thing's taught the boy and ev'ryone around. About that balance.*

*Me I see lotsa young people tryin' to live like traditional Indyuns. Got braids and going around to ceremonies, drummin' an' singin' and callin' themselves traditional on accounta that. But they're foolin' themselves. See, traditional people are the ones who know all the prayer songs. The songs you sing when you tie together the ribs of the sweat lodge. Songs you sing when you gather sweetgrass or cedar for smudgin'. Songs you sing for each part of the preparation for big ceremony like rain dance or sun dance like them prairie Indyuns do every year. Real traditional people know all about the why of things, insteada just the how. Until you know all that, can't really call yourself a traditional Indyun.*

*The truth is that most of us are movin' between Indyuns. Movin' between our jobs and the sweat lodge. Movin' between school and pow-wow. Movin' between English and Anishanabe. Movin' between both worlds. Movin' between 1990 and 1490. Most of us are that kinda Indyun.*

*It's not a bad thing even though some figure you're not so much of an Indyun when you're tryin' to find that balance. Them that think that way are ignorin' them two truths I was talking about. See, the old man told me one time he said, us we only think of our culture as bein' the old way. Old-style Indyun way. But it's not true, he said. Culture's what you find yourself doin' day in and day out, he said. Culture's the way of livin' and us we gotta admit that these days our culture's made up of sweat lodge, TV, radio, huntin', school, fishin', sweetgrass, cedar, work and all sortsa things. Whatever we find ourselves doin' day in and day out. That's our culture now and that's why most of us are the movin'-between kinda Indyuns. Movin' between the pickup truck and the sweat lodge, movin' between the office and the wigwam, movin' between school and the traditional teachin's.*

*But we can always get more and more traditional by learnin' them teachin's and puttin' them into our lives. Or we can get less and less traditional by ignorin' them teachin's. That's why balance is such a big thing. We need a balance between worlds today. Guess in a way the boy got more traditional than most right away on accounta he kept on askin' about things and learnin' them and puttin' them into his livin' day in and day out. That's what's important. Do what the world asks you to do but do it with the spirit of the teachin's. You'll never get lost that way. Never. You can go and be whatever. DJ, hockey player, businessman, lawyer, anything as long as you carry them traditional teachin's with you wherever you go. That's balance. Us we learned that good with that radio. Made it part of our lives. Used it like a tool. Another horse we learned to ride.*

White Dog was hosting their annual pow-wow and as usual had invited every reserve in the area to come and dance and celebrate the powers of nature. By the time of the opening Grand Entry—that's where all the dancers line up and dance in together for an opening prayer by elders—there was about two hundred people here from other places. That's an awful lot of folks for a tiny place like this and people were bunked in with relatives and friends or else camped out in tents and trailers all around the pow-wow grounds, which was really the ball diamond. It's a big thing and White Dog folks take a lotta pride in giving their guests their best hospitality. Lotsa fresh moose meat, warm blankets given away, stories swapped and all kindsa things that are seen as being special.

This year was different and things were going really well up until the very last night of dancing. There's another part of pow-wow that's not really an official part but part and parcel of every pow-wow in Indian country anyway. It's called snaggin' and it means that the young people are all around on the lookout for that special someone to snuggle up with. Another word for it is "teepee creepin'." You're considered snagged if you're seen in the company of a young man or young woman holding hands, smooching or making them big wet goo-goo eyes at each other. Next to hockey it's the biggest sport in Indian country. Come to think of it, it's ironic that we have our pow-wow on the baseball diamond since mosta the young people are all trying to get past first base and score.

Anyway, dancers save their best moves for the benefit of the person they're interested in. The snaggee I guess you'd call them. And singers all sing their best when their target is near, et cetera.

Well, Wally Red Sky had his eye on this young jingle-dress dancer from the Rat Portage reserve, and I have to admit that old Wally had a pretty good eye. Not being a dancer or a pow-wow singer meant Wally was a little low on the totem pole when it came to attracting any attention to himself so he was forced to be creative. They were sitting right in front of me on the bleachers that night when Wally made his big move.

"Sure dance good," he said. "Come here often?"

I winced.

"No," she said with a little grin and a wiggle that sent a shiver down the jingles or her dress and a real big one down Wally's spine.

"Betcha don't know that I'm the chief radio executive here on White Dog, eh?" Wally said, slowly skulking in for the big snag.

"No," she said, and turned her head real coy-like and

looked away at the men's fancy dance competition going on below.

"Yep." Wally said, getting all puffy in the chest like a male partridge going into his mating ritual. "I'm the one brought the world to White Dog. Hooked us up to the twentieth century. An' I'm also the special musical guest ev'ry night too. Gonna be a big country singin' star real soon. Headin' for Nashville really."

He leaned in a little closer while he told her this so she could get a good whiff of his Brylcreem and Old Spice.

"Really," she said.

"Really," said Wally.

"Bet you're really good," she said with a little bat of her big brown eyes and a roll of the shoulders.

"Betcha," Wally said with a fairly good sized gulp.

"Wanna show me your set-up?" she asked.

"Well," Wally said, getting all puffy again, "only a very privileged few ever get to see somethin' as big an' important as that. The radio station, I mean. I don't let just anybody in on it."

"Oh." She gave another bat of the eyes.

"But I can tell that you're the kind of lady who appreciates the finer things in life. Someone who appreciates the sight of a first-class operation, so maybe we should just waltz on over there an' I'll show you what I got."

"Oh, I don't know," she said. "how far are we going to go?"

Wally gulped so loud I thought the dancers could hear him and he brushed back his hair and wriggled his shoulders while he shopped for a good comeback.

"No way of knowin' till you get there, is there?" he said finally, standing up and offering his hand to the little dancer. "But come with me an' I'll show you somethin' you ain't never seen before. An' maybe I'll show you the radio too."

She batted those big brown eyes again and giggled, and they disappeared in the direction of Wally's while I smiled, shook my head and turned back towards the dancing. I caught a glimpse of Chief Isaac walking with a visiting chief off towards his house. Probably going to show him his new satellite TV set-up and pump him for information on the latest developments in native politics in his area. Lotsa different kinds of snagging goes on at pow-wows, see.

About an hour later after the dancing had shut down I was sitting at Keeper's having a late-night game of checkers and some tea. Keeper almost spilled his mug all over the board when Wally's voice burst from the radio speaker beside us.

"This is the seat where all the magic happens, baby—If you lived here I'd be slidin' through your window ev'ry night for four hours of uninterrupted bliss."

There was a shy little giggle in the background as Wally started to explain how he played the records and then went live with his own electrifying country singing.

Then he played a slow, inviting version of "Back in the Saddle Again" while Keeper'n me almost choked with laughter. When he finished singing Wally asked her if she might like to join him at the broadcast desk and we could hear soft smooching and the occasional giggle.

Guess what happened was, old Wally forgot to turn his amplifier off. Most folks were home now too and it wasn't too long before big Barry Kingfisher almost tore the door off Keeper's cabin rushing in to tell us the news.

"Keeper Keeper Keeper!" he yelled. "Wall's on the radio with some girl an' it sounds like he's going for it!"

Meanwhile Wally's voice was whispering through the speakers about how the Red Sky men were known far and wide for their prowess in the lovemakin' department and how the White Dog women just wouldn't or couldn't seem to leave him alone. Letting them down easy without breaking their hearts was a skill he'd had to learn over a number of years on accounta Wally was saving his vital energy and juices for that special someone somewhere. By this time there was about ten of us all huddled around Keeper's speaker in varying states of helpless laughter. We could hear roars of laughter coming across from other cabins and figured that old Wally was really going prime time that night.

All of which would have been fine by White Dog standards, except that by this time Chief Isaac and his guest had browsed through the 147 available channels on the chief's satellite TV and now old Isaac was about to show off the latest in White Dog technology. As they walked into the kitchen they caught the sounds of Wally's more amorous advances.

"Mmmmmm, so where'd you say you were from there, sugar lips?" he asked to uproarious laughter from all across the reserve.

Chief Isaac would later explain down at the store how they too suddenly got interested in the romance of the airwaves and pulled up chairs around Isaac's kitchen table.

"Rat Portage. You know, down south a little?" she said softly.

"Hey, that's one of the girls from my band," said Isaac's guest, suddenly more interested.

"Heard it's good fishin' down there," Wally whispered. "I can see it now. Moonlight . . . a canoe . . . me . . . and you. Mmmmm."

"Mmmmmmmm," she sighed. "Yeah. Mmmmmm. Yeah."

"What's your name anyway, honey?" Wally asked. We all heard frantic shuffling from the speaker.

"Audrey," she said shyly. "Audrey Two Canoes."

Now there are those who claim to this day that you could hear the scream that came from Isaac's that night clear across the townsite, even over top of all the laughter that was rolling openly between houses. We didn't hear anything at Keeper's but we sure were glued to the radio that night. Chief Isaac later said his guest nearly hit the roof when he heard her say her name. Turns out, you see, that his visitor was Chief Oscar Two Canoes of Rat Portage and Audrey was his youngest daughter up at White Dog to compete in the jingle-dress competition and whom he believed to be with her mother at a cousin's house.

"Where is he? Where is he?" Chief Oscar screamed at Isaac. "I swear I'll beat him within an inch of his life. Where is he?"

He charged out of Isaac's kitchen, grabbing the wire leading from the speaker and following it down the road all bent over like a garbage dump bear. All the while he was shouting her name and Wally's name at the top of his lungs and describing in perfect detail the harm that was about to befall radio's chief executive once he located the White Dog One studios.

All hunched over and squinting in the darkness Chief Oscar felt his way along that wire up to each and every house on White Dog. Maggie and Ben Stevenson almost jumped out of their nightshirts when an enraged, sweaty, somewhat ugly Indian appeared at their bedroom window screaming all kinds of vile things in their direction and then disappeared into the night. Ben grabbed his partridge shotgun and headed out the door in full pursuit, the tail of his nightshirt flapping away in the wind behind him.

When Chief Oscar's greasy, bush-torn face appeared at Len and Clarice Bird's window they too screamed and took off after him. House after house joined the parade chasing Chief Oscar across the reserve. By the time they reached Keeper's there was about fifty Indians in full pursuit of what they believed to be an evil spirit come to kidnap their children in the dark.

Chief Oscar's head appeared at Keeper's window just slightly ahead of the angry mob. We were still busy listening to Wally's major moves and Audrey's enthusiastic replies when they burst through the door.

"Come on, you guys!" Len Bird shouted at us. "Need ya with us 'cause we got a bad spirit chasin' the kids around tonight!"

Keeper jumped up all startled, grabbed his coat and headed out the door. By the time the ten of us joined the parade of people stumbling through the dark after the barely visible hunched-over shape of Chief Oscar, there was about sixty people involved.

Out past the cabins on the edges of Shotgun Bay and back through the bush towards the townsite we crashed and tumbled after Chief Oscar, whose bellowing could still be heard a long ways off. He did sound like an enraged spirit and some of the language we heard that night made us awful grateful we weren't the ones this evil being was after.

Things kind of got settled down once we hit the dirt road through the townsite again and Chief Isaac pulled up in his four-by-four and told us about Chief Oscar. As many of us as possible crammed into the back of the truck and headed off to prevent disaster at the White Dog One Radio Network. Turned out that Chief Oscar beat us by about a heartbeat.

All we heard as we pulled up was a loud pair of screeches followed by one heck of a lot of banging and crashing before Wally Red Sky burst through his open window, shirtless, shoeless and barely managing to zip up his Levi's. He took off down the road faster'n I seen anyone move around here before or since. Chief Oscar flew through the window head first and roiled in a big heap at our feet before jumping up still screaming and headed off in pursuit of the rapidly disappearing Wally. He had Wally's guitar held up in both hands over his head and he looked pretty intent on braining him a good one if he could get close enough.

For his part Wally was hightailing down the road like a jackrabbit from wolves, little puffs of dust being kicked up by each footstep. He was screaming back over his shoulder at the fast-approaching form of Chief Oscar.

"Radio play! Radio play! Wasn't real! Wasn't real!" we heard him scream as he turned sharply off the road and headed into the bush.

"Radio play, my ass!" screamed Chief Oscar as he too crashed into the bush, swinging Wally's guitar like a machete at the bushes and limbs in his face.

All we could hear was loud crashing and screaming through the timber and Wally's voice fading further and further away in one long continuous "AHHHhhhh-hhhh . . . !"

By this time of course we were all rolling around on the ground laughing as hard as we could. We could hear laughter from all around us and no one even bothered calling out to Audrey as she slipped out the door of Wally's and headed off towards her cousin's. By the time things settled down enough for people to breathe again we could hear only faint crashings deep in the bush.

"Oh boy, that Wally," Keeper said, holding his belly with tears streaming down his face. "Always managin' to stay one step ahead of his audience!"

Wally's fear eventually outran Chief Oscar's anger. Either that or being a local he knew the area better and managed to lose the chief in the darkness. But Oscar showed up about four in the morning all bush-torn and sweaty carrying what was left of Wally's old guitar. He was nodding and mumbling about all sorts of things and then just as he was climbing into his pickup he burst out in great rolling waves of laughter. That's what woke us up actually. Huge spasms of laughter that kinda echoed off the lake. When Ma'n me looked down the hill towards the townsite all we could see was the burly shape of Chief Oscar rolling around on the dirt road by the ball diamond shrieking and shrieking with laughter.

By the time any of us reached him he was sitting in the middle of the road with tears streaming down his face.

"Ah-hoo, ah-hoo, ah-hoo!" he sorta coughed and laughed at the same time. "Where you from there, sugar lips!" he said and burst out in rolls of laughter again.

"Me'n you, a canoe . . . ah-hoo, ah-hoo-hoo-hoo!" he laughed and started to climb into the cab of his truck. "Funniest damn thing I ever heard in my life. Ah-hoo-hoo-hoo-hoo!"

He looked out at the little group of us standing there and wiped his eyes with a handkerchief. "Best damn pow-wow I bin to in a long time.

"Funniest thing I ever heard. Tell that kid he's okay in my books. Little weird maybe, but okay. An' tell Audrey when she comes outta hidin' that it's all okay too. Damn. Gotta get me some of that radio thing down home too. Ah-hoo-hoo-hoo. Fast little bugger too that Wally Red Sky!" He slammed the door and took off down the road in a spray of dust and laughter.

There was just Stanley'n Jackie'n me standing there after a while and we were all still smirking about it when Jackie suggested coffee at his place. He clapped me on the back and laughed real big and loud.

"Downtown enough for ya or what?" he said.

"Yeah," I said. "Yeah. Damn good thing I didn't talk to Wally about disco!"

"Brother, man," Stanley said in his best downtown brown imitation, "brother, man, y'lla gotta be watchin' watchu layin' on the brothers here. We be dyin' laughin' you keep up that rap, hear?"

"Yeah, I hear, I hear," I said, putting my arms around the shoulders of my brothers and heading off towards whatever this day was gonna hold. "Just tryin' keep things moving around here, that's all!"

There's something I do for myself still these days. When that sun's starting to go down on those long, calm summer evenings, I'll walk down to the dock, climb into my boat and head out across the lake to watch it. You can motor out about five miles before you reach what's probably the middle and I just kill the engine and lie across the middle of the boat. Got my feet dangling over one side and my head on a seat cushion against the other. Then I just sit there. It's nice. Watching that sky kinda explode into a thousand different shades and bobbing up and down with the waves can take you on incredible journeys inside.

I sit there and watch that sun go down and then I sit there and watch the night take over the sky. Me I call it my magic time. There's a moment just before the dark really takes over that still gives me a thrill when I see it. See, there's a shade of blue in that night sky that there's really no name for in our language or any other that I ever heard. It's hard to explain that color, it's so magical. Deep and dark and light and metallic and silver and purple all at the same time. It's a blue that seeps inside you and makes you wanna cry and laugh and smile and dream. It's right at the edge of that line between dark and light. It's there in the winter and it's there in the summer except it might be even more powerful on those long summer evenings alone on that lake. I sit there and wait and wait and wait and when it finally slides into view there's a part of me inside that just goes, Mmmmmmmmm. A peaceful, silent blue. The only word I ever heard that comes close to explaining how that blue feels inside me is "eternal." Eternal blue. My favorite color and my favorite feeling. There's an Ojibway phrase that comes close. Goes, Wass-co-nah-shpee-ming. Light in the sky. That eternal blue's the big light in my sky and my world these days on accounta it reminds me of where I want to be mosta the time. Peaceful, silent, alive inside.

So I go out on that lake to get some of that blue inside. And I watch it as it grows and then fades into the purple of night and I think about my life here and the thousand other lives I lived before I came home. I sit there and I drift across that lake, bobbing up and down on the waves, them stars coming closer then moving away with each lift and drop, and it always feels like the universe is alive and moving around me, above me and below me. As Keeper says, I become part of it. And I drift and I drift until finally the boat will nudge up against the shore and I'll have to get my bearings and head for home. I do that for myself lots still.

Biggest reason is that blue feeling's a lot easier to take than either the big empty I used to feel or the hunger for the fast life I still get sometimes. Helps me balance my insides really. The other big reason is I really remember lots when I'm out there. Lots of things that help me keep in balance with the way my life's going.

There's still lots of changes going on and getting in touch with that blue sure keeps me moving the right way. Most of what I've been telling you was brought back by long nights in that boat and whenever I need to remember something important I usually head out on the lake at night. Winters I just stand outside looking at it till I get too cold.

I thought I was really missing out on something until one night on the lake. Keeper'n me had spent all that day talking about the drum and how important it is to the ways of the Anishanabe. He told me about the woman side and the man side of all of us and how we gotta learn to lie in balance with both those sets of gifts to really be happy in this world. It all sounded strange to me at first but as I sat there in the middle of the lake that night it began to fall together inside of me. Inside out. Keeper was always talking about how nothing in this world ever grows from the outside in. Growth only ever happens from the inside out. So finding a balance inside myself as a man and as an Ojibway meant that finding a balance with the outside world was gonna be a whole lot easier. Funny how something as simple as a drum can unlock the universe for you once you get taught how to look at it.

There was nothing at first, just the soft sound of the waves on the side of the boat, a little whistling of the breeze. The full moon was rising in a big orange ball at the east end of the lake. It was huge. The trees looked like long fingers and I remember thinking that right at that moment the land really was alive, those fingers reaching up and trying to touch the moon. I watched it as it slid upwards into the sky and just as the thought came to my mind that it looked like a big orange drum in the sky, I heard it.

Softly at first and then getting steadily louder and clearer from far off past the far end of the lake. A drum. Boom-boom, boom-boom. Boom-boom, boom-boom. The heartbeat rhythm. For the longest time that's all I heard, and then . . . a voice. It was a man's voice and it echoed off everything, the hills, the rocks, the water, until it was impossible to pinpoint where it was coming from. I'll never forget that song. It was pure and clear and filled with respect, awe and power.

"Soo-wanee-quay," the voice sang. "Soo-wanee-quay." That's all. A single phrase over and over again as that moon rose higher and higher into that purple sky. That drumbeat lulled me into a deeper peace and as I drifted over that lake that night I could feel the power of the earth all around me.

I could see the flicker of half a dozen fires out back of people's homes. There were the racing shadows of the kids playing some game and I pretended I could hear their teasing and their laughter. I saw the quick shadow shapes of dogs chasing around after them kids and a few seconds after their yapping barks reached my ears. I could see the hunched-over shadows of the old ladies bringing tea out back and now and then I could make out a young couple strolling hand in hand alongside the lake. All of it just kinda sat there that night like some big moving painting with a background of purple treetops like fingers reaching up towards that moon. As that drumbeat carried on and that voice kept singing what I knew inside to be a hymn to the earth, I bobbed up and down on that lake and smiled. I bobbed and bobbed and my insides filled up with that hymn, that scene and the belief that if there really was a thing called balance in this world I wanted this place to always be the balance point.

I thought about Ma's belief in a common magic born of the land that heals us and I smiled. There was magic that night and on many of the other nights I've drifted alone across that lake watching the lives of my people fill the shadows of the land.

Nights later when I told Keeper about it he just smiled.

"Someone gettin' balance themselves, sounds like," he said. "Soo-wanee-quay's a Cree sayin' comes from the sweat lodge. Means somethin' like power of the woman. Whoever was singin' that song out there was recognizin' the power of the woman in everythin' out there and thankin' it. Recognizin' the woman's gifts inside himself and singin' so he could join himself up with it."

We never ever did figure out who was singing that song. Ma and my uncles tell stories about the shadow people. Shadow people are people who lived before us who kinda watch over us all the time. Always hanging around to help us learn things, and Ma says she's seen one or two in her time and even heard a couple when she's really been needing some help. The way my family figures it is, on accounta no one else heard what I did that night, that I must of heard one of the shadow people singing his blessing over the land, its powers and for me too. Big gift, Ma says, and I believe her. Big gift. Ever since that night I been okay with my life here.

Whenever that feeling creeps into my insides about maybe leaving and checking out the action again or whenever I feel myself getting all tied up inside, I head out on that lake in my boat. I find the middle. I cut the engine and lean back across the center of that boat and start bobbing up and down. When I feel the up and down rhythm of that boat kinda like a drumbeat itself, I look up and around at the land and the universe around me and I sing real soft and low, "Soo-wanee-quay, soo-wanee-quay." Feels like coming home.

*Hmmpfh. Sometimes these days old guys like me be wonderin' all the time whether there's any magic left in this world. Old people talk about times before the whiteman when magic was all over. Midewewin were big makers of magic an' the powers of the land could always be counted on for big teachin's. Nowadays with not lots believin' anymore, well, we wonder whether that magic mighta moved on somewheres else.*

*Me I figure the boy's been kinda my key to callin' back a little of that magic around here. Us we all need someone or somethin' to guide us. Sometimes that guide's funniest-lookin' guide you can imagine an' lotsa the time they don' even know they're guidin' you. That's what the boy's been for me. Unknowin' kinda guide for me. He guided lotsa us back then. Dug in so hard tryin' to learn an' be parta us he helped us see what we shoulda been doin' ourselves. Hmmpfh.*

*Learned good, him. Learned good. Us we laughed like crazy over Wally'n that radio thing. Still do lots. Thing about us Indyuns, laughin' kinda frees up your insides an' you remember lot more things than if you get all sad an' weepy over somethin'. Nothin' to cry over with that little adventure though. 'Cept maybe that Wally's still singin' nights on that radio. Heh, heh, heh.*

*But hey, me I learned lotsa good sayin's for next time I'm out there snaggin'. Heh, heh, heh. Old man like me gotta have a good line or two now, can't just lean on my good looks an' sleek physique. Heh, heh, heh.*

*Anyway, what I mean by the boy kinda bein' a guide for me goes back to a couple weeks after all that settled down. He come around one night askin' more about this balance. Wonderin' how he was supposed to know what he didn't need no more and what he was supposed to keep of that old life. Helped me remember what the old man told me one time too. So that's what I told him that night, same thing.*

*See, me I come to Harold one time, musta been about ten or eleven. I really wanted to be like him. Real old, kinda all gentle an' soft an' kind but strong too an' I didn't know how I was ever gonna get there. Just didn't know. All confused about what I should be doin' and what I shouldn't. So I asked an' he told me this story.*

*Way it goes is, a young man was walkin' around his village one day lookin' around at his people. He stopped an' watched everythin' they were doin' an' started to notice how real quiet, gentle an' good they were with each other. Kinda felt the first stirrin's of love for them deep in his chest. More he walked around lookin' more love he felt for them.*

*So the young man walked over to the old woman of his village an' started to talk to her. He told her about walkin' around seein' the life his people led, the way they were with each other an' how he loved them for their ways. Told that old woman that he wanted to become a great warrior. Told her he wanted to be a warrior so he could always protect them from anythin' that might hurt them or make them change. The old woman watched him as he talked an' she just knew that his words were comin' from a true place.*

*Then the young man asked that old woman, he said, "I wanna be the greatest warrior for my people that I can be. And to do that I need the medicine power of the most respected animal in the animal kingdom. If I can have that I will really be a great warrior."*

*That's what he said.*

*And the old woman looked at the young man, kinda had a tear in her eye, an' she told him, she said, "I can tell that your heart is pure an that you're askin' for this on accounta you really do wanna be a protector. No other reason. So I'm gonna give you this. But first you gotta be able to tell me who this animal brother or sister is that's got the most respect of all the animals. Do that an' I'll give you that medicine power."*

*Well, I guess that young man just kinda got all happy on accounta it sounded like such an easy question. So he yelled out, "The animal that's got the most respect from its animal brothers an' sisters is the grizzly bear! It's the grizzly bear on accounta he's fierce an' strong an' fearless."*

*But that old woman just shook her head real sad-like an' told him, "No. It's not brother bear. There's another."*

*So the young man thought a little longer an' then he said, "Well then, it's gotta be the wolverine on accounta the wolverine's a great fighter, fearless an' scary."*

*But one more time the old woman shook her head all sad an' told the young man, "No. That's not the one. There's another."*

*One by one the young man named all the most fearless, strongest, biggest, fiercest animals he could think of but each time the old woman just shook her head an' said, "No. There's another."*

*Finally, after a long time the young man hung his head real depressed an' told her, he said, "I don't know who this is. So I guess I can't have this medicine power an' I guess I can't be a great warrior."*

*But the old woman reached out her hand an' touched the young man, looked deep into his eyes an' said, "No. Because your heart is so pure I'm gonna give you this one's name an' I'm gonna let you have this great medicine power because I know you'll use it in a good way.*

*"The animal that's got the most respect from his animal brothers an' sisters . . . is the mole. Tiny, blind little mole that lives in the ground is the greatest warrior in the animal kingdom."*

*Well, the young man could hardly believe his ears. "But how can that be?" he asked. "The mole's so small, can't fight, can't even see."*

*The old woman smiled. Them old people they always smile*

*when they're gonna lay some learnin' on you, even now. She smiled an' told the young man, she said, "Reason the mole's got the most respect is on accounta he lives in constant touch with Mother Earth. All his life always stays in touch with her. That way he gets wise. Gets wise so that even though his eyes are bad he learns to see another way. The way of the spirit.*

*"Other reason he gets most respect is on accounta when the mole's busy burrowin' through the earth like he does he's always gettin' vibrations from the surface from whoever else is movin' around up there. So in order for him to learn when he's in danger or not that mole will dig his way to the surface an' have a quick look around. That way he learns when a rabbit runs over him or when there's even a fox chasin' that rabbit. Knows the way a bear walks across the ground, a man, knows the way of everythin' on accounta he's gonna up to take a sniff whenever he's felt somethin' movin around.*

*"An' that's why the mole's got the most respect of all his animal brothers an' sisters. That's why.*

*"Because even though he might get eaten, even though he might be injured, even though he might feel a great deal of pain on accounta it, that mole always takes the time to investigate what he feels. That's why. And you gotta have that same medicine power to be a great warrior."*

*The young man went away to think about it. Thought about it long time an' he went on to become a great warrior who was loved an' respected by all the people for his kindness, fairness an' softness as well as his strength, fightin' and brav'ry. That warrior always took the time to investigate his feelin's before he did anything.*

*That's what I told the boy that day, just like old Harold told me. He sat there for a while thinkin' it over an' when he looked up there was kinda tears in the corners of his eyes an' he was smiling. He didn't say anything then, just sat there smilin' all glitter-eyed an' happy.*

*An' you know, ever since that day that boy's always walkin' around checkin' out his insides whenever he's gotta make a choice. Sometimes it takes days but he's diggin' for the surface just like that mole, kinda sniffin' around, investigatin' what he feels. An' he ain't really been wrong yet. Still listens to that blues music an' dances around all crazy sometimes, still talks big dreams an' still likes to go to town an' check things out, but he always comes back. Comes back for more learnin'. Comes back for more of himself an' for more home inside.*

*Told you he learned good, didn't I?*

BOOK FOUR

# LOOKIN' JAKE

The land is a feeling. That's what Keeper says all the time and I was just beginning to get an idea of what he meant by the second fall I was home. See, according to Keeper all the fuss and trouble the government has with us Indians is on accounta the land. They call it "the Indian problem" and they figure it's all about us wanting our own governments and to be able to run things on our own. But it's not, according to Keeper. This so-called Indian problem is really a land problem. It's always been that way, he says. The way Keeper tells it is that most of them politicians are pretty much aware of the way the land was taken on the sly. So ever since then they've been carrying around big blanket of guilt, he says. They put us on reserves telling us we could live the old way there, hunt and fish and trap, do all the things we used to do before the whiteman got here. Said it was for our own benfit. But according to Keeper it was for their benefit, not ours. He says putting us on all these reserves kept us Indians from talking a lot to each other. Couldn't get together and couldn't put together any really big plans. Still afraid of a big Indian uprising, I guess. Way Keeper sees it, the government came along and told all the Indians if they put down their arrows and went off to live on these reserves and were good little Indians then maybe one of these days we'd be able to get some of those arrows back. Down through the years they gave us a few back but they kept all the points and feathers and only gave us the shaft. And we been pretty much getting the shaft ever since. Funny guy, that Keeper.

Anyway, what I was meaning to say was that the land is a feeling. The reason the Indians want all these land claims settled is on accounta they wanna protect their connection with the land. It isn't on accounta they want all of North America back like some people believe. Keeper says nobody in their right mind wants something back that someone else has already wrecked. They just wanna protect their connection. Land is the most sacred thing in the Indian way of seeing. It's where life comes from and all the teachings and philosophy that kept Indians alive through everything that happened to them all over all these years comes from the land. Lose that connection you lose yourself, according to most people around here. Lose that connection you lose that feeling of being a part of something that's bigger than everything. Kinda tapping into the great mystery. Feeling the spirit of the land that's the spirit of the people and the spirit of yourself. That's what I was learning all along but I needed to get a lot closer to it and that's kinda what happened that second fall I was home.

See, there's something I do even now that I first done that second fall. I don't know why I started really, except that it felt like a good idea at the time. Keeper says it was the first stirrings of that woman side of me calling out directions. Intuition, the gift of the mother. Anyway, it's kinda become a personal ritual and every fall at the same time everyone here knows that I'm gonna disappear across the lake in a canoe for four days of living on the land all alone. Usually I paddle in for a whole day, find a good campsite, set up and just wander around out there, looking around, studying things. There's a huge silence you discover when you get way beyond things like houses and roads and motors. It can be kinda scary at first but once you get used to it it's like the most beautiful sound you ever heard and it fills up your insides until you think you're gonna pass out from the pressure. A beautiful, roaring silence. A silence that's full of everything. When your ears get used to it you start to hear things you never ever heard in your life. Things you never knew were there. Things like the whispers of old people's voices when the wind blows through the trees.

Little gurgles and chuckles like babies when the water from a creek rolls over the rocks. The almost holy sound of an eagle's wings when it flaps above you, kinda like he's breathing on you. Even something as quiet as your paddle moving through the water's got a silky sound like the ripple of a lady's shawl in a fancy dance. Far-off thunder sounding like a big drum in the sky and all the snaps and crackles, rubbings and scrapings that goes on in the bush at night when you can't see anything. A thick blanket of sounds that tells you that darkness has a life too. A beautiful silence. The most beautiful music I ever heard. Full of all the notes of life and living we miss when we get away from it too long. The sounds that connect you to yourself and your life.

That's why I go. On accounta when I get back and start moving around with people again I always got that silence to fall back on when things get strange. That silence gets to be a part of me by me going out there and being a part of it. I didn't know that then, that first fall. All I knew was that there was a feeling telling me it was a good idea to go. I wanted to head for that area just beyond the other side of the lake where I was born. The traditional land my grampa trapped. The beginnings, I guess. Something inside me was telling me that I needed to go there. So I talked about it with Keeper and Jackie and Stanley'n Jane to see what they thought and everybody figured it was a good idea.

Course Ma was all worried when I told her. Being a bush woman all her life, Ma knows how tough it is to get by out there if you don't know what you're doing and how fast things can change out there when you don't know how to read the land or the signs it gives you.

"Sure you wanna go alone, my boy?"

"Hey-yuh. Been spending lotsa time with Gilbert and Charlie this summer. Been watching how they do things and they showed me lots. I'll be okay."

"How far back you gonna go? Not far, I hope."

"Kaween," I said. "No. Not far. Other side of the lake, maybe one portage back, two maybe."

"Holee. That's far. Lotta wolf an' bear around out there."

"Hey-yuh. Lot."

"You know your grampa's old trapline land starts back there?"

"Hey-yuh. That's a big part of the reason I wanna go there. Being home's great, Ma, it really is, but I feel like if I don't go there and see for myself where it all started for me, it's not really gonna be like I've come home at all yet."

"I know. Us we can only give you parta yourself back here. Help you learn about this place an' us. Yourself. But's a big parta you out there in that bush. Maybe now's the time you went there an' picked it up an' brought it home."

"Yeah, that's what it kinda feels like. I don't know why I gotta go there. I only know that I do."

"Still, maybe Jackie oughta go with you first time? Good bush Indyun, that Jackie."

"Kaween. Jackie's one of the ones said I should go alone in the first place."

"Really?"

"Hey-yuh. We both figure I'll be okay. And I just kinda need some time alone for a while. To think. Get away from things. Fish. Walk around. Find something."

She was looking at me kinda different by this time, nodding her head real slow like she does when she starts to understand or see something she missed the first time around. Her eyes were smiling now and she reached out to touch my cheek with one warm brown hand.

"Hey-yuh. I know. Your papa useta do the same thing every year too. Useta just get up real early, load up a canoe and paddle off by himself. Us we never knew where he was going, just that he was going off alone again. Never said much about it when he got back but he was always more, bigger kinda when he got back. You looked just like him there for a minute," she said, stroking my cheek real soft. "Hey-yuh. Lot. So I guess it's okay. Runs in the family, I guess."

"Hey-yuh. Jackie said him'n Stanley do that too all the time. Says our uncles go off alone too lots. Jackie says it helps him. Gets him kinda peaceful inside."

"Yeah. I know. Maybe you ask Keeper sometime to tell you about it. Been a parta what us Indyuns do for a long, long time."

"So you're not gonna worry?"

"Oh, I'm still gonna worry. Oh yes, me I'll worry. But

I know too that you gotta do it. You'll learn lots out there you're gonna need. Lots."

"Wanna help me get ready then?"

"'Kay. How much you wanna take?"

"Not lots. Wanna travel light."

"How light is light?"

"Light light. Just what I'm gonna need."

"'Kay then. Only thing is . . . how you gonna get across that lake with a stove and stereo in that canoe?"

If you ever wanna get the idea of how it feels to fly, all you really gotta do is paddle a canoe alone across a northern lake when it's calm. When there's no wind and no waves it's like moving through glass. You look over the sides and it's like you're suspended above everything. Water so clear you float over the rocks and boulders and logs on the bottom like an eagle over land, seeing the fish kinda scatter and picking out their favorite hiding places as you pass. If you look out over the front it's like a magic curtain of cloud. Big shiny silver curtain that parts with the tip of the canoe, revealing the lake like you've never seen it. Things coming into view all slow and gradual, quiet and peaceful like you're soaring over all of it. Paddle faster and it's like you're flapping your wings harder and the land passing beneath you moves by like a dream. It takes your breath away and really makes it hard to travel very far very fast. One of the rewards of being alone in a canoe early in the morning is that feeling of flying.

I discovered it that first morning that fall. It was one of them foggy mornings when the mist over the lake kinda makes all the sounds sharper and clearer. Me'n Ma could hear loons and herons across the bay and the yap of dogs from somewhere back in the bush like they were right beside us. We could hear Keeper coming even though that old guy moves pretty quiet in the bush, so we weren't surprised when he appeared out of the fog.

"Ahnee," he called from the top of the steps leading down to the dock behind Ma's. "Minno gezheegut. It's a good day. How's things?"

"It's okay, Keeper. You?" Ma said.

"Oh, not bad. Gonna miss that bacon, Garnet, you make sure and get back okay on accounta I need my breakfast chef."

"Yeah, right," I said. "You'll find some way of arranging an invitation to someone's for breakfast. What's that you got there?"

"Oh, this?" he said getting that surprised look on his face that he always does when he's about to give something away. "Just somethin' you're gonna need out there. It's not much."

"Well, what is it?"

"Tobacco, white pieces of cloth, string. That's all."

"So what do I do with this?"

"Pray."

"Pray?"

"Hey-yuh. Pray."

"How?"

"Lots," he said, and we all laughed.

"No, really. What's it for?"

"It's for the land. You gotta give it back to the land. It's an offering. Gratitude offering. Us we do this. Those of us tryin' to live the Indyun way, we do this couple times a year. Called a tobacco offering. You take this tobacco and you wrap a small pinch of it in these little white pieces of cloth, tie 'em up with string. Make up a long circle of them."

"Why?"

"Well, it's on accounta us we sometimes forget what all we got to be thankful for. Forget that everythin' comes from the land. Food, home, health, everythin'. So the old ones made this ceremony an' taught everyone to do it. Don't need to be an elder or a teacher to do it, it's for everyone on accounta we all gotta show gratitude to stay humble.

"So you go out there. When you're all set up, you find a place that feels kinda special. Maybe up on a big, high rock or at the foot of a bay. Smudge first. Pray. Then you take that tobacco an' wrap it an' tie it. When you do this you think of somethin' or someone in your life you're grateful for an' say a prayer of thanks. Pray for their happiness, health and harmony. Then you think of somethin' else an' say the same kinda prayer. Keep on like that till you run outta prayers or tobacco. Then you take that circle of prayers you just made an' you leave it in the branches of a tree or at the top of that big rock. Give those prayers back to the land an' the spirits. Back where they came from.

"Might take you long time. Should. But you take as long as you need, give thanks for everythin'. When you're done you'll feel real good an' you'll treat everyone an' everything with lotsa love an' respect. It's hard to be unloving an' disrespectful towards things you prayed for."

"Do you do this, Ma?" I asked.

"Hey-yuh. Couple times a year ever since I was a girl. It's good. Keeps you real."

"Anything else I gotta do?"

"No," Keeper said. "Just pray for all you're thankful for. It'll be good for you an' it's time you got movin' in this way now. 'Specially where you're goin'. Findin' that special place is not gonna be hard for you, I think." He handed me the moose-hide pouch.

Ma gave me a big warm hug and looked real proud at me for a long time as I got ready to shove off. I remember feeling like I was about to discover something really big in my life and I couldn't wait to find out what it was.

"'Kay then," I said when I got seated in the canoe. "Be back in four nights, round sundown, I guess."

"'Kay then," Ma said. "Careful."

"Hey-yuh. Will be."

"Oh, an' Garnet," Keeper said, kinda mischievous. "You gotta try'n light a fire only usin' two sticks when you're out there."

"I do?"

"Hey-yuh. It's traditional."

"Really?"

"Hey-yuh. Only for you we're changin' it this time."

"Yeah?"

"Gonna let one of them sticks be a match!"

I looked back once I got a hundred yards or so out on the lake. They were still standing there with their arms around each other's waist watching me head out across. It's one of those Kodak moments, only these kind we keep in our hearts instead of some photo album. I got the idea that I knew what prayers those first two pouches were gonna be for.

As I paddled across that lake that morning, watching the sun start to burn the mist off the water, it was like seeing the light being born inside me again. By the time I reached the northern shore it was midmorning and I hugged the shoreline as I worked my way east to where I knew a portage to be. That's when I discovered the feeling of flying. I was lost in it for miles. Those who say there's no magic in the world anymore have never taken a solitary paddle on a northern lake in the morning. That feeling of being on a cushion of air was pure magic. Only the shadows of the trees and cliffs on the water kept me earthbound and by the time I reached the cairn of stones that marked the portage, my whole being felt like it could detach itself from earth and soar off somewhere into the wild blue of that morning sky. In a way, I guess, it did.

*Watchin' the boy headin' off across that lake that mornin' reminded me of myself one time. I must have been about twelve.*

*Me'n the old man been hangin' around together about a year by then. Me I'd learned lots but had a real long way to go yet. Old man told me it was time I went out to feel the power. That's all. Go and feel the power. So we spent a coupla days gettin' me all ready for this trip. It was gonna be four days. Wasn't all romantic like them movies. Me I had a fishin' pole, knife, rifle, food an' blankets, just like the boy's canoe. Them Westerns wanna make you think us Indyuns go out with nothin' but a blanket and spend a long time fastin' in the wilderness. Sometimes we do. Sometimes we do for special reasons like gettin' ready for a big ceremony but most of the time we go out there all alone so we can greet the world again. That's what it's all about. Greetin' the world again. See, us we get all busy with our lives. Gotta go here, go there, do this, do that, all the time. Get so busy we forget to look around an' see the world. Forget to spend time with our best teacher. We start thinkin' maybe we're kinda important or too busy or both. So we go out there where no one else is around an' we sit there. Most of the time that land'll give you something to bring back. No big dreams or visions, although some get lucky an' have them, but mostly you just see somethin' in the land itself that'll get you thinkin' right again. Me, I forgot toilet paper one time an' I seen a vision. Or at least I thought it was. Old man told me, he said, I only see somethin' strange on accounta I was all constipated an' my vision was blurry after four days. Hey, heh, heh. Funny guy, that Harold.*

*Anyway, I paddled long time, made a portage, went way to the end of this long lake I found. Made camp. First time I ever did things old way makin' camp. Spruce boughs on the floor of the lean-to I made, sayin' prayers for everythin' I used, leavin' little tobacco offerings by the trees an' all. It was nice. Felt safe. Was real quiet there. Couldn't find no sign of other people havin' been there before an' I felt kinda special. Like this was my spot on the earth kinda. And that's where I stayed for four days. I still go there now an' again an' it's still as quiet an' untouched as it was way back then. Still get that feelin' of bein' connected again when I go there.*

*No big thing happened. Me I was lookin' around for a big message or vision but nothin' big happened. Except for the eagles of course. See, the old man told me about makin' my tobacco offering too. First time I did it then. So that second morning I was way up on this big rock cliff, sittin' on this ledge lookin' way out over that lake an' the land. Started makin' those tobacco ties an' prayin' like I was told. Kinda got lost. Didn't have no idea of time so I was surprised to look around finally an' see it was midafternoon already. Kinda hungry, you know. I was thinkin' about leavin' an' goin' to eat, maybe come back next mornin' to keep on with it. But I looked around an' there was a big eagle sittin' about four yards away from me on the top of this dead pine tree. Just sittin' there lookin' at me. Didn't move. I looked the other way an' there was another one sittin' in the top of another tree about the same distance away. Me I figured they were a pair. Thought maybe I was close to their nest or somethin' but they weren't actin' too upset so I figured it was just one of them crazy coincidences. Kept on watchin' them watchin' me for a long time. Finally kinda got too hungry so I got into sayin' one last prayer to thank the Creator for sendin' me up there an' for the day I was having. When I looked up them eagles was gone.*

*Next day I'm up there early doing more ties an' prayin'. Soon as I looked up from that first prayer them eagles were back in the same trees right up close to me. Hmmpfh. Kinda felt strange all of a sudden. Stayed there all day an' every time I looked up from prayin' them eagles were watchin' me.*

*Third day same thing. Only when I got up there they weren't around. Hmmpfh, I figured. Wasn't no sign, just lucky. Waited about half an hour before I said that first prayer an' them eagles weren't anywhere to be seen. Looked up after that prayer an' there they were, sittin' there lookin' at me. Really felt strange then. Stayed there again all day them birds. Never moved. Just sat there.*

*Finally that last mornin' before I loaded up the canoe I went back up there to finish off. Had a big long circle of prayers to give back an' I wanted to leave it there on that big rock cliff. Climbed up an' no birds nowhere. Smudged up an' prayed. Looked up an' sure enough, there they were, same trees. By this time I'm okay with it. Me I figured I just made some friends. So, I said a big long prayer an' offered my circle of prayers back to the land an' the spirits. When I looked up them birds were gone. So I tossed that circle of prayers across an' they landed near the top of that one tree where I saw the first eagle. Left it there an' went back to get ready. Figured that was the end of it. Got all packed up an' headed out in the canoe. Only got about ten feet off shore when I heard this sound an' saw this shadow on the water. Looked up an' seen them two eagles soarin' around in a great big circle over my head. Way up there circlin' around. Sat there in the canoe watchin' them for a long time, screamin' their eagle cries an' circlin' above me. Finally I decided*

*I better get movin' so I started to paddle again. But I heard this long cry an' looked up real quick. One of them eagles was just tuckin' his wings under and startin' to dive right at the canoe. Hmmpfh. But me I wasn't scared. Kept lookin' up even when that bird started to power dive right at me. No fear. When he was about ten feet above the water he spread his wings real fast an' flapped them four times. Stopped him right in midair above the canoe. Flapped four times an' then screamed one last time an' flew off. I sat there an' watched the two of them disappear over the far end of the lake towards home. Felt real happy inside. The sound of them wings was like a blessing to me and I felt real happy inside. Boy, I sang all the way home. All this time I never forgot them two eagles. Sometimes even now when I feel low I think about the sound them wings made an' I feel okay again. Been back there since an' never seen them again either. Hmmpfh.*

*Told the old man all about it. He never said nothin', just smiled an' walked away. Hmmpfh. Crazy old coot I figured. Next day he come an' brought me two eagle feathers tied all together with moose-hide thong. Said I earned them. Then he talked to me about them two sets of gifts we all carry. Told me them two eagles were signs to me about livin' in balance with them two sets of gifts. Mother's and the father's. When I was prayin' I was in balance an' that's why they came. Both sides comin' together with my prayers. Man side and woman side. Sacred union comin' together when I pray. Sacred union inside me. That's what he told me. Said the reason they disappeared over the end of the lake leadin' towards home was to remind me that I gotta take that teachin' back into my life. Can't just use it when I'm out there. I gotta live it. It's gotta be parta of my livin' all the time. Whenever I needed to find that balance for myself I just need to pray. That's what them eagles were a sign of. So he gave me them two feathers tied together and told me keep them somewhere where I can see them all the time, to kinda remind me. Me I still got 'em. Hangin' on the wall of my cabin. They're a big sign of how I'm supposed to live. A big teaching I forgot for a long time. One I walked away from but awful glad I managed to walk back into again.*

*That's what seein' that boy headin' out reminded me of. Me I just knew he was gonna come back with somethin' that would fill up big corners of his insides. Somethin' that was gonna be just for him. The land's like that. Let yourself be a part of it an' it's always gonna give you back a part of yourself you never knew you had. Good friend that land. No wonder it's brown. Heh, heh, heh.*

Grampa's trapline was about eighty miles long when it was running full tilt. The hydro dam had drowned most of it but the one end's still there and that's where I was headed. Jackie'd given me directions so I pretty much knew how to recognize the place where one of the old line shacks used to stand. I had to make two easy portages, cross one small lake and look for a place where a little creek dumped into the lake in a waterfall about five feet high. I found it by about midafternoon. It was beautiful. The little falls made a big wide pool in the end of one little bay that was surrounded by tall jack pines and there was a stretch of level ground all mossy and grassy where I would camp. Lot of cool shade and the pool was deep enough to swim in. Looked like someplace I could spend the rest of my life and never worry about anything. Kinda felt like home.

Watching my uncles had taught me pretty good how to set up a camp so doing that was really no problem and I had a good fire going by the time that sun started to go down. Guess you don't have to be an Indian to appreciate a good fire in the middle of the wilderness. Keeper says there's something in all of us human beings that's attracted to a good fire. On accounta we all started out the same, he says. All of us were tribal people at one time in our history and sitting by fires late at night's a big part of who we all are deep inside. That's why fires are so popular, even in big fancy homes in the city. All of us got a secret yearning for our tribal past. The simple past, according to Keeper, and fires kinda spark that for us no matter who we are. Says that's the way the problems of the world and between people gonna be solved someday. Once we remember about the common fires that burn in our pasts. Hmmpfh.

I sat there long into the night. Every now and then I'd lay some sweetgrass or cedar on a red-hot piece of wood and the smoke'd kinda calm me down when I got sort of freaked out by that feeling of being out of control. All around me was a huge land. Empty but full. In the middle of it all I felt pretty small and inside me there was a growing feeling that I was pretty powerless in the face of it. I imagined big bears, wolverines or cougars sneaking out of the bush and ending things for me and there wasn't anything I could do. Or a big storm coming up and blowing away the canoe, drowning my fire and soaking my camp, or a sudden snowfall that would bury all the signs and directions. The land could pretty much do whatever it wanted and I couldn't do a thing. Guess that's really when I woke up to the idea of where the real power in this world is. It was in that lake, the trees, the rocks, wind, sky and ground. Me I was just there trying to find my part in it. By the time I hit my bed I fell into a deep sleep and never moved until morning.

And what a morning. The sun was just coming up and the purple light was fading off, revealing mist on the bay and the circles of rising fish. There was more birds in the trees than I ever heard before and just beyond the mouth of the bay was a beaver hauling a long branch of poplar to his den somewhere further down the shoreline. The long dwindling Y in the water sent ripples right up to where my camp was. By the time I got the fire stoked up and going again the sun was completely up.

For me, breakfast in the bush is the greatest thing in the world. There's nothing quite like that first big slug of campfire coffee and the smell of bacon and eggs against the cold crispness of the air. I fished awhile and hooked a nice little pickerel from the pool and ate him up right away too. When I finished I remembered what Keeper'd told me and left a small pinch of tobacco by the water's edge as thanks for the food. It felt kinda nice doing that.

According to Jackie the old cabin would be somewhere back in the bush to the east of where I was sitting now, near another small bay like this on a smaller lake. Probably wouldn't be too much left of it after all these years and I'd have to satisfy myself with a few old timbers. Didn't matter. I just needed to see the place. All those years of wandering around shopping for a story for myself, some hook to hang my life on, had finally brought me here to where it all started. Somewhere back in those trees was the history I never had. Most people got them photo albums got pictures of their past. Me I never had that. Seen some snapshots that Ma'n Jane kept but there weren't any of those days when it all started for this little flock of Ravens. I kinda needed to have one of them Kodak moments for myself right back here in the bush. Needed to touch a part of myself I never knew was there. I felt like one of them salmon that's gotta go back upriver to where it was hatched after a long time at sea. I was at sea a long time myself. The only difference being that the salmon's gotta go back so it can die. Me I had to come back so I could live.

I grabbed a fishing pole and knife, threw a small pack on my back with the moose-hide pouch and some food, matches and fishing hooks and headed eastward into the bush.

There's a moment in this life that I love every time it happens. It's that moment when you step into the bush and feel it close itself behind you. Kinda like the door to a favorite room. Only this room's the biggest one in the world and it's full of everything you want around you.

You look straight ahead of you at that moment and all you can see is the power of the rough and tangle. Something as important as direction gets all erased by the power of nature, the land expressing itself. The rough and tangle. You take a hundred steps and stop. In every direction there's only the law of the land. Those areas where there are no paths, no blazes on trees, no sound of roads or motors to comfort your city senses and no end to it all, are those places where that magic happens. The door to nature's room closing behind you. I love it more than anything these days and it started for me that morning. Funny that I always felt like I was being threatened on the streets of them cities even though I thought of them as home all the time. Surrounded by all the comforts of civilization, all the so-called safety, and I still always felt threatened. But that morning, feeling that door close behind me, knowing there probably wasn't another human being for miles and miles, no one knowing for sure where I was, no gun, no outside-world security, felt like the safest place in the world to me.

Something caught my attention and I started to move. It wasn't much. Just a shadow through the trees, but I started off in that direction looking behind me for a latch on where I came in. I climbed a small rise all strewn with fallen logs and found myself looking at all the little plants that were growing in the shadows. Snakeberries. Mint. The small ferns the old people used to strip and tear long shreds off for weaving and sewing. I started to see things that I remembered the uses for, the tea plants, the mosses, the bark of trees. As I moved through that bush I felt like I knew my way around. It was strange. Not so much like I knew where I was going, because at that time I didn't, but more like I knew what was growing around me, from the names of trees to the places where I knew I could look for skunk cabbage and berries. It was an eerie kinda feeling.

All through that morning I moved through that bush and that feeling of knowing kept getting stronger and stronger. I picked out the almost invisible trails where the deer move. Rabbit runs. I identified bear sign, fox sign, felt the change in direction of the wind on my cheek and looked up to check it with the way the branches were moving. When I came to another small bay I knew where I was gonna be able to catch fish by the shadows on the water, knew the beaver slides, where the muskrat den should be, all of it just by looking from the edge of the bush. It was strange but comforting at the same time. This was the bay I was looking for.

I sat down and pulled the moose-hide pouch out of my pack and offered a pinch of tobacco to the land for allowing me to travel safely through it and for getting me here. I proved the fishing theory by pulling out two big jackfish with a couple of grubs I found under an old log. Then it was lunch and a nice short nap in the sun by the edge of the water. Sleep, dreamless and easy.

I found the cabin without any problem. It was sitting back of the bay about thirty yards, in the shade of two really big birch trees. Calling it a cabin's doing it a favor. It was only a crumple of rotted logs but the outline was still there in that heap. There was grass and small saplings growing up through the middle of it all and no real sign of a trail leading up to it or away from it, but it was the cabin, all right. My heart told me that. I sat down against one of them big birch trees and stared at it for a long, long time.

There's no word in either Ojibway or English that describes the feelings that were flowing through me that afternoon. Maybe flowing's the best word of all. I was sitting there like a big open channel on the water when them waves are pouring over it, rolling and rolling and rolling. They're moving so fast on the top that they churn up things that've been resting down there a long long time. That's how it felt. Churning. Old feelings, images and dreams all churned up into motion again as I sat there leaning on that old birch tree. I closed my eyes real tight and I imagined that I could hear four small children running and playing in the shadows. The voices of adults laughing and yelling for them kids. My name. Garnet. Garnet. Peen-dig-en. Peen-dig-en, Garnet. Come in. Come in. I imagined I could see the faces of those who I would never know in this reality. My grampa. Long gray braids and deep-set eyes in a wrinkled, weathered face of many seasons. My granny. Kerchief framing another wrinkled face with a gap-toothed grin and eyes the deep, deep brown of the land. And my father. John Mukwa. A face like mine. Big broad cheekbones with curlicues of laughter at the edges and a quiet strength born of the land

and all its motions. A bush man's face.

I could hear their voices there. The ghosts of voices that filled those shriveled timbers with love and hope and happiness. The voices of an Ojibway family alive forever in a time beyond what the world could do and did not so far from then. Voices from a history that got removed. A past that never got the chance to shine in me. A glittering, magic past that was being resurrected right there in the crumpled heap of an old cabin that had given itself back to the land a long time ago. It was part of me. And there in those rotted lengths of mossy, gray-black timbers was the thing I'd been searching for all my life. The hook to hang my life on. The hook that hung on the back of a cabin door amidst the rough and tangle of the land, the past, the heritage that was my home, my future and mine alone forever. I cried.

And as those tears swept my face I offered a pinch of tobacco to the skeleton of the cabin that had become the bones of my life, to the power of the land for keeping it here, to the Creator of all things for his plan and I knew that there would be no need to search for that special place to offer my circle of prayers. And I knew that when it was time to leave this place, it would be sacred land. Sacred land. To carry it in my heart forever was my responsibility, my destiny and my dream. The land, you see, is a feeling.

I beached the canoe and moved all my things across to the site of the cabin. It took the better part of the rest of that second day and all the while moving through the bush I couldn't shake that feeling of knowing my way around it all. Funny. Kinda like déjà vu but stronger. A memory you carry in the hands and feet. Turned out that little bay was full of fish and supper was a virtual feast of pickerel and jackfish. I made my first open-fire bannock beside that bay and felt like the great chef of the outdoors by the time I was finished. I had a few hours before sundown so I figured I'd walk around in the bush for a while and see if I could remember anything about that early life of mine.

It was easy to see why my grampa would've picked this spot for a cabin on the trapline. Water was good and fresh, lots of fish and instead of being real marshy and full of mosquitoes, this was one of them pothole lakes the glaciers made with a shoreline of trees and rock. Little streams flowed into it from out of the back country and I could see the notch in the shoreline a ways off that marked the runoff stream. All around it were hills. Not the big unclimbable hills this country's full of but smaller rolling hills that were covered in trees and thick acres of berry patch. Meant there'd be a lot of bears around but I wasn't worried about them. Around here bears still act like bears. Not like them bears out west that get fed from cars and campsites all the time and got more and more bold as the years went by. These bears here still gotta lotta respect for humans and pretty much keep their distance. I saw all that from the hill back of the camp I made by the cabin. Saw the big thickets of trees where the deer would lie in the daytime and saw stretches of shoreline that would make perfect watering places for them if I had a mind or a gun to hunt them with. All around me I could see signs of life. Knew there were foxes, raccoons, porcupine, skunk and wolf trotting around this area regular. Knew that from the signs they left on the ground and from somewhere inside me that I couldn't identify then. Grampa knew it too and that's why he picked this place for a line cabin on the trapline.

That in itself was strange. I'd been city-raised mostly. My way of seeing and knowing was city. I'd learned a lot from my family since I'd been back but as this was the first time I'd ever really been in the boonies it was strange that I knew how to read the country like I was doing. Now there's lotsa people walking around that when you ask them how come they know so much about living in the bush and all, they'll say on accounta I'm an Indian, but in my case this wasn't true. Sure, I'm an Ojibway, but back then I sure didn't have a whole lotta knowledge about what that meant. More than what I did when I first got here but I still had lots to learn. I knew enough to get by for a few days alone long as I brought most of what I needed with me, but I knew I couldn't go it alone for long empty-handed. But there I was reading the land and knowing what it would take to survive. It was the first thing I was gonna ask Keeper about when I got home.

If there were any physical signs of my childhood around there, the land had pretty much taken them back by then. I wandered around for an hour or so and then headed back to the cabin. The shadows were getting long by then and it was time to leave the land to the creatures of the night. I made a pot of tea and settled back to relax and think this day over. My four days were half over already. I kinda wished I could stay longer but I knew if me'n that canoe didn't appear on White Dog Lake by sundown of the fourth day there was gonna be a whole bush full of Ojibways tracking me down real quick. Comforting to know that really.

That's when I remembered about the tobacco ties. I piled a few logs on top of each other and leaned back against them while I opened the pouch. There was a big pile of loose tobacco, about three dozen square little pieces of white cloth and a spool of white thread. If I took about a fingernail's worth of tobacco it'd fit into one of them pieces of cloth. Then I could just wrap the ends tight with the thread and go on to the next one. That part was easy. The hard part was gonna be the praying.

I didn't wanna go into it just because Keeper said it was something I oughta be doing. I didn't wanna go into it just because I figured it was Indian to be doing this either. And I sure didn't wanna go into it without believing in what I was gonna do. Especially here by the old cabin.

So I sat there again long into the night. I watched them stars wheel around the deep bowl of the universe and the moon skate across it in a big arc. I listened to the land around me. I could hear the quick little movements of the smaller animals drawn by the shiny light of the fire and from further off the howl of wolves saluting that moon. Every now and then a fish would jump in the bay and the splash would echo over the lake. Me I sat there by that fire listening and thinking. Listening and thinking. Feeling safe in this full and empty land with that blanket of darkness covering all of it. Feeling safe beside the remains of this cabin that was full of my history. Feeling safe beside this fire that burned like Ojibway fires had been burning for thousands of years. Feeling safe because of that growing sense inside me that I was really a part of all of it. Really a part of it. And the longer I sat there listening and thinking the more I started to feel and believe that it was a part of me too. The heartbeat of the land beating inside my chest. That feeling of gratitude was burning as warm and bright as that fire by the time my head fell against my chest and I collapsed into the land of dreams to run with the wolves across that full and empty land that had become my home.

It was a dream like any other. I was running. Long, loping strides that floated me over the land. My legs felt free of anything as restricting as muscle and it was like I had wings. I ran and ran and ran, seeing the trees and rocks and lakes passing by like those movies you see where they got the camera latched onto the belly of a plane flying low. Running. Effortlessly running. Bodiless almost. Then suddenly I was in a canoe. I was standing up and paddling really slow around a big point of land. The point of land was nothing but a huge rock cliff. There were trees growing out of the face of that cliff like you see around here all the time. The bigger ones were dying from the top on down but the smaller ones were still a bright green and thick with branches. I paddled real slow and squinted to look at the sun shining on the face of that calm water.

As I rounded the curve of that point there were two big skinny jack pines standing there against that cliff. I stopped paddling to look at them. Suddenly, I noticed there were two eagles there. One at the top of each of those trees. They were looking at me. Not moving just looking. I watched them watching me for a long time and the canoe drifted in and bumped against the shore. There wasn't any fear, not in me and not in them birds. We just watched each other. There was a big silence like you always feel in dreams and I could feel the wind against my cheek while I watched them birds.

Just as my neck was beginning to ache from all that looking up they started to move. First one then the other. Not moving like they were gonna fly away, not like that. One of them started shrugging its shoulders around. Then the other. Kinda bouncing their shoulders around. Bouncing them forward and back. Pretty soon they were moving together, in rhythm. Shoulders moving forward and back and their heads bobbing up and down, side to side too. I watched from the canoe in that thick silence of dreams.

All of a sudden they both kinda popped offa the tops of those pine trees. Jumped. They spread their wings and drifted down to the ground in big sweeping circles, coming close together then circling further apart and then coming close together again until they landed on the ground. When they landed they kept up that shrugging and head bobbing with their wings still spread apart. Their backs were towards me when they landed but as they turned to face me I could see that they weren't eagles any longer. They were an old man and an old woman. On their arms they wore the wings of eagles and on their heads bonnets of eagle feathers that hung down over their eyes. They wore ceremonial costumes and as they danced they kept on watching me. They danced for a very short time and then when they stopped they turned to look at me one last time. They looked right into my eyes, smiled, nodded. When they leaped into the sky they were birds again and I watched them as they slowly disappeared over the far end of the lake. I could hear the soft flap, flap of their wings against the sky and it was that sound that woke me. When I opened my eyes it wasn't to the wings of eagles but to the soft lapping of the waves against the shore. The water curling over the rocks. Flap, flap, flap.

There's those that call us Indians the people of the dream. That's on accounta we spenda lotta time and energy seeking vision. Back in the old traditional times the old ones would send young guys like me out on a four-day fast in the hills. No food, no fire, maybe a little water. They'd sit out there and pray and pray and pray. Sometimes they'd be lucky enough to be blessed with a vision sent to them by the Creator or the ancestors in the spirit world. That vision could be just about anything and was meant to be a sacred and private thing for the seeker. Gave a direction for their life. Called it a vision quest. Nowadays with the traditional ways getting left behind more and more there's not so many going out on vision quests as there used to be. Fact, when you hear about it these days it's a pretty special thing. Anyway, we Indians spent a lot of time seeking dreams and visions to give us direction and strength. One of the things the elders tell you nowadays is to try real hard to remember all your dreams, write them down even to help you. Remember them and talk them over with an elder to try and figure out what they're telling you if you can't figure them out yourself. Us we put a lot of stock in dreams. This dream of mine was powerful and I'd be talking to Keeper about it as soon as I got home. In the meantime I was sure one humble kinda guy by the time I got to moving around that third morning.

After another good breakfast of fresh fish, bannock and good old-fashioned Ojibway bush tea I started making those tobacco offerings. It was sunny and still that morning. As I sat there in the shade of those big birch trees, staring at the remains of that old cabin, I could hear the orchestra of birds all around me. Sat there for a long time with my eyes closed listening to the sounds of creation shrugging its shoulders and moving back into life again. Was nice. Left me feeling really peaceful and as I set out all the parts of that little ceremony there were no ragged edges in my belly.

This was gonna be the first time I ever did anything without Keeper. All the time I'd been home he'd been directing me and giving me all the background to the things I was doing. My guide like he says all the time. Now, Keeper was a day's paddle away and I was about to do something important on my own and I wanted it to be done right. For Keeper and for myself.

I found a thick piece of smoldering wood in the fire and set it down in front of me. This would be my smudging stick. I took a bit of dried cedar and a little twist of moss and placed them on the hot end of that stick. When the smoke started curling up off it I began smoothing it over my head with my open hands. Keeper'n me smooth that smoke over our heads, shoulders and body four times when we smudge. He says it's on accounta four's a strong traditional number and on accounta when we smudge we're purifying ourselves and we gotta purify all of us. Meant our mind, body, spirit and emotion. Get centered. Each pass of that smoke was a purifying pass over one of them areas. It worked. I always feel more centered and positive when I smudge.

"Our bodies are the Creator's house," Keeper said one day when we first started. "It's his house an' us we're only livin' in it for a while. Got everythin' we need to survive in this world in that house with us. Thoughts, muscle, yearnin's an' feelin's. Mind, body, spirit an' emotions. Got it all in that house we're given to live in.

"Us we gotta take care of it. Clean it so we can live good. That's why we smudge every day. Clean that house. Purify all of it so we can live in a good way."

Keeper says when the ancestors in the spirit world smell that smoke it makes them happy on accounta they know that someone in this reality's a believer and trying to live in a good way. They remember to watch over us and protect us. And that smoke as it drifts up and up and up and finally disappears is carrying our prayers into the mystery where the Creator can hear them. According to Keeper, praying's as much a part of being Indian as breathing. Gotta do both to live, he says.

So I smudged up real good that morning and then sat back with my eyes closed trying to feel my breathing. When we do that we reconnect to the sound of our heartbeat. We can feel that boom-boom boom-boom boom-boom in the center of ourselves and when we can feel that, we can feel the heartbeat of life all around us. Tells us we're never alone and that we're part of everything. Kinda hard to feel lonely, lost or afraid when you can feel part of everything around you. Learning that was one of the biggest things I learned from Keeper. That way we're always gonna feel at home in the house we were given to live in. Hmmpfh.

When I opened my eyes I felt ready to start. I lined up everything by my crossed knees and started thinking about all the things I was grateful for. I remembered what Keeper said about this one day when we were walking in the bush. He pointed all around us in a big sweeping motion and nodding his head like he does.

"Us we think funny lots," he said. "Think we're bein' thankful for all the right things. Think we're doin' right by bein' grateful for our home an' health an' family. It's okay. It's right to be that way about them things. But there's more. Just gotta learn to use our eyes different and we see lots to be grateful for. Lots. Gotta look around, really try'n see this world around you. Do that you see lots you're gonna be thankful for an accounta you're gonna see lots that taught you something sometime. That's what this gratefulness is all about. Not just for now. Grateful for all your life."

So I started thinking back as far as I could. Started sending my mind and my eyes back through my life, trying to see things I hadn't looked at in years. Trying to find the gratitude for things happening the way they did. Sat there with a little mound of tobacco in my hand and thought about everything. Never ever thought there'd be a day when I'd see myself saying a prayer of thanks for living the kinda life I'd led but there I was that day wrapping tobacco in little pouches and tying them off with thread, saying thanks for the teachings. Thought about them schoolyards, the teasing, the fighting, the lost feelings. Thought about the streets and how grateful I was to have survived out there. Thought about the pen and how grateful I was to not have to be there anymore and for coming through that kinda whole too.

Lonnie and Delma and faces of people I met that I gave up thinking about a long time ago came up in my mind and I tied up my gratitude for them and what they taught me in a little pouch that I was gonna offer back to the land that day. I sat there for a long, long time, thinking, crying sometimes and being grateful. When I lifted up my eyes finally the sun was telling me it was midafternoon. I had quite a long string of prayers already but there were more waiting to be born inside me. Gotta be strong to give birth I figured, so I broke for lunch and a walk.

By the time I got back it had to be about four-thirty. I recall these days how quiet it all seemed around that old cabin that day. Kinda like ev'rything around me was joining in on the process.

I sat back down in the shade of them trees and smudged and centered myself again. This time I didn't have to travel so far back in things. I thought about coming home and all the people I'd met, things I'd learned, seen and done, and being grateful for all of that came real easy. Then I started looking around me at the trees, water and animals I knew were there but couldn't see. Thought about the land itself, the air, the rocks, earth and sky. Everything went into little pouches and onto that length of thread that was getting longer than I ever expected it to be when I started out. Just about the time I was thinking about the cabin and the grandparents I never got to meet was when I ran out of tobacco. I said a good long prayer for them away and then gathered everything up to go look for a place to offer back my circle of prayers.

Just then I heard that familiar cry of an eagle. When I looked up I saw one sitting at the top of a big jack pine across the bay. Must have been close to suppertime for him and he was scanning the open water for rising fish. When I moved to the edge of the water that bird just looked over at me standing there with my long circle of prayers. We watched each other for a minute or two and then he cried out again and flew off, crying that eagle song. I started walking around the bay to the tree where that bird had been sitting. Kinda like in my dream, I thought, except there was only one of them.

When I got to the tree I sat down at its base and breathed in and out real deep and long for a few minutes. When I felt right I offered up a prayer of thanks for being able to come out here and do this thing and for the opportunity to see the place where I'd lived when I was a baby. I asked for a part of this place to always travel with me so I could remember that I always had a home and I wouldn't have to leave anywhere again in search of it. I prayed for Keeper and my family and asked to be taken home to them safe and sound in the morning. Then I started to climb. I climbed up that tree until the branches started to get a little thin to hold me. I reached out to put that circle of prayers on a higher branch and I came face to face with a big eagle feather just sitting there nestled in the branches. After I made sure that prayer circle was secure I picked up that feather and held it in my teeth as I scampered down that tree. When I hit the ground I sat down again to have a look at it.

It was beautiful. That eagle must have left it when it flew off. Right then and there it didn't really matter where it came from. Eagle feathers are a real honor with us Indians and here I was being offered one by the bird itself. I held it in my hands and looked it over really good, feeling a feeling kinda like honor itself for the first time in my life. Honor and humility all rolled up in one big, shiny, swell-in-the-chest package.

"Us we give feathers when someone's done somethin' needs honorin'," Keeper said one time. "Someone shows courage, faith, humility, love, anythin' like that. Any one of them spiritual qualities meant to help people, we give them a feather. It's a big thing. Somethin' you gotta earn. Earn by livin' right and good."

I thought about that all the way back to the cabin. Thought about how even though I felt kinda afraid when I first got out here that I managed to stay anyway. And about how good I felt about following directions and doing this tobacco offering in a good way. Thought about how for the first time in my life I'd done something really important just for the opportunity to do it and learn. Thought about how it felt to be out here, to be a part of it.

The northern lights were dancing like crazy as I lay there by my little fire. In the morning I would be heading home and right then and right there was when the word "home" began to mean more to me than just four walls and a door. Meant everything around me and in me. Something I could take with me wherever I went, like the eagle feather I clutched to my chest while I slipped away again into the land of dreams.

*Wanted to tell you why it's so important that the boy go out there by himself. Me I knew that he was ready. Ready not like being able to live out there for four days but ready to face the feelin's he was gonna have bein' there at that cabin. Face them with humility an' respect. Face them for growth. That's the way we been teachin' young people for long, long time. Stick with 'em and know when they're ready for more learnin' and ready for findin' their own way too. It's the same at twenty-six as it is at twelve. You gotta be ready. If you're not ready you won't learn. Simple as that. You gotta be willlin' too.*

*Anyway, it was his time. The tobacco offerin's pretty much an individual thing. No one can tell you what you gotta be grateful for on accounta no one really knows your history but you. How things touched you. So you go out there an' pray your own prayers for your own lessons in life. It's a good thing. Makes you walk back over your own territory. Go back down some trails maybe you forgot. Forgot on purpose even sometimes. Him he'd been learnin' real good and it was time he took that walk back through his life. See, bein' grateful's hard when the hurtin's fresh or when the scars have been on the wound a long time. But he worked hard that first year he was here an' found stronger parts of himself. He wouldn't fall apart inside by goin' back there. Was gonna be able to see the teachin's. See 'em and be grateful for 'em. It was his time.*

*An' that tobacco offerin's the way we prepare people for learnin' more. More about ceremony an' ritual. You go alone out there, don't matter how old or young you are, go alone out there when you're not used to it an' you're gonna feel real humble real soon. Gonna find where the real power in this world is at. Gonna see you ain't that much in the scheme of things. Us we needed that humble feelin' workin' in us all the time and out there's where you find it. So we send people out there to find the humility an' respect they're gonna need to appreciate ceremony. Get that an' ceremony's gonna always mean more. Teach you more.*

*Anyway, the boy needed to learn that on accounta he was gonna be led to more. Go in deeper. So headin' out was good timin' and an all-around good idea.*

*See, that's the way. It's the teaching way we been usin' for our young people forever. Start 'em off learnin' respect and humility. Good base for learnin' and workin' as a member of the band. Old man told me he said, us we gotta learn that way, gotta learn that what we do touches everybody, every action, every move touches everybody. Then he told me about fire.*

*Back in the real old days, long before people started markin' human time, Anishanabe had firekeepers. The firekeeper's duty was to keep embers from the campfires alive so they could start another one when they needed it if the people were movin' around. Kept 'em in big moss bags. Moss was cool an' damp so it wouldn't burn but was just dry enough for the embers to keep smolderin' all day long. Soon as they come to a campin' place the firekeeper started cookin' fires and warmin' fires from those embers. Got them goin' right away. Back then it was real big thing. Time went by and our people learned to capture the secret of fire. Learned how to start 'em from scratch in a lotta different ways, under all kinds of conditions. So the firekeepers kinda got lost in that learnin'. But the old ones just knew there was big teachin's in that old firekeeper way. So they started lookin' for a way to use it.*

*Found it in the fire. They saw how the people loved sittin' around them fires tellin' stories and laughin' together. Saw the young ones at the edges of them fires takin' it all in too. Saw 'em tryin' to be a part of it. So they started teachin' them about fire. They told those young ones back then about them old firekeepers an' how important their job was to the people at one time. Said firekeepin' was a big tradition an' real important. Told them how the old ones in camp needed them fires to keep their bones warm an' how if there was no fire the people couldn't eat that day. Told 'em how fire was as big as huntin' in our way. Make a good fire you're takin' care of the people same as hunters are, they told them kids. Big thing, that fire.*

*Well pretty soon, kids bein' kids and all, they started lookin' at that fire different. Started wantin' to be the ones to start 'em. So the old ones started teachin' 'em how to make good fires. Smokeless fires and big roarin' winter fires. Pretty soon them kids were takin' real big pride in their firemakin' skills. Kinda pushin' each other to learn it better. Found big honor in that simple thing. They learned how to make good fire because they learned to hunt. All through that they were learnin' how every action touches everybody. Respect. Learnin' that there's big honor in takin' care of people. Humility. Learnin' that bein' responsible starts with the simple things and leads up to the bigger ones. All the same rules but it starts with the simple.*

*So they started teachin' them all that by teachin' 'em to make campfires. Kids would be runnin' around gatherin' wood as soon as it got to be that time of day again. Started learnin' real young about workin' together for the benefit of the people. Was a big lesson they were gonna need forever. An' that's how we been teachin' our kids ever since. Same with the boy. Just a big kid him. Came here as innocent of our ways as them other kids. So I started him off the same way an' this tobacco offerin' was somethin' he had to do in order to learn more. Simple lessons first.*

*See, our way's simple. Us we see power in everythin' except ourselves. Them trees an' rocks an' things are all blessed with power comin' in. Us we gotta look for it. So we go to the land an' see where the real power is. Get humble an' respectful in the middle of it all. Pray'n ask for help. It's the start of findin' your own power. Seein' you got none but knowin' where to go to connect up to it. Simple, eh? If you ain't got no power you gotta connect up to the power source. Plug in. Hmmpfh. Don't ask me where that came from. Me I can't even plug in at home. Some of us Indyuns ain't never gonna have no power on accounta the hydro lines don't reach that far. Heh, heh, heh.*

*That's why me I say the land is a feelin'. You go out there and stand in the middle of it an' you're gonna feel it. You're gonna feel it. That's why all them city people are always headin' to the country every chance they get. Somethin' deep inside 'em's hungry for that feelin'. Lost it lots of them and want it back. Us we got it all the time. Learn it early. Keep it inside us. Then no matter where we go we always got that feelin' in us. City, town, don't matter. We got that connected-up feelin' workin' inside us. That feelin' of power that we looked for an' found.*

They were waiting around on the dock trying to look casual when I started back across White Dog Lake. I made real good time coming back so it was about an hour before sundown but they were still hanging around trying not to look like they were scanning the lake every minute or so. Keeper'n Ma, my brothers and sister, Gilbert, Charlie and even old Doc Tacknyk were crowded onto that little dock. By the time I reached them they were all smiles.

"Couldn't tell if it was you or not," my uncle Charlie was saying. "Kinda got skinny out there. Maybe we shoulda give you a couple of hand grenades."

"What the hell for?" I asked.

"Easier huntin'," he said, to wild laughter all around.

"Doesn't look all too malnourished to me," Doc said, reaching down to ease the canoe against the dock. "Must have been the ten pounds of groceries he carried in with him!"

"Yeah, amazin' how long that frozen fish stays froze," my uncle Charlie said, winking at me as he reached for my pack.

"Didn't have no frozen fish," Ma said, kinda pouty-like. "My boy knows where to camp to have regular food all the time, that's all. Where'd you set up anyway, my boy? Downtown Minaki?"

Everyone laughed but I could tell they were all pretty relieved that I'd made it back on time and okay. Keeper was grinning away and letting the family pretty much have their greetings first and he winked at me too while Jane grabbed me up in another of her big wraparound hugs.

"Prouda ya, bro'," she said and wiped a little tear from her eye.

"Yep. Bagga antlers. Lookin' pretty jake," Jackie said before hugging me too.

I asked, "What's jake?"

"Jake's the cool, hip, together, you know?" Stanley said, rubbing his hand through my hair. "Lookin' jake's the way you wanna look when you go out on the town. Except maybe right now you'd consider havin' a bath before you hit town tonight!"

"Hmmpfh," Ma said, hugging me and giving me a real big kiss on the cheek. "Nuffa this talk. Boy could use hot tea, stew an' bannock, an' me I got some goin' right now."

We laughed and walked into Ma's where a big pot of stew was simmering on the stove and a bannock the size of a seat cushion was waiting on the table. There wasn't much talk for a while as we all filled up bowls and headed out to where Jackie had a fire going right away. As I looked around at those people I sure was glad to be home and real grateful to have been met by all of them.

"Did ya find it?" Jackie asked, over the rim of his teacup.

"Hey-yuh. Right where you said it would be."

"How was it? Standin'?"

"Kaween. Down. Not much left anymore really. Just a big pile of rotted logs with trees and stuff growing up out of it."

"Figgers."

"Someday I wanna go there too me," Ma said, looking out across the lake towards that first portage. "Someday maybe you take me there, my boy?"

"Sure, Ma. I'll be back there lots."

"How did it feel, Garnet, being away off by yourself for the first time?" Doc Tacknyk asked. "I know the first time I was out there alone I felt very intimidated."

"Yeah. Me too at first. That first night felt like I was a thousand miles away from anybody. After that though it was okay. Felt like home."

"Was your home," Uncle Charlie said. "Long time ago when you were just crawlin' around. Couldn't even talk then. Just howled lots you."

"Hey-yuh," said my uncle Joe through a big mouthful of stew and bannock. "Always gonna be Raven land there. Our footprints all over that area. Now yours are there too. It's your home again now."

"Well, that's how it felt, all right. Like I'd been there not all that long ago. In fact, I could almost swear that I knew where I was going all the time. Like I knew what and where everything was. Weird."

"Not weird," Ma said. "Not weird. First thing you learned from your grampa an' your father was that land."

I sat down on a log with Jane, who put her arm

around me and her head against my chest. Stanley and Jackie came across and sat down there too looking at Ma, who was sitting on her favorite stump with a big mug of tea.

"First present you ever got from them two was the land, my boy. See, us we were always fightin' over who was gonna take care of you when you were still a car-ryin'-around baby. Us women, we wanted to be around you all the time, breastfeedin' an all that. Me'n your granny'n your aunties we wanted you close. But them two wanted you around 'em too. So we'd all the time be fightin' over who got to take care of you for the day. Lotta the time they won out.

"Your grampa or your dad'd strap you to their chest an' head off into the bush to work the line. You'd be all wrapped up warm'n safe in that cradleboard an' they'd walk around all day with you on their chest. All that time they were walkin' through that bush they'd be talkin' to you even though you were so small and couldn't understand nothin'. Still they talked to you.

"When they seen a bear in the bush they'd tell you his name. Mukwa. Then they'd tell you all about that mukwa. Where he went, what he done all day, what he liked to eat'n where you should look for him. Everythin'. An' they'd call your name out to that bear too before he disappeared. They'd say, this is my son. His name's Garnet Raven an' he's Anishanabe. Then they'd tell you that the bear was your brother and you didn't have to be afraid of him. Same thing with fox, raccoon, weasel.

Introduced you to each other. Same thing with water, tree, rock, fish, everythin' out there. Plants, insects, all of it. Told you all of it was your relative an' the land was always gonna be your home.

"Introduced you to the world that way, my boy. Told you everythin' an' introduced you to all of it. So that whenever you went there anytime in your life, you'd never feel like a stranger. Days'n days they carried you around till you met everythin'. They introduced you to the world. Gave it to you as a gift.

"But even though you were too young to understand, somewhere inside you it stuck. Never went away all this time. Reason you could see all that'n know all about it. Same with all you kids. That's the way we did things back then. It's our tradition. Introduce you to the world. It's our way."

No one said a word for the longest time. Right then and right there I chose to believe it and believe that it took an awful lotta love for someone to take the time to offer the world as a gift. To take you around and introduce you to it all. Explain it, give it size, give it direction. And my heart swelled knowing I was loved that much. Still was too, judging by the way everyone was looking at me.

"Wow," said Jane. "I didn't know that, Ma. That's really cool."

"Cool ain't the word, sister," Stanley said. "Strong maybe."

"Dad told me about it one time," Jackie said, looking up at the sky. "Told me it was what I should do one day if I ever had any kids of my own. Told me it was my responsibility."

"That's right," Keeper said really quietly, "that's right. It's your responsibility. First, though, it's your responsibility to get to know that world yourself. Reach out, touch it, feel it, get to know it, be a part of it. Find yourself in it. Find it in you. The only time you can give it away's when it's part of you. That's what our way's all about. Feelin' that universe inside and givin' it to someone else sometime."

"That's very beautiful," Doc Tacknyk said, "and very, very true. Makes me wish I was an Indian."

"Hmmpfh," Keeper said. "Some Indyun you'd make. First time we had you out to smoke fish you had to ask me which end you were supposed to light!"

We all laughed. As I sat there on that log with my brothers and sister, looking across at the fire throwing big shadows on the face of our mother, I thought of how something that started way back in that bush a long time ago had been rekindled like a fire inside me and I knew suddenly that in our own ways, in our own time, we all of us are firekeepers like Keeper talks about, lighting the fires of love and home and family for each other. Firekeepers. A responsibility and an honor.

"Ever hear what happened the first time Keeper cleaned a fish?" Doc was saying.

"No," Jackie said. "What happened the first time Keeper cleaned a fish?"

"He started crying because he couldn't find the ears and he wanted to make sure he scrubbed behind them too!"

Would have made a good Indian after all, that Doc.

"It's a gift," Keeper was saying the next morning after we'd prayed and sung and I told him about the eagle feather. "Big gift. Bird wants to honor you for what you done there. Left that for you to remind you all the time what you done. Help you remember the teachin's that come from it."

I was busy getting breakfast ready and he was leaning back in his chair with his feet propped up on the stove, smoking his pipe and watching me. When I caught his eye he winked at me and smiled real big.

"So . . . see anythin' special out there?" he said, sly-like and slow.

"Kaween. Nothin' special." I handed him his dish full of bacon and eggs.

"Hmmpfh. Thought maybe you seen somethin'."

"Like what?"

"Don't know. Somethin'."

"You mean, like a vision?"

"Maybe. Vision. Dream. Strange animal. Somethin'."

"Well, I did have a kind of strange dream one night. Night before I did the ceremony."

"Hmmpfh," he said with a mouthful of bannock. "Kinda dream?"

While he ate I told him about the dream of the eagles. He watched me all through the telling and his eyes moved between surprise and understanding. When he finished he relit his pipe and rocked slowly in his chair while I finished my breakfast. It was quiet for a long time.

"So what do you think it means?"

"Hmmpfh. Hard sometimes to tell with dreams. Sometimes you gotta live with 'em for a long time, goin' back over 'em and over 'em. More gets shown that way. Deeper meanin's, bigger teachin's, more messages. Still, there's somethin' big there. Somethin' big."

"Like what?"

"Well, eagle's a strong symbol. Water's a strong symbol. Paddlin' alone's a strong sign too. Lots there. Gonna take you long time to sort it all out for yourself, but dreams work that way. Always gonna be more there the longer you look. But here's what I think one big part is.

"See, you went out there lookin' to link up with yourself. Go home, find somethin' there maybe. Somethin' you been missin' you don't even know the name of. Somethin' you figure you lost might never get back. So you find that old cabin. Sit there. Thoughts go way back. Kinda start feelin' part of that old cabin even though it's only a pile of logs now. Kinda feelin' like home inside. Fall asleep, start dreamin'. When you were runnin' at the start was like your life before you come home. Always runnin' lookin' for shelter. Someplace safe. That canoe's kinda like your shelter. Our way. The Indyun way. Anishanabe. What you always were. You found it here an' you're workin' hard at lookin' for more. Feelin' kinda safe but wantin' more. The calm water means you're trustin' your surroundings. Me, us, this place. That's how you are when the eagles let you find them."

"Let me find 'em?"

"Hey-yuh. Let you find 'em. See, us we're always thinkin' we're discoverin' something out there. Truth is nature's allowin' us to see her secrets. Them birds were waitin' till you found 'em. Wanted to give you a message."

"I didn't hear no message."

"Two eagles turnin' into an old man and old woman means the grandfathers'n grandmothers are lookin' out for you. Long as you stay in that canoe they're always gonna show you which direction to take. That's why they flew off one way together. You gotta live with that dream for a while, try'n remember which direction they flew. Go talk to a teacher then. They'll tell you all about that direction. What it means. What kinda work you gotta do. What kinda journey you gotta take."

"Grandfathers'n grandmothers?"

"Hey-yuh. See, that old cabin gave you back big sense of where you come from. Never had that before. Got a little bit from bein' around here but not so much as you got there. Grandfathers'n grandmothers mean them that went before. Ancestors. Spirit world ancestors. Always lookin' out for you now on accounta you were brave enough to go look for them'n yourself too. Also means tradition. The old way. Indyun way. Follow tradition where it leads and you'll never be lost again. That's what it means."

"And the dance?"

"Don't know. Not my dream. Maybe means ceremony sometime you gotta do. Maybe means you're gonna be a dancer yourself. Dance that dance sometime. Don't know.

"But you'n me got a lotta the same things in our paths. Need to learn same things too. That's why we're together. To teach each other. You gotta learn to live the same way as me. See, we got two sets of gifts inside, an' us we gotta learn to use 'em both. Man gifts and woman gifts. You wanna be Anishanabe, live the Indyun way, you gotta learn to be whole that way. You'n me. Both of us the same. Hmmpfh. Who'da figured?"

"Figured what?"

"Two guys so diff'rent bein' able to teach each other. Goes that way, I guess."

"So what I do now?"

"Keep on goin' back to that dream. Write down stuff that comes to you. Live with it. Try'n see what it's tellin' you. Try'n live it all the time. Got lotta responsibility havin' a dream like that."

"Responsibility?"

"Hey-yuh. Big gift. Same as that feather. Tellin' you to always look an' remember the teachin's in it all. Do that you get more dreams. More lessons. But always gotta remember one thing."

"What's that?"

"Always gotta remember . . . dream and vision without action ain't nothin'."

"Hmmpfh. You mean always keep lookin' for more. Don't take them lightly."

"Hey-yuh. Teachin's always gonna come to you different ways. Dreams sometimes. People sometimes. Animals. Different ways. Quit lookin' for teachin's you quit growin'. No such thing in the Indyun way as gettin' wise. Gettin' wisdom. Wisdom's a path you decide to take'n follow, not someplace you get to."

"Hmmpfh. You mean I'll never get to be full of wisdom? That there's always gonna be more? Stay on the path there's always gonna be more to learn?"

"Hey-yuh. That's what the Indyun way's all about. Stayin' on that good red road."

"Red road?"

"Yeah, red road. Path of the heart. Stay on that path you learn to be three things."

"What three?"

"Stay on the path of the heart, the red road, you learn to be a good human bein' first. Then you learn to be a good man, or good woman dependin' on who you're born to be. Then because you learned to be those things sometime you find out you learned how, to be a good Anishanabe, a good Indyun. That's the way it works. Learn to be good human bein' everythin' else follows. Learn to be complete. Your life's a prayer. That's our way. Way it's always been."

"So what I do with that feather?"

"Same as me. Put it up someplace where you're always gonna see it. Someplace close to you. More you see it, the more you remember what you're supposed to be doin'. One of these days you'll find someone comes your way you wanna give it to maybe. Someone tryin' to follow the same path. Someone showin' same kinda courage."

"Lot to it, eh?"

"Lot to what?'

"The Indyun way. Our way."

"Hey-yuh. Lot to it. More all the time too."

"Are we ever gonna be able to learn everything?"

"Nah. World changes all the time. More teachin's all the time. Always gonna be more. Rules always the same, though. Rules always the same."

"Rules of tradition?"

"Hey-yuh. Rules of life. Follow 'em you get through anythin'."

"Funny. Remember how scared I was coming here the first time? Scared about not being able to be an Indyun, scared I'd never be able to be one, scared that I was always gonna be on the outside?"

"Yeah. Scareda that still?"

"Nah. More scared of not being enough of one now. Not living up to what I learned, y'know?"

"Hey-yuh. I know. But don't worry. You're doin' good. But there's somethin' you're gonna need."

"What?"

"Gonna need those two feathers the old man gave me long long time ago. Me I wanna give 'em to you on accounta you done somethin' took real bravery. An' on accounta they're a big part of who you are. Big part of that old man. Big part of me. Big part of our way. That's who you are now. Goin' to that cabin, doin' that ceremony hooked you up to our way. Put it inside you. Made it into a heartsong. You listen to that song. It's yours. It's made up from your life. Everythin' you went through to get here right now. This place. This moment. So me I wanna give 'em to you to help you always remember who you are."

He got up slowly and made his way across the cabin to where those feathers hung on the east wall. The drum hung beside them. As he turned back to me I could see big tears rolling down his face and he was smiling at the same time. He walked towards me really slowly looking at those feathers in his hands. Touching them, running his hands down the edges and moving his fingers through the soft plumage at the bottom where they were joined by the moose-hide thong. I stood to meet him.

It felt like forever. An old man'n me. Keeper'n me. Two friends joined by the spirit of another old man who'd moved through our lives in different ways but left his footprints on our hearts anyway. My grampa. When he handed me those feathers we never spoke. Just looked long and deep into each other's eyes, nodding our heads slowly.

"They're yours now, Garnet. Always were I guess. Me I was just the keeper of these feathers too. Take 'em. You earned 'em. Honor 'em. Honor 'em by tryin' to live a good way. Our way."

"Meegwetch, Keeper. Meegwetch. I will. I'll try."

"Hey-yuh. I know you will. I know you will. You're a good boy. It's only right you should have these."

"Why's that?"

"Might look like eagle feathers right now but me I always believed they were always . . . Raven feathers."

We laughed. Laughed good and deep and then we collapsed together in a great big hug. We stood there rocking back and forth with our arms wrapped around each other for the longest time. Feeling that feeling that's got no name in our language or any other. The feeling that happens when two spirits collide and soar. Kinda like those two eagles in my dream. Two hearts and two lives joined together by that common magic born of the land. A common magic we carry within us always, bringing us together with the ones who'll be our guides in this life, the ones we travel that good red road with.

The path of the heart. The path of the Anishanabe. The path of the human beings.

"That's the thing with hugs," Ma was saying later that day when we were hanging all three feathers on the east wall of her cabin. "Make you feel real good all the time. But there's a reason. When we hug someone an' really mean it, we get given a gift by the Creator who sent that person our way. That's the gift of another heartbeat. We feel it on the empty side of our chests when we really squeeze that person close. The old people say when we're really happy that extra heartbeat we feel when we're huggin's helpin' us celebrate. An' when we're full of hurt or sore that extra heartbeat's givin' us the strength we need to get through whatever it is. That's the old way of seein' it. Makes sense to me."

"Yeah," I said real slowly, "yeah. Makes sense to me too. Thanks, Ma."

"Oh, you're welcome, my boy. Now c'mere. Your old ma wants to feel another heartbeat . . . help me celebrate these feathers."

She was right. There is another heartbeat when you stop to try and feel it.

Thing with us Ojibways is, we can't stand holding onto good news for very long without sharing it with somebody. Strange how word gets out so far and so fast sometimes. Around here it's called the moccasin telegraph. Word is that the moccasin telegraph's a faster means of communication than any scientist will ever discover. All it takes is one whisper and pretty soon everyone's in on the news. Sometimes I think us Indians got what you could call satellite ears. We can pick up the frequency of whispering a mile or more away and that's why the moccasin telegraph's such an amazing thing to watch. Ma'n me weren't the least surprised when Chief Isaac and old Doc Tacknyk knocked on the door just after noon.

"Heard the good news, Garnet," Chief Isaac said, stretching out his hand in congratulations. "Long time since anyone earned an eagle feather around here. Especially two. Prouda ya.'

"That goes for me too, Garnet," Doc said, patting me on the back with them icy fingers. I could feel their chill right through my wool sweater and was kinda grateful I didn't need a check-up in the near future. "Isaac and I figure this calls for something special. Don't we, Chief."

"Hey-yuh. We do. Fact, we were talking down at the store about it an' we figure it's time we had a big feast. Get everyone down to it. Get the drummers to sing you an honor song. Get everyone nice'n fat. Party it up, y'know?"

"You were talking about this down at the store?" I said. "Didn't happen but this morning."

"Yeah, an' we're all real happy for ya," Isaac said, sitting down in a chair with a hot mug of tea he'd grabbed off the stove. "Everybody is."

"Everybody?"

"Hey-yuh. It's the talk of the reserve today."

Ma giggled in the background and I saw her'n Doc trade a big wink. They both settled into chairs to hear the rest of Isaac's plan. I just stood there leaning against the door frame, shaking my head. Even when you're kinda used to it, the moccasin telegraph'll amaze you sometimes.

"So what I figger is this," Isaac said, setting his mug on the floor and leaning forward with his elbows on his knees and hands wide open in front of him. That's his favorite political stance. Figures it gives him that honest, just-your-neighbor politician look. "Huntin's been good, lotta fish being smoked, everyone's in pretty good shape foodwise, so we can all pitch in. Band office'll throw outta buncha money for extras. Maybe we can get the drummers'n singers from Shoal Lake to come'n do us a big old round dance, party right into the morning. Sound good to you?"

"Sure sounds like a dandy idea to me," Doc said. "Been a while since this place had a good old-fashioned round dance. Even longer since we had a feast."

"Hey-yuh," said Ma, her eyes gleaming at the prospect. "An' I jus' know my brothers'll bring out their fiddles'n guitars. We can do us some jiggin' too."

"Good. I'll make the arrangements. Figure three days to pull it all together. So Saturday night at the community hall startin' about seven. Be there or be square!" Isaac said. He swilled back the rest of his tea and stood up real official like.

"Be there and be round will be more like it, eh, Garnet!" Doc said, giving me another icy slap on the back.

"Oh good!" Ma said, dancing a little jig step or two beside the stove. "Best way to head into winter's to have a big feast'n round dance. Jiggin' too, you watch!"

"'Kay then," Isaac said, and he and Doc headed out the door. "See you."

"Hey-yuh," I said, glad to squeeze a word in. "See you."

We stood together in the doorway watching them make their way down the hill towards the road. Doc was walking in that straight-kneed stork walk he's got and

Isaac was leaning in with his hands all busy, gabbing on about something. Kinda looked like Stan and Ollie and when I pointed it out to Ma we both howled. Isaac and Doc looked over their shoulders and Ma'n me howled even louder. They disappeared down the hill and Ma'n me went back inside.

"What's this feast thing about anyway, Ma?"

"Well, goes back long way. People'd get together every once in a while to celebrate. Sometimes just the change of seasons. Sometimes like now when they wanna honor somebody for somethin'. Sometimes just on accounta they wanned to show their gratitude by gatherin' for prayers'n ceremony. Different reasons. But feast's a special thing. Brings people together."

"Do I have to do anything?"

"Kaween. Nobody does. Just come. Be with the people. Party it up like Isaac says."

"Well, I know how to do that!"

"Hmmpfh. Ain't gonna be none of that blues down there that night. Gonna hear some good Indyun playin' You save that crazy stuff for your room."

"Crazy stuff? Thought you liked it?"

"Do. Some anyway. Got a good beat. Lot like Indyuns, them black people."

"How you figure?"

"Got that music in their bum'n feet. Got the drum in their heart'n soul too. Like us."

"There's another way we're alike too."

"And how's that?"

"Well, I was in town one time and heard one of them rednecks call us a bunch of cotton pickin' Indians."

I barely dodged the pillow she threw my way.

When word got out about the feast you could feel the energy level climb to an all-time high. For us Indians all you need to really do is say three little words to get people moving. Those words are usually "bingo," "pow-wow" and "food." There was more bannock being baked, rabbits skinned and stewed, deer meat roasted and berries cleaned than anytime before in recent White Dog history. It was a virtual cultural revival and all because somebody'd done what our people had done for centuries really. I was walking around feeling kinda proud and a bit unsettled at the same time. I brought it up the next day when Stanley'n Jackie'n me were heading out to hunt up a couple deer for the feast.

"Can't see it, really," I was saying. "I don't feel like I done anything real special, y'know? Mostly I was out there for myself, my own reasons."

"That's the way of it," Jackie said, stopping to scan the area for a good spot to enter the bush. "Funny thing about followin' our way is you're always kinda out there for yourself. Don't matter what, really. Simple thing like tobacco offering or fastin' out there. You always go for yourself but it always touches other people what you do. Example kinda."

"Maybe it's special on accounta it's you doing it this time," Stanley said, checking the load in his rifle and rubbing the barrel for luck like he always does.' Biggest talk around the fires this last summer'n fall's been how much you changed. Almost like a real Anishanabe now."

"Hey-yuh, bagga antlers, lookin' kinda jake, all right. Lookin' kinda jake," Jackie said, slapping me on the back.

"And another thing," Stanley added, looking at both Jackie'n me with that wide-eyed head-tilted look he offers up when he's really being thoughtful. "People really been needin' an example of how following our way can help somebody. Really needin' it. Been forever since anyone's really got into it and done it the right way. You comin' here the way you did, lookin' the way you did, actin' like a James Brown Indian and then latchin' onto Keeper'n doing what you been doing the last year's really made a lotta people look. Really made them see what they been missin' themselves. You kinda become a leader, and this feast's all about showin' how much they respect what you been doin' since you were home. That and just wantin' to party like crazy."

"That's right," Jackie said. "It's about honoring. See, us we find it hard to just come out'n say things like we're prouda you, we respect you. Timid that way us, I guess. Rather show it. Means more to us an' to the one we're doin' the showin' to. Always been our way to show the things we feel about people instead of sayin' them. Ceremony, you know. Old people say that the words disappear too fast'n we sometimes forget we said them. But displayin' our pride and respect for people is gonna last forever. You'll remember this feast as long's you live. Us too. Watch."

"Hmmpfh," I said. "Who woulda figured?"

"Figured what?" they said together.

"Figured I'd be being held up as an example of living the Indian way. Didn't mean to. I was just doing what felt right all along."

"That's what it's about," Jackie said. "All you ever need to do to follow our way's to do what feels right."

"Hey-yuh," Stanley said. "All you gotta know. Ceremony'n ritual'n customs are just there to help you go deeper once you feel that way. Go deeper, learn more. All starts with feelin' right inside about something."

Jackie said, "You follow that teaching and you'll be lookin' jake all the time. Lookin' jake on the inside's a whole lot better'n bein' all cool-lookin' outside. You know that by now."

"Hey-yuh," I said, looking at my brothers with pride and doing a quick James Brown spin. "But damn, brother, can I help it if I be lookin' jake all the time on the outside too?"

We laughed.

"Lookin' jake. Hmmpfh," Stanley said. "Still ain't got no butt. How are you gonna look jake when you ain't got no butt?"

"That's right," Jackie said. "Look at you, my man. Narrow-assed Ojibway. Straight line from your shoulder blades to the back for your heels. Can't look too jake like that!"

"Reeee-leee!" Stanley said, stretching the word out on purpose to sound like some of the old ladies and eyeing my rear end. "Ho-leeee! Gettin' kinda ripped off when you buy jeans, ain't ya?"

"Whaddaya mean, ripped off?"

"Well, it's like your friend Lonnie told you in T'rana—there's gotta be two square feet of unused denim back there!"

We laughed again, wrestling around and collapsing onto the ground. The three of us. My friends'n me. My brothers'n me. My family.

When the laughter and wrestling died down we looked each other over and stood up kinda embarrassed.

"Ah-hem . . . well . . . done a good jobba spookin' any deer in this neck of the woods. Better move on down the line a little," Jackie said.

"Yeah, right. Gotta get one anyway," Stanley said.

"Hey. Did you guys know that I knew how to make a deer stew before I even got home here?"

"No way. City guy like you? Hmmpfh," Jackie said, all disgusted.

"No, really," I said. "I knew how all along."

"How do you make a deer stew, then?"

"Sneak up on him and whisper in his ear, it's hunting season, it's hunting season. He'll stew over that for days!"

They chased me into the bush uttering ugly threats.

*Me I like a good feast. Get to be my age there's only a couple things really get to be important. One's a good story'n the other's free food. Heh, heh, heh. Yeah, them feasts are good things.*

*Mostly on accounta they feed the old ones first. Heh, heh, heh. Sorry. Kinda gettin' all excited just thinkin' about it. But them feasts are good an' us we been doin' that long time now. Feastin' an' celebratin's big part of the Indyun way. Any time there was somethin' to be recognized or even any time the people all wanted to get together they had a feast. Wanna keep an' Indyun happy, keep him round, I always say. Heh, heh, heh.*

*I remember when I was a boy. Us we feasted lots. Change of ev'ry season, birth of kids, weddin's, good hunt, good fishin', anythin' was good reason to celebrate together. Lotta things changed real big when we got too hooked into the speed of the outside. Got too hung up in the shiny an' forgot the simple. somethin' like feastin' got washed away on accounta we started to thinkin' we had to be somewhere, do somethin' or see someone. Community kinda got spread apart from each other even though we were still livin' in the same place. Thing like feastin's what helps bring us more together. Reminds us we're all part of one circle. Got responsibilities. Need each other. Nothin' big'n mysterious about it. Just people sittin' down and bein' grateful for things'n eatin'. Givin' thanks to the Creator for the food'n all the things around 'em. That's all.*

*Simple ceremony but kinda sly in how it works on you. See, we all throw in together. Everyone brings what they can. Deer meat, rabbit, bannock, moose. Mmm. Moose meat. Little wild rice on the side. Hot bannock, lotsa lard. And it all gets offered to the people. But it's how it's offered that's the sly part. See, the thing with ceremony is, after a while you get used to it. Been doin' it so long it gets to be too easy. Somethin' you take for granted lots. Not just us. Me I seen lotsa different belieivers got the same problem. Too familiar with their ceremonies and they don't mean nothin' after a while. Somethin' you do on accounta you figure you gotta on accounta you're a certain kinda believer. That's where all the lostness comes from. Makin' the moves but not feelin' it. So us we feast and remember.*

*Old man used to tell of times when the people'd gather from all over in big feasts'n celebrations. People'd paddle in from way long ways. Days sometimes. Comin' together for honorin' or just praisin' the earth for the gifts been comin' long time. Big celebrations. Hand games, lacrosse, target shootin', foot races, story-tellin', lotsa stuff goin' on all round there. Hundreds of people maybe, sometimes more. When he was a boy he said there wasn't a season went by there without a feast to celebrate. Always happenin'. Me same thing. Lotsa gatherin's all the time. Maybe not so big as that but always somebody feastin'. It's on accounta rememberin'. Rememberin' where it all came from and gettin' centered on that again. Rememberin' how we're supposed to be with each other. Simple ceremony but big teachin's.*

*Happens like this. Feast gets talked up. Everyone hears about it, starts gettin' somethin' ready. Hunters hunt, bring fresh meat, people go fishin', bake bannock, everywhere there's people gettin' ready. That's the first sly part. Gettin' ready. Everyone wants to make up their best. Best moose stew, best bannock, best deer roast. Right away they're thinkin' of somethin' outside themselves. Thinkin' of the people. That's what our way's all about. Thinkin' of the people. Right away that simple ceremony's workin' on their thinkin'.*

*Then the gatherin' happens. People come together. See each other headin' together reminds 'em of how important they are to each other, Maybe how much they miss someone they ain't talked with for long time. Gets that feelin' movin' inside 'em.*

*Once everyone's there they all get seated in a great big circle. Old man says he seen one circle one time big as the townsite here. Big as the townsite'n seven deep. Lotta people. Dangerous too. Bad enough gettin' two hungry Indyuns together but try bein' close to five hundred Ojibways in a feedin' frenzy. Heh, heh, heh. Anyway, they get seated down in a big circle. Before the food comes one of the elders'll get up'n say a big prayer. Big long prayer. Me I remember one time that old woman who was prayin' prayed so long I kinda fell asleep. It was all the rustlin' around woke me up. Gladda that. Never wanna miss no feast. Heh, heh, heh. Anyway, the elders, men or women, they pray and give thanks for the food, the land, the people, the gatherin', everythin'. That's another sly part. Big reminder of where it all comes from. Everythin'. Hunters remember that it wasn't them that brought the deer, wasn't fishermen brought the fish. It all came from the Creator. That's what that prayer tells 'em.*

*Then the big part happens. Instead of everyone running up'n grabbin' plates'n divin' into it, somethin' real big happens. Big but simple, eh? Young men, warriors, braves, whatever you wanna call 'em, get up outta the circle'n start servin' the people. Drummers'n singers are singing an honor song for the people an' the young men start servin' 'em. Start with the elders. Old guys like me and the old women get to eat first. It helps us remember that we gotta respect the wisdom of them that lived long time. Respect their vision. What they seen'n learned from. The teachin's they hold. Reason the young men serve the people's to remind them of their place. Be humble. Warrior's gotta be people's protectors. Biggest part of protectin' is nurturin'. Helpin' the people. Bein' humble enough to feed 'em first. It's another sly part. Reminds 'em that warriors gotta learn to nurture before they learn to fight or hunt or anythin'. Biggest part of protectin' is nurturin'. Feedin' the people first. Takin' care of 'em. Mother's side workin' in them young men. That's why they do that.*

*After the elders are served the young men feed the women'n children. Once everyone's served they sit an' feed themselves. Women get up after'n fill bowls up. Go around'n round again and again until all the food's gone. Sly again. Reminds us there ain't no such things as better or bigger. Equal. Share the responsibility. Men'n women got to be equals. That's what that simple sharin' of responsibility reminds us of. Equals. Two sides balanced in that circle. Makin' it complete. Two sides balanced inside us too. Makin' us complete. It's another simple teachin' that kinda gets forgot lots. Nobody gets up'n talks about all this. Nobody gives big speeches about the teachin's that are happenin' durin' that feast. Us we don't do that. Eyes gotta grab teachin's on their own in order to keep 'em, and them feasts sure open lotsa eyes again on the way us Anishanabes gotta be. That's why they're such big things and that's why we keep 'em so simple. The only thing I ever learned by someone tryin' to hit me over the head with somethin' was how to duck good. Heh, heh, heh.*

By the time Saturday evening rolled around this place was full of energy. Kids were screaming around all afternoon chasing each other around the community hall.

Adults were wandering around too looking like they couldn't figure out what to do up until it came time to head for the feast. Me'n Ma went for a long walk ourselves just to get a stretch of the legs and could see the drummers and singers arriving from Shoal Lake. People were pulling into the townsite like clockwork every five minutes and their relatives would met them at the porch of Big Ed's store with hugs and laughter. Looked like it was gonna be a big gathering. When Ma'n me headed out towards the hall that evening there were about thirty cars and trucks parked around the townsite and people were heading down to the hall in big meandering lines from everywhere. We could hear the sounds of drumming and singing already.

"Oh boy!" Ma said, picking up the pace a little and tucking a big pot of roast duck under her arm. "Gonna be a hot time in the old town tonight!"

I laughed. It was good to see Ma all excited. My brothers and I had tracked down a couple deer once we'd quit laughing, and I was carrying a big roast under my arm too. I figured if everybody there had something like Ma'n me there was gonna be an awful lotta stuffed Indians lying around tonight.

The hall was crammed. The circle of people went right around the room and I could see where Bert Otter and his helpers had moved all the usual tables and things out back of the building to make room. There were only four tables left at the front of the hall where the food was stashed. All around the room people were laughing and talking. Kids were running around crawling between people, and a large group of older ladies were arranging the food on the tables while everyone else was craning their necks trying to get an idea of the size of the pickings. One group of drummers and singers was wailing away pretty good and people were moving their arms and shoulders to that old beat all around the room. I felt real warm inside looking at it all and I guess Ma knew what I was feeling by the way she wrapped her free arm around my waist and gave me a big squeeze.

"Kinda nice, eh?"

"Yeah, Ma. Kinda nice. Lotsa people. It's nice."

"Here for you, you know. Most of these people who drove in are your relatives from Grassy Narrows, Rat Portage an' Whitefish."

"Really?"

"Hey-yuh. Second cousins'n such. Been wantin' to meet you since you been home but never got around to it. Wouldn't miss no feast though. Good reason to come see you."

"Wow."

Jane'n Stanley'n Jackie appeared from out of the crowd and steered Ma'n me towards an empty spot in the front part of the circle. There was a big blanket spread out there and we all sat down together. Jane wrapped her arm around my shoulder and smiled at me.

"See those people right there?" She pointed to a group of about eight people all clumped together on another blanket a few feet away. "That's our dad's brother Harlin. Never comes here, him. First time him'n his fam'ly been here in years."

She spent the next twenty minutes or so pointing out people I'd never seen before and telling me about their place in our family. All the while she was doing this we kept on meeting people's eyes and they all smiled over at us and nodded their heads towards me real shy-like. I never knew how big our family really was until that night. Big flock of Ravens. Big.

It wasn't long before Chief Isaac came in wearing his chief's clothes, followed by Keeper and an old man I'd never seen.

"That's old Lazarus," Jackie said real respectful. "Lazarus Green. Midewewin teacher from Rat Portage. Gonna be real special prayer said tonight."

The three of them made their way towards the open space beside us. Keeper nodded and winked and old Lazarus looked at me with a wide-open look that made me feel kinda funny inside. Like he knew me. Chief Isaac was really into his chief role and made big gestures to everyone he made eye contact with. Us Indians we talk with our hands a lot but old Isaac was really playing it up that night. Probably because of old Lazarus being there, I figured. When they sat down Isaac gestured with his hand and the drummers stopped.

"Meegwetch, meegwetch," he said in their direction. "Welcome. Real glad everyone could make it to our feast. First time we had a feast here in a long time now.

Good to see so many friends from all over. Share with us. Help us celebrate. Help us strengthen the circle. And afterwards, once we ate, maybe come on over here and help me stand up!"

The room erupted in laughter. One thing about Chief Isaac, he kinda gets caught up in the politician thing sometimes but he never forgets the Indian way of doing things. There's always time for a good laugh, and Isaac was right there with the first funny of the evening.

"We have a very special guest with us tonight. One you probably already know but for those of you who don't, let me tell you a little bit about Lazarus Green.

"Lazarus Green is from the Rat Portage Reserve. He's been a respected teacher and leader of his people for longer'n most of us have been around. He's ninety-four years old and the way he tells it . . . you young women better be on the lookout . . . he gets a little frisky once he's ate!"

The old man cackled, and when I watched his wrinkled old face crack up in a toothless grin I found myself liking him right away. Some of that eerie feeling in my belly eased away.

"Anyway, Lazarus is here to help us celebrate. Celebrate the undertakin's of young Garnet Raven here, who's become a well-liked part of our service since he's been home with us an' also to help us celebrate comin' together like this. It's somethin' we need to be doing more often. So I'd like to ask Lazarus Green to say our openin' prayer for us tonight."

We all stood as the old man rose to his feet. Lotta the time us Indians will stand for prayers at ceremonies. Showing our respect for the person praying and to show that we're not afraid to stand before the Creator in prayer. Ma took my hand while we all bowed our heads.

Lazarus cleared his throat and began to pray in Ojibway. He prayed for a long time and although I only understood a small part of it I could feel the sincerity in his voice. Been around a bit with Keeper since then and heard a lotta old people pray and them old languages really stir something up inside me every time I hear them. Heard Sioux, Cheyenne, Cree, Blackfoot and it always hits me the same. Every now and then Ma would give my hand a squeeze and when I heard my name come outta the jumble of Ojibway words she squeezed even harder. Lazarus's voice rose and fell, rose and fell for a long time, and that room around us was as quiet as I ever heard anywhere. Not even the little kids were squealing around all that time. When he finally finished and began to sit down I could see people nodding their heads towards each other and smiling. He grinned at me when I sat down and gave me the Indian sign for "travel well."

Keeper was busy arranging a big smudging pot in front of old Lazarus. Pretty soon cedar smoke began to fill the room. With a quick little signal from Keeper, Stanley'n Jackie and a handful of other young men got to their feet. I started to get up too but Jackie pushed me back with one big hand. He smiled at me and shook his head. For the next while the young men brought each of the dishes over to Lazarus, who passed them over the smudging pot, which was a large shallow clay bowl with intricate designs around the outside. The men then moved around the circle offering food to all the elders and then the women and children. It took about half an hour to get everyone fed before they filled their own bowls and sat down. All the while the serving was going on the drummers and singers kept up a steady stream of songs. When one drum group stopped to eat another took up the singing.

There were smiling faces everywhere. People busied themselves with the meal and visited all around their little areas. Some sat crosslegged, others lay on one elbow, some on their stomachs.

"More smackin' of lips goin' on around here than at your average drive-in movie," Jane said.

"Hey-yuh," Stanley offered in agreement. "Only here when you get more goose it's a family thing!"

"Ojibways're the only people I know can eat'n gab at the same time without missin' a beat," Jackie said, with his mouth full of moose meat just to prove his point.

"That's why we got such big cheeks," Ma said, getting all our attention right away.

"Oh yeah, Ma? Why's that?" I asked, knowing it was a set-up.

Ma smiled real big. "On accounta's not polite to be stickin' food in your face when someone's talkin'. So us we can stash a bunch in the sides of our face'n keep right on chewin'!"

We all laughed. Keeper waved me over to where he'n Isaac'n Lazarus were sitting.

"Garnet Raven, this is Lazarus Green," Isaac said, waving a piece of bannock in Lazarus's direction.

"Meet'cha," Lazarus said, offering his hand.

"Ahnee," I said. "I'm happy to meet you."

Elders got a way of shaking hands that's real comforting. They take yours in both of theirs real soft and shy-like and hold onto it all the time they talk to you. Used to surprise me lots when people around here did that but I got used to it after a while. Still, old Lazarus holding onto my hand like that felt really good, like there was a current there.

"Harold'n me, we did lots together. Long time friends us. Your dad, he'd come see me now'n then. Good man. Be prouda you today. Both of them." He looked into my eyes with that wide-open look I first noticed about him.

"Thank you. Meegwetch," I said.

"Welcome. You keep listenin' to this one here." He hooked his thumb Keeper's way. "Him'n me are gonna be workin' together for the next while. Gonna be away lots now. But you listen what he tells you when he's here. Same road. Only now's time to go further. Both of you. So you listen. Do what he tells you. This thing you done, it's good but it's only the start of the trail. There's more."

"I'll listen," I said, realizing that the current I was feeling from the old guy was a current of kindness. Pure. Purer than any I ever felt before or since. "Keeper'n me are friends now. I . . . I trust him."

"That's good. That's good. Trust gotta be there when you travel this road. He told me your dream. That's what you gotta work on now. That dream's the key to your road. Stick with it till you run outta questions. Then wait for another one. Another teachin'. Another dream maybe. They'll come if you want 'em. Them they always come when you want 'em. When you work for 'em."

"Lazarus?"

"Hey-yuh."

"My grampa'n my dad . . . am I . . . like them?"

"Hmmpfh. If you got courage in you, if you got lotta love, if you got a feelin' for the land inside you feels warm, if you get scared, doubtful, worried'n ain't afraid to tell about it, an' if you move more towards the gentle than the tough . . . then maybe you're like them. Ain't for me to say. Ain't for you to say. Ain't for anyone to say right now on accounta no one gonna know till you're done walkin' this road what you been like. That's how we stay alive forever, you'n me'n Keeper here. Everybody. That's how we stay alive forever."

"How do you mean?"

"Stories get told about us when we're gone. People feel same way inside when they hear them stories as they felt when we were with 'em. Nice. Safe. Warm. Loved. That's how we stay alive forever. Make a good story of our life right here. People always gonna wanna tell it then. Part of us gonna be alive in the hearts of our relatives years'n years from now. Like your grampa'n dad are alive in you right now. That's how."

"So us we're all storytellers?"

"Hey-yuh. Right now. Story of our life. One thing, though."

"What's that?"

"Them they always asked questions too. Do that you'll be like 'em all the time."

"Hmmpfh. Meegwetch."

"Welcome. You come see me any time with this one here. I'll be expectin' you."

"I will. Gotta go now. Get busy."

"Busy?"

"Hey-yuh. Got a story to work on."

They laughed. Good and long and deep. As I walked back to my family they were all smiling. Sitting down on the blanket with them felt like the most natural thing in the world.

"So what'd you'n old Lazarus talk about?" Jackie asked.

"Not much. Storytellin'. That's all."

"Kinda storytellin'?"

"Don't know yet."

"Don't know yet?"

"Hey-yuh. Kinda startin' to get an idea, though. Kinda startin' to get an idea."

"Too much bannock ain't good for some people!"

We laughed but as we met each other's eyes I knew we all understood. Funny how that works sometimes.

It took about an hour before everyone had eaten their fill. The only things left on the four tables at the front of the hall were a few scraps of bannock. There were the sounds of happy burping and the flick of matches and lighters as people got ready to enjoy an aftersupper smoke. It wasn't long before Chief Isaac stumbled to his feet. His cheeks puffed out like they do when you wanna keep a big burp to yourself and he adjusted the belt on his trousers as he stood. The drummers stopped.

"Well, that was fun! My mouth ain' been that busy since I made that speech for fundin' last year! Ahem . . . anyway. Movin' on here. We wanna get Garnet Raven to come over here. Garnet's been here with us for about a year'n a half now. You all know about him bein' taken away when he was a baby. Twenty years he was gone. Made it back last year and has been livin' with his ma'n his family here ever since.

Most of you know how different he was when he got here. Fact, it's been the talka the town ever since! Heh, heh. Kinda looked like somebody spray-painted Gumby all glow-in-the-dark and glued an sos pad to his head! Heh, heh. Anyway, most of you know that he's been really workin' hard at bein' one of us. Fact, he's put lotta us to shame for learnin' as much as he has. Been workin' with Keeper here'n doin' lotsa smudgin' and learnin' about our ways. Old ways. Somethin' I guess we get too busy for sometimes but somethin' a lotta us need to pay attention to. Garnet here's been an example to all of us how important them things are. So we wanna get him over here. The Red Eagle drummers from Shoal Lake have brung an honor song especially for you, Garnet, an' they're gonna sing it now. It's your song. Always gonna be sung in your honor now. While they're singin' I want you all to stand and those of you who brung gifts for him can come and offer them to him while the drummers sing. Garnet?"

Everyone stood at the same time as me. Walking across that floor that night felt like my feet were concrete. Every step was a chore. It was the most nervous I'd ever been in my whole life. I never expected gifts. I figured we'd just dance and sing and celebrate. It was all getting to be a bigger and bigger surprise as we went along. People were looking at me and there were more than a few shiny eyes that night. Isaac motioned me to stand between Keeper'n Lazarus. As I took my place they both reached out to shake my hand and give me a big warm hug. Standing there that night between those two old guys felt like the safest, most comfortable place in the world despite my nervousness.

I never knew too much about the differences between honor songs and other pow-wow songs before but that night I felt it. There was a note of celebration ringing through those Ojibway words that reached inside and touched a special place in me and I felt the tears coming. When I looked over at Keeper he just nodded his head like he knew how I felt and was telling me to just let 'em go. I did. Pretty soon people started coming up to me carrying things. They placed them at my feet and then stood to shake my hand and hug me. The song went on and on and that pile of gifts got bigger'n bigger. The warm feeling inside of me from all those hugs, all those other heartbeats, was almost overwhelming. Every face was a tearfilled face that night. By the time the song was over and I saw my ma reach over and pick something up and head my way I thought I'd pretty much had it all as far as honoring was going. Turned out I was wrong.

Her eyes were all sparkly and them tears streaming down her face were like little creeks of silver. She was carrying something bright yellow that looked almost familiar. She handed it to me and then collapsed in my arms crying and kissing my neck over and over again. The room was quiet again. When she finally let go she looked me deep in the eyes.

"Prouda ya, my boy," she said. "Prouda ya. These people're prouda ya too. You're one of us now. Always gonna be no matter what or where you might go. Always gonna be one of us. Them twenty years? Gone now. You're home in our hearts. So me, I want you to have this shirt I made for you. Us we call 'em ribbon shirts. Special kinda shirts we wear for special occasions, like ceremonies, feasts'n stuff. Got colored ribbons on it remind us of things. You ain't got no tribal colors yet but me I sewed on these blue'n green ones on accounta they were your grampa'n dad's colors. Wanted 'em to remind you of where you come from'n how you wanna be. Think you'll recognize the shirt."

She hugged me again. As I unfolded the shirt the material felt familiar. It wasn't until I had it all held out in front of me that I knew what it was. It was the balloon-sleeved yellow shirt I had on the day I arrived at White Dog. The sleeves were cut back regular, the long pointed collar was gone and the ribbons ran across the chest and back and down the arms. It was beautiful.

"You saved this thing?"

"Hey-yuh. Always kinda wanted to remember how you looked. Didn't know it'd come to be like this though. Not till a while ago anyway."

"Thanks, Ma."

"Wanted to make it up for you on accounta now it's like your life. Our way got built onto the way you had to grow up. Where you come from is always gonna be part of where you go now. See?"

"Hey-huh. I see. Don't know what to say, though."

"Don't say nothin'. Put it on."

"Now?"

"Now. Then dance me around all night. Look pretty jake with that on."

When I slipped that shirt over top of my T-shirt the whole room erupted in applause. It fit perfectly, of course, Ma being the expert sewer that she is, and it felt like an old friend. Lazarus'n Keeper came over to give it a good feel and me another handshake. When the drummers started their first round dance song of the evening Ma'n me were the first ones on the floor. Round dance is where everyone gets together holding hands in a big circle. It's the big social dance at all our gatherings and a big favorite everywhere I've been.

Most everyone there that night joined in right away. When that first one was over Ma'n me headed over to check out the other gifts.

There were handmade moose-hide gloves, a tanned buckskin jacket with really beautiful flowered beadwork across the back, moccasins, a deer-hide pouch that I knew would be perfect for holding my smudging stuff, bullets, fishing line and an old beaver fur hat with big earflaps.

"Gonna look real jake in all that," Keeper said, peering over my shoulder.

"Really," I said.

"No more James Brown Indian, I guess, eh?" Stanley whispered in my ear.

"No more, bro'."

"Might wanna look at the linin' of that jacket," Jane said.

I wasn't surprised. It was the lime green trousers I'd worn with that yellow shirt. Everyone laughed.

"I shot the deer'n tanned the hide," Jackie said, squeezing my shoulder hard. "Jane did the beadin'. Was my idea to use the pants. Were gonna save it for Christmas but this seemed like a better idea."

"Do you know what kinda underwear you were wearin' that day?" Keeper blurted out.

"No. Why?"

"On accounta they just might surface in that beaver hat!"

We all laughed and there was a big circle of hugs again in that little group.

The rest of that evening was spent talking with people who wandered over one after another. I met cousins twice removed, nephews'n nieces, uncles'n aunts and a lot of people who knew my family. We laughed and talked and danced long into the night. By the time the people started winding their way towards home and their beds I was wearing all those things I'd been given to wear. Felt real good and I still prefer the smell of smoky tanned hide to any other perfume in the world.

"Lookin' jake, Garnet! Lookin' jake!" I must have heard that about fifty times from different people. Somehow I knew they weren't just talking about the things I was wearing.

"Wanna go home now, my boy?" Ma said, looking pretty worn out by this time.

"No, Ma, I think I wanna take a little walk by the lake for a while. I know I'll be warm. Got gloves'n everything."

"You okay?"

"Hey-yuh. I Just need to think about all this for a bit."

"'Kay then. Don't be long. That old Keeper's gonna wanna be having his breakfast cooked up same as usual, you know."

"Hey-yuh. I know. I won't be long."

"'Kay then."

"'Kay then."

"See you."

"See you, Ma"

She walked off towards home and the rest of my little family followed her. I watched them walk across the light that was thrown from the hall until they disappeared into the night. When I felt the hand on my back I knew it was Keeper.

"Okay?"

"Yeah. I'm okay. Kinda feelin' humble though. Wanna go have a little walk by the lake."

"That's good. You go. Feel what you're feelin'. Remember it an' keep part of it inside you. Save it. Sometime you're gonna need it. It's good."

"Lazarus gone?"

"Hey-yuh. Too old to party it up all night no more. Sleepin' at Isaac's. Gonna head home early."

"Good man, that Lazarus."

"Hey-yuh. Good man."

"He's gonna be your teacher now, eh?"

"Hey-yuh. It's time. Time to carry through on that deal I made with Harold. Start really bein' a keeper."

"Keeper?"

"Yeah."

"I love you, man."

"Hey-yuh. I know. An' me . . . I love you too, Garnet Raven. I love you too."

We put our hands on each other's shoulders and stared into each other's eyes through the tears that were there. It was a look as pure as the current I'd felt running through old Lazarus when he took my hand. No words. Wasn't any need for them anymore. We stood there looking at each other for a long time while the last of the people filed past, unashamed of showing our feelings for each other, unashamed to let others see us like that and as connected as those two eagle feathers that hung on the wall of Ma's cabin. Finally, we sniffled and nodded at each other real slow. He gave my shoulder one last squeeze and turned towards Shotgun Bay and his little cabin in the bush. I watched him move across that same stretch of light until he reached the edge of the darkness. Then he stopped and turned to face me.

"Garnet?"

"Yeah?"

"Mornin'?"

"Yeah. Mornin'."

"'Kay. Jus' checkin'."

"Keeper?"

"Yeah?"

"Dreams."

"Hey-yuh," he said with a wave. "You too. Dreams."

The moon is a hand drum that hangs in the sky. It hangs there on nights like that night of the feast, lit up forever by the spirits of people who search the sky for magic. The dreamers. The believers. The ones who know that power lives in the things we see'n hear'n wonder about. The ones who come to stand upon the land and search for stories. Teachings. The blazes made by them that went before. The signs that mark the path we're all supposed to follow. The path of the heart. The path of the Anishanabe. The path of the human beings. The red road.

They used to tell me in that life I lived before that there's only four directions. North, south, east and west. They were wrong. That red road's got seven of them and for a human being to learn to travel well, like old Lazarus signaled to me that night, they gotta learn to walk all seven. Seven makes the circle. The complete journey. The whole human being. In our way there's the four usual ones I mentioned but it's the other three that make the road so tough to travel. Them three are up and down and—inside.

The old ones say that there's a fire for each one of them directions. A fire where the travelers sit when they reach it. Warm themselves. Rest. Reflect on the journey. Gather with the old ones who sit by that fire forever, waiting for the stragglers, the lonesome and the afraid.

Travel each direction, you learn to see and hear and feel more. Sit by each of those fires and gather your strength. East is the place of light where the sun comes from. You travel that road you learn illumination. The beginnings of knowing. South is the place of innocence and trust. Southern travelers learn to listen to the teachings with an open heart and open ears. West is the look inside place. Investigating what you feel. Growing. North is the place of wisdom. You pause. Look back along the path you followed and see the lessons, the teachings. Reflect. And the up and the down is the motion of life. The day-by-day things we get so hung up on all the time. The things that make us forget how far we traveled. The lessons that came from breathing. The teachings built into the power of choice we picked up along the way. That's where we practice the wisdom we found from traveling the first four. Through the motions of that up'n down. And that last fire, that last destination on that red road, is inside. The place of truth. The warmest fire. The fire that chases out the darkness. You gather there with all the travelers who made that journey too and you are alone no more. There's feasting and celebration. Great stories are told and you learn that you gotta keep that fire going on accounta there's more to come. There's always more to come. Travelers who are gonna need a guide because we're all tourists really. And you never get a map until you reach that seventh fire.

I thought about that journey that night. Watching that hand-drum moon hanging over White Dog Lake reminded me how far I'd come. How far I'd come since the night that old man'n me watched it float across the sky. The night I found my guide. The night I took that first step along that red road. The night I started home.

Learn to be a good human being, he said. Learn to be a good man. Then sometime along the way you start to realize that because you done those things you learned how to be a good Indyun. A good Anishanabe. You learned the *why* of this life instead of just the *how*. You found your way to that seventh fire. Hmmpfh. Who'd have ever figured this? Looking jake, they said. Looking jake. Sitting under that moon that night I knew for the first time what it was all about. Looking jake was sitting by that seventh fire. Sitting by the fire that burns on the fuel of your own truth. The logs and kindling you picked up along that red road.

It's been five years since I came home along that bumpy as hell gravel road. Just over three since the night of that feast and I'm still a tourist. Got a good guide though. Got a good guide. He's been workin' with old Lazarus ever since that night and teachin' me as he goes along. We spend a lotta time going over those old teachings, them old ways of seeing, and it's funny because there's always this feeling coming up inside me when we talk long into those nights, that somewhere, sometime I heard it all before. Like it's not so much being taught to me as reawakened. Rekindled. Like I sat by that fire before. Hmmpfh. Maybe the old coot's right all along. We do carry the embers of those old fires inside us. Something inside us keeps those embers glowing and it just takes a good guide to lead us back there and teach us how to stoke them up again. Firekeepers. Tourists. All of us. Hmmpfh. Who'da figured it, eh?

We still go sit by the edge of Shotgun Bay and watch that big orange hand drum of a moon float across the sky. Still walk over through the frost and snow and rain to pray and sing and cook breakfast. Still having adventures and laughter. Still learning. Looking more'n more jake all the time. Be a storyteller, he told me. Talk about the real Indyuns. About what you learned, where you traveled, where you've been all this time. Tell them. Tell them stories on accounta them they all need guides too. Hmmpfh. Guess we're all Indians really. Heh, heh, heh.